ON BOARD WITH THE SECRET BILLIONAIRE

ON BOARD WITH THE SECRET BILLIONAIRE

CAENYS KERR

RED AVENTURINE PRESS

Copyright

This is a work of fiction. The characters, incidents and dialogues in this book are the work of the author's imagination and are not to be construed as real. Any resemblance to actual events or persons, living or dead, is completely coincidental.

First edition: 2025

Cover art by Qurat ul Ain

RED AVENTURINE PRESS

**Logo design by
Courtney Taylor**

Dedication

For David,
whose planning is thoughtful and meticulous for every one of our
adventures together.

Other books by this author

Return to Calypso Station
Merry Christmas Liebchen
Rosettis series:
    Her Holiday Fling
    Happy with the Millionaire (due for release 2026)
The Heritage Series:
    The Salignac Legacy
    The Beaulieu Birthright

Contents

Chapter One

Tristan Sinclair balanced a tray with two gold-banded coffee cups as she battled the stiff winter breeze funnelling through the canyon of high-rises in Melbourne's bustling central business district. Damn, it was cold. Maybe she should invest in a decent coffee machine for the office and save herself the hassle of fighting the elements for a caffeine fix.

Shuffling her heavy tote higher on her shoulder, she adjusted her grip on the drinks and pushed through the door to her office building. A gust of wind whipped from behind her bringing with it a tail of heavy caramel fabric that snagged the tray, upending the cups, and sending a cascade of coffee onto her favourite skirt suit.

What the heck?

"Scusi!" A deep, masculine voice cut through the commotion.

Tristan spun, irritation zipping through her like a live wire. She was drenched in coffee, in the middle of a workday, and all this tourist had to say, was 'Scusi?' Seriously? Her usual even-tempered approach evaporated in the city's high-density wind.

She tensed, frustration bubbling beneath her skin. Facing him, she glanced up, then higher. There weren't many men she needed to look up to, that, in itself, gave her pause.

Startling honey-brown eyes met hers. A fresh gust caught a lock of dark chestnut hair sweeping it across his brow.

He glanced around her feet at the mess he'd caused, seemingly unperturbed by the breeze. Her bare left hand remained outstretched on the door as other city workers bustled past eager to escape the cold.

"Scusi," he repeated, raising the arm carrying the coat in explanation. "The coat, the wind." He shrugged, as if that were enough.

God, he's beautiful. The sensitive part of her brain sighed. Her sanity, however, was less impressed. Her lips parted, ready to unleash the tirade he had coming.

His lips twitched.

Oh this was funny for him? He was about to learn she wasn't willing to accept limp, non-apologies.

He raised one hand, fingers curled except for his upraised index finger. "Ah, mi dispiace. Er, my apologies, signorina. Please, don't scold me." Shifting the coat from his right arm to his left, he pulled a pristine handkerchief from his trousers pocket. He hesitated, dithering for a moment as if debating whether he could or should touch her suit. Making his decision, he wedged the handkerchief into her hand beside the cardboard tray. "Ancora, signorina, I am so sorry. Ciao."

Just like that, he was gone.

He glided through the very door she'd stepped through moments before, his coat, the instigator of this whole mess, billowing behind him like a dismissive wave, as he strode through the security barriers to the bank of lifts for the upper floors of the building.

What? Wait. How did that happen? Tristan glared at the tray still in her hand. The empty tray. She should get more coffee. A quick scan of her ruined suit put an end to that idea, at least until she'd mopped the dark stain from her clothes.

With a sharp pivot, she stomped in the direction the man had taken, veering across the marble flooring to the reception and security desk in the foyer.

The middle-aged security guard smiled as she approached.

"Hey, Tristan. You good?" he asked.

"Sort of, Frank." She held her arms out from her sides. "I've had a bit of an accident, as you can see." She jerked her head toward the entryway. "There's a mess by the doors, now. Can you get someone to deal with it? It'll be a slip hazard otherwise. I'd hate to see someone injured because of me."

"No problem. I'll get maintenance onto it straight away." Frank picked up the telephone handset.

"Thanks. You're an angel," she said, a wisp of gratitude easing a little of the tension in her chest.

On her first day in this building, she'd checked in with security to ask directions, nervous as a cat. Frank had noticed the understated lapel pin on her jacket.

"Navy vet, huh? Persian Gulf? Did you join straight from high school?" he'd asked.

"I did, stayed for six years." She rarely spoke about her time in the Navy, but she was proud of her service. There, nobody cared that she'd been abandoned to the welfare system as a two-year-old, only that she was committed to doing her best job no matter the circumstances.

"Good on you," he'd said, giving her two thumbs up. "Don't you let any of those useless wannabes upstairs get you down. They'd never understand what you've been through—or even what you've done on their behalf. Whenever you need sanity or fellow feeling, come on down and have a cuppa in my hidey-hole." He'd given her a smiling wink and keyed her through the barriers. They'd been friends ever since.

Raising a hand in farewell, she strode to the mid-range lifts, pressed the button for her floor, and rode up.

Celia, her forty-something secretary, peered over her glasses at the crushed cardboard in Tristan's fist.

"Melbourne's run out of coffee?" she asked, her trademark dry humour intact.

"There was this guy..." Tris trailed off.

"Tall, dark, incredibly handsome?" Celia batted her eyelashes in an exaggerated swoon.

"Actually, yeah." Tristan scratched her forehead with the edge of the empty tray.

Celia slid her keyboard forward into its hidden shelf above her lap, rolled the chair back from her desk—clear except for a monitor in front of her and a handset to her right—then rose gracefully onto four-inch heels.

"Ah-huh. I see." She smirked. "Leave the coffee to me. You go clean your outfit." Before Tristan could protest, Celia spun her toward the inner office. "I'll be back in a jiff," she added. "Then you can tell me all about it. Are you okay?"

At Tristan's nod, Celia grabbed her purse, threw a final questioning look, then strode to the lifts.

Tristan glanced down at her stained clothes, let out a frustrated sigh then stomped into her office.

She crossed the thick pale-grey, short-tufted carpet and flopped into her ergonomic leather chair—her mind still on him. He was as exactly as Celia described, self-assured, exuding an air of control over his environment, spilled coffee notwithstanding.

Tristan wanted to reject the sharp jolt of awareness she'd felt when she met his gaze. The arrogant klutz thought a hanky was an acceptable attempt to help? She'd love the chance to tell him exactly what she thought of that. With a huff, she slammed the coffee tray into the trash bin beneath her desk. She bent to rescue the handkerchief that had gone with it. *What the heck am I supposed to do with this?*

Her gaze dropped to her outfit. What had been a strawberry-ice-cream-pink, was now blotched with dark brown stains. As a redhead, pink didn't always suit her, but this particular shade worked. She'd chosen it after seeing an Aussie movie star—one with similar skin and hair tones—pull it off flawlessly.

In this work environment, projecting a softer image had its uses. This suit had worked wonders in that morning's meeting where competitors for 'her' job had slithered out of the woodwork.

It was her strategy suit. Blast it.

At least she didn't have to scramble for something to wear tonight. Her dress for the evening's event already hung in her tiny office closet. Building management held soirées every three months—part networking event, part update on renovations and maintenance issues. Normally, she'd attend with John, her mentor and direct boss. Tonight, though, he had a gallery opening with his partner. She was going alone.

Slipping off her matching pink heels, Tristan padded across the carpet, closed the door, and locked it.

Ignoring the scudding clouds beyond her office window, she shimmied out of her clothes, rolling the skirt, jacket, cami, and handkerchief together, into a neat bundle on the closet floor. Standing in nothing but a silky pink G-string and balconette bra, she grabbed the red dress from its hanger and tugged it over her head.

Deceptively simple in design, the dress skimmed her figure in all the right places—emphasising her not-so-tiny bust, trim waist, flat stomach, and rounded hips. It wasn't her usual business-day attire but given the state of her suit right now, it was the best option. Besides, it would save time between her late meeting and the party.

She gathered her hair into a ponytail letting the tie rest at her nape, then touched up her makeup using a mirror affixed inside the closet door. With her feet slipped into heels that matched the dress, she was back in control.

Unlocking the door, she left it ajar. There was no sign of Celia or the replacement coffee yet.

Tristan strolled to her desk, turned to her computer, and stabbed at the keyboard to bring up her emails. A message icon blinked in the bottom corner of her screen. Siena? You're in Italy. Why are you awake at this hour? The muscles in her forehead tightened, and she tapped the lightning bolt logo.

"Call me. ASAP!" The short message was enough to raise hackles of alarm on the back of Tristan's neck.

She clicked on her friend's image, triggering the familiar, rippling ringtone.

A moment later Siena appeared on the screen, looking frazzled. Her dark hair was a mess, her usually luminous pixie face drawn and her bright-blue eyes rimmed with red.

"Why aren't you asleep?" Tristan asked.

"Too much on." Siena frowned. "Listen Tris, I need your help," she began, then stopped abruptly. Her expression shifted—alarm flashing across her features.

Tristan straightened in her chair. Siena never asked for help. She was one of the most self-contained people Tristan knew. A murmur of caution and concern stirred low in Tristan's gut.

"Now I know you're available, I'll call you." Siena disconnected.

Tristan's handbag rang. The black phone? Her stomach tightened.

Years ago—back when she, Siena and Beth were cadets at the Defence Force Academy in Canberra—they'd bought prepaid mobile phones. This was long before the Australian government mandated that all new SIM cards be traceable.

Their phones were strictly for their inner circle, used only amongst the three of them or in case of emergency. They were as far off the grid as technology allowed. In TV terms, they'd be called burners. Though she and her friends weren't criminals dodging detection, the phones gave them a level of anonymity they hadn't realised they might need one day.

Every Sunday night, Tristan followed the same routine: check the phone's credit balance, make sure it hadn't timed out, and put the phone on to charge. Come Monday morning, it went back into a hidden pocket in her daily handbag, despite her wondering why she kept it. Beth had been missing, presumed drowned, for five years, and Siena was safe in her job with a cruise ship company in Italy. There didn't seem to be much point in carrying it around anymore.

Yet here it was ringing.

With a sense of foreboding curling in her chest, Tristan rummaged through her handbag—past wallet, lipstick, tissue packets, two reusable shopping bags and a handful of stray pens—until her fingers closed around the small, lightweight device. It was old, practically obsolete, but at least it was ringing.

She pressed 'accept'. "Siena, what's going on?"

"Oh God, Tris. There's something fishy in the state of cruise shipping that I need to uncover." Her voice hitched on a distressed hiccup. "But... I've done my knee, so I'm off on sick leave."

Siena panicking?

Not good.

Tris focussed on the mundane giving herself a moment to process and time to ground Siena. "How did you injure your knee?"

"Silly. Rookie mistake. You'd be ashamed of me." Siena let out a shaky breath. "I was out on the deck in the rain, slipped, and my knee slammed into a railing. History."

A pause.

"You'd think I'd know better after Beth's accident," she added, her voice dropping, "but it wasn't even a storm—just drizzle."

"You still like singing in the rain, huh?" Tris teased, the memory momentarily easing her unease.

"Yeah," Siena said, her voice softening. Tris could hear the way her friend's lips would quirk to the side along with a subtle shift in her gaze—her classic 'mea culpa' tic.

"How long are you off work?" Tris asked.

"Three weeks. I'll miss this sailing, and then the ship goes into dry dock for six weeks for refurbishment, which means I may never get to find out what's happening and why." Frustration edged her tone. "If the bosses figure it out before I do, I'll cop the blame—new on board, an easy scapegoat." Her voice rose with each word. "The runes warned me. So did the tarot. Hagalaz—crisis, and The Tower—destruction. Did I listen?"

Tris exhaled. Siena had read rune stones and tarot cards for every question in her life for as long as Tris had known her, so their mention was nothing unusual.

"Whoa. Slow down," Tris said. At least Siena sounded more angry than scared. "What exactly is the trouble?"

"I need more time," Siena said, "or someone I trust, to figure it out for me."

Tris rubbed the bunched skin on her forehead. "Figure what out?"

Siena took a breath. "We're understaffed but payroll is inflated; understocked on wine and liquor but our invoices are over the top. Money's haemorrhaging somewhere, Tris. I'm worried there's serious embezzlement happening on my watch. I need to pinpoint when it started on the Dorata Laura, how it's happening and who's behind it."

Tris straightened. "The Dorata Laura is the ship where you work, right? You're the Crew Purser. How is any of this your responsibility?"

Siena let out a humourless laugh. "The same way it worked in the Navy—we handle everything around what the staff are doing. If there's a problem, it lands on my desk. Fights? My problem. Theft? Also mine. I don't know if I can trust anyone on board to help me sort it out. My boss, his boss... they could be involved. If that's the case, someone else is being set up to take the fall." The sound of hair being scraped back. "The whole situation has the stink of organised crime. I've gotta tread lightly."

Tris's gut twisted. "Where do I come in?"

"I need someone I can trust to take my place when the ship sails on Wednesday," Siena said.

Tris swallowed. "Wait, what?"

"They'll need an emergency Human Relations Manager-slash-Crew Purser since they don't have a spare on the books. You have the skills. You're way more forensic in your approach than I am, and, most importantly, I trust you. You'd be perfect if you were willing to give up your holidays and spice up your life with a bit of cloak and dagger—like the old days."

The old days.

Tris took a sharp inhale. Those were long gone, thank God.

Back then, she, Siena and Beth had been deployed to infiltrate dockside bars to keep their ears open for political intrigue—pirates appearing off the coast of Ethiopia, movement of illegal arms, or sudden shutdowns in places like the Suez Canal. Three young women, out for a good time, had seemed like no threat to the sailors who frequented those places.

There had been a few close calls—some men wanted more than just conversation—but the strategy had worked. The intel they gathered had gone straight up the chain to the higher-ups making strategic decisions.

The three of them made sure to stick together, no matter what, for overwatch and protection. Taking risks was what they did—then.

This? This felt dangerously close to now.

"I'm not great on ships anymore," Tristan said, swallowing against the flood of images she'd tried so hard to suppress—stormy chaos, Beth's slipping grip and the sheer helplessness as her friend vanished into the black sea.

The scar on the inside of Tris's right arm, slicing through the tattoo inked there, was a permanent reminder. Beth's nails had clawed for traction, tearing skin as she fought to hold on. If Tris could have, she would willingly have traded places, suffered anything to save Beth. Siena's iron grip on Tris' belt ensured the two of them survived.

The captain of the suspected arms dealer's yacht circled the area in a cursory attempt to find her, before making the call there was no hope of finding Beth alive in the rough seas. Siena had the presence of mind to throw over a lifebuoy, just in case, despite the crew's irritation with the waste of resources. At the time, it felt like the captain had shrugged his shoulders, redirected the boat and Beth was left behind. Forgotten. Expendable. Siena wrapped Tris's wound as best she could then they'd held each other all the way back to port.

Tris forced herself to focus as Siena kept talking.

"You're only afraid of storms, Tris. Big ones. We don't get those in the Adriatic Sea at this time of year—nothing like that night off the North African coast." Siena's voice softened. "Ships were your life. Maybe, this could be... I don't know. Therapeutic."

Tris almost laughed. That was the problem with old friends. They knew exactly where your weak spots were—and how to prod them.

"Therapy isn't the word I'd use," she said with a growl. The thought of being trapped on a ship in open water made her skin prickle with cold sweat. "I can't."

The words were barely a whisper.

Siena sighed on the other end. "Tris. Sister, sword and shield, one heart forever. If there was another way, I wouldn't ask. I really need you."

One heart forever.

Tris' gaze dropped to her arm. The ruined tattoo. A heart with the initials S, T and E at the corners. The E for Elizabeth, Beth, had been shredded by Beth's own hand in those final moments. One heart forever meant they would be there for each other when needed. The shield surrounding it and the sword diagonally across it symbolised their promise to always protect one another. Whenever, wherever, whatever the cost.

She closed her eyes and swallowed hard.

"I'll come if it's crucial." The words croaked past the tightness in her throat. She cleared it, forcing a steadier tone. "I was supposed to spend my vacation preparing for a promotion interview. I guess I could do that anywhere." Heaving a breath, she said, "What qualifications do I need? I haven't done anything in HR since I left the Service four years ago. Even then, my title wasn't 'human resources'. What makes you think they'd even hire me?"

Was it totally wrong to hope they wouldn't?

Her friend was in trouble, and yet, deep down, Tris wasn't sure whether she was more afraid of failing Siena... or stepping back onto a ship and facing herself.

"You have serious staff management skills, a business degree and forensic accounting experience. We'll keep the last part quiet, so we don't tip off the bad guys," Siena said.

"I don't use that anymore either. I'm straight middle management now, keeping the business functions ticking over in the world of cleaning supplies." Not for much longer, if she had her way. The promotion she was eyeing was her chance to change the company's culture, bring real recognition to the people, mostly migrant women, who did the work the company's reputation relied on.

"Okay, so I'm a little out of touch. You still know how to do it, right? That's what matters. All I have to do is email Freda Higson at head office, send her your name and qualifications, and bingo, you're my temporary replacement. Are you in?"

Tris rested her forehead in the palm of her hand, exhaling sharply. "Siena..."

"Before you answer, I checked flights." Siena's voice turned sly. "My finger is hovering over a business class seat for you. There are only two left."

Classic Siena. "Melbourne might be at the other end of the world from Naples, but we have international flights all day, every day."

"Yeah, yeah. This one is perfect. You leave Melbourne at ten-thirty on Friday night, a quick layover in Dubai and arrive in Rome by lunchtime Saturday. I'll meet you, we crash in Rome for the night so you can shake off the jet lag, then we head to Naples on Sunday. You start work Monday—meet everyone and get up to speed, then sail on Wednesday."

"Wait. How long is the cruise? Stop—just stop! I have to consider the implications. Are you railroading me on purpose?"

"Yep." No hesitation. "You overthink everything. That makes you great at finding clues, but dreadful at making decisions for yourself. If I give you even one inch, you'll talk yourself out of it."

For the first time in the entire conversation, Siena laughed—genuine, relieved.

"Besides," she added, "you're on holidays anyway. Why not spend the time on an eight-day Adriatic cruise? You'll need some glad rags. Officers have to mingle with the high-profile guests at formal events."

Tris pinched the bridge of her nose. Her gut was already warning her—this wasn't just a favour. This was going to cost her. She also acknowledged the truth in Siena's words. Given the chance she would talk herself out of it.

"Humph. You know what I think about those sorts of people." Her gut clenched with remembered humiliation.

"How many times have I told you to forget that arsehole. He was Navy days. History."

Easy for Siena to say. Would Tris ever get over the hurt of it?

A fellow officer from a wealthy family, who'd promised her everything. Love, stability, the family she'd never had growing up. He'd painted a golden future, swearing his parents would adore her, spinning a dream so perfect she'd let herself believe.

Right up until they'd docked in Sydney, where his actual wife—blonde, polished, adoring—waited for him with open arms.

He'd had the gall to introduce them. "This is Tristan," he'd said, with an easy grin. "She's one of the boys."

Tris had shaken the woman's hand, her chest suffocated by the weight of shame, bile burning her throat. The poor woman had no idea of her husband's rampant infidelity.

That was the moment Tris erased anticipations of love from her future. No fantasies, no long-term commitments—just a career. Work had a far better return on investment.

She shook herself free of the past to focus on Siena—the single, unwavering constant in her life.

"What can I say to persuade you?" Siena's wheedling sounded desperate. "Come for the holiday?"

"A holiday where I'll be working in a job I haven't done in years, and feeling like a fraud?"

"I need you, Tris." Siena's voice softened. "You're the only person I trust in every way."

Tris sighed. There was the button only Siena could press.

"And your big selling point is that it might be dangerous?"

"Only if the bad guys are really bad guys... I'll fill you in when you get here. It'll be great to see you." A beat of silence, then Siena's teasing tone slipped into her voice. "May I press the button now?"

Chapter Two

Luciano Ricci sat behind a heavy mahogany desk, its polished surface gleaming under the office lights. His company prided itself on old-world values—solidity, tradition, respect. The furniture echoed the ethos.

Work beckoned, but his mind lingered on the moment outside. Melbourne's July winds were fierce. He should have worn his coat, but the short walk from the restaurant, where he'd lunched with potential dockside providers, hadn't warranted it. Instead the darn thing had created havoc, tangling around the woman trying to bring in her coffee.

She was tall, almost eye-level with him. Strands of bright auburn hair had escaped her ponytail, whipping against her cheek. Her glare had been sharp. Mossy green eyes locked on him, her temper primed for explosion.

He'd raised a single finger in an instinctive move, and she'd hesitated, her eyes flickering with curiosity.

It had been a long time since he'd felt that whump—the unmistakable collision of challenge and attraction. He wouldn't mind seeing where it led.

A brief association would be good. Longer relationships came with expectations of commitment and permanence. More often than not, those expectations had little to do with him and everything to do with his money.

Cynical? Maybe, but he trusted his own experience far more than his mother's insistence that some grand, enduring love, like the one she shared with his father, was waiting for him.

Settling down was a problem for future Luciano—a problem he'd shelved until he was too old to care.

He should have asked for coffee-girl's number. Not that she would have given it to him. More likely, she'd have decked him with her handbag. Luc chuckled.

How could he find out who she was? She must work in the building, given she'd been carrying coffee inside, but with fifty-eight floors of offices, tracking down one staff member would be impossible. Unless...

He could wait near the main doors around five in the evening, to see if she appeared. It was a long shot, but...

His private phone rang, slicing through the thought.

Only one person had this number. Luc's spine tingled in premonition. His father never called unless it was urgent, let alone at two-thirty in the morning. Ettore Ricci worked all hours, but the timing was odd, even for him. Luc stabbed the button to answer.

There was no greeting, just his father's clipped voice. "You need to come home and find the trouble on the Dorata Laura."

Luc exhaled slowly, relief replacing the initial spike of fear. The Laura was one of the newer cruise liners owned by the family company, named after his grandmother. Each ship bore the 'dorata' prefix as a mark of the fleet's 'golden' luxury.

"I'm more useful here," Luc said. "Today, I negotiated a new dockside deal so we can send a cruise ship to Australia, New Zealand or even the Pacific Islands."

"Good, good, but I can hire a manager to do those things. Wilhelm Broek tells me you did a fine job finding the troublemaker on the Nautic Noble," his father said.

Ah, there it is. His father wouldn't say it outright, but Luc heard the unspoken addition loud and clear. *Come home. Work for your own company as you should have been doing since you left university.*

Luc pinched the bridge of his nose.

"I am not Wilhelm Broek's son. No one on his ships expects to see the heir to a billion-euro shipping empire scrubbing decks, so they don't see him."

Ettore snorted. "You're a billionaire too, mio figlio. We are joint partners in every way— thanks to your doting grandmother's besottedness."

Luc sighed. The conversation was far from over. The inheritance was another sore point Luc didn't want to dwell on.

"What I'm saying is when I work for someone else, crew and customers might see a cleaner, if they see anything at all." He raked a hand through his hair. "In our company half the people have known me since I was born."

"È vero," Ettore conceded, "but they think of you as a teenager, not a man pushing thirty. Besides, you wear disguises for everybody else—why not for us? No one expects to see my globe-trotting son on board unless it's in the Owner's Suite."

Luc scraped his fingernails across his forehead. His father wasn't going to let this go.

"I need you here." Ettore pressed the point. "I need someone I can trust without question. Money is vanishing. Negative reviews are popping up on travel sites. The ship is supposedly fully staffed but the managers say they're short-handed. I don't know who is behind it and I don't have time to find out when I'm running a freight company and five, nearly six, other cruise ships. You know how these things work, and it will get you back into the business."

There it was—the real argument. The not-so-subtle pull toward the empire his father intended him to inherit, a job Luc had avoided for years for damn good reasons.

He drew two fingers down the stubble on his cheek. It'd been three weeks since he'd wrapped up the Nautic Noble case. He was ready for another challenge. It may as well be for his own company.

After all, he was an equal partner with his father. His grandmother made sure of that. Staying away had been his strategy to avoid conflicts over leadership. Divided loyalties killed businesses faster than bad investments.

If he was doing this, he needed a starting point.

"Do you have any suspects?"

Ettore didn't hesitate. "The trouble started right after we appointed a new Human Relations Manager, McFarlane," his father said. "Maybe you could start there."

Luc filed the name away. "Are there any current vacancies on board?"

"There's about to be," his father said. "I'm sending the accountant on leave. That's what you trained for, even if you don't use it much these days."

Luc ignored his father's complaints about a wasted university education. His accounting degree had served him well, giving him a formal understanding of business, strategy and management—invaluable skills in his undercover work. It wasn't just about finding offenders but uncovering their motives as well.

Over the years, he'd taken various cover jobs from deckhand to gym instructor working aboard cruise ships, bulk carriers, and freighters across the world. His real work was discovering where chinks occurred in otherwise smoothly run businesses. He'd dealt with cases as minor as petty cash theft which bred distrust amongst cruise ship activities staff, to more serious disruptions, like his last job on the Nautic Noble where he'd uncovered the instigator behind brawls among the engineering crew.

"How will you get the accountant to take leave?" Luc asked.

"Since we had trouble with a deckhand a couple of years ago going stir-crazy, we made it company policy that all team members must take adequate rest time away from the ships. This guy has been working non-stop for two years, moving from one of our ships to another, so I can enforce the policy. He transferred from the Isabella to the Laura a few months before we appointed the new HR manager. He was an applicant for the job but wasn't as qualified as she was. She had experience managing large teams. Now I wonder if I made the wrong choice if this woman is siphoning money from us or, worse, working with someone to take us down."

"Don't jump to conclusions, Papa," Luc said. "We need more information before throwing accusations around or even making assumptions. When is the next sailing and how long is it?"

"It's an eight-day voyage on the Adriatic route from Naples to Venice, leaving Wednesday. Can you get here in time?"

"If I tie up some projects, I can come on Friday or Saturday. I'll check the flights and let you know. What will you tell Mama? I can't go home to see her until afterwards if we don't want anyone to know I am around. She won't be pleased if she learns I'm back and haven't called in," Luc said.

"Leave your mother to me." His father chuckled. "She won't find out you're here if you stay under the radar."

"Will you organise cruise identification, or shall I do that?"

"You won't need it. I'll tell them you're a stand-in, so you won't need papers. If you're asked, you can say we have not transferred them from the Isabella. You can handle it." His father was confident. "I'll send the jet for you."

"Not if you want me to be anonymous. I'll travel commercial and it won't be in first class."

"Alright, alright. Get here as soon as you can." Ettore ended the call.

"Che sfiga." Luc swore under his breath, slumping in his chair. He'd entertained hopes of finding the woman he had (not) met and discovering what went with those lips. Leaving Melbourne without identifying her was indeed rotten luck.

He would have loved the opportunity to woo her for a whole evening to see where his instant attraction might lead. There goes that fantasy. He turned his attention to the tasks to be cleared for him to leave on the weekend. He should be back in a fortnight. Finding her must wait until then. He called his secretary to organise his flight home. He should be ready by Friday night.

As the afternoon wore on, he didn't see the point of rushing to the meeting of office tower tenants. The report would be on his desk in the morning because his family held a considerable stake in the real estate. Nevertheless, as the company's representative in Australia, he had a responsibility to show his face. Technically, he was a tenant, too, since the Australian headquarters of their cruise line, Eleganti Crociere nel Mediterraneo, and his current office, were located there.

Mild sunshine struggled through scattered clouds as he ambled to the premier hotel adjacent to the office. The tower block's body corporate committee insisted on holding their meetings in the hotel ballroom rather than the large communal boardroom in the main building. "For the prestige," his secretary had said.

He deposited his coat with the concierge on the way through the foyer, leaving it for the laundry staff to clean the coffee stain from one sleeve. Housekeeping would return it to his suite by the end of the evening.

Smoothing his left hand over his hair to tame the breeze's effects, he strode down the wide, ground-floor passageway. The sounds of clinking glasses and lively conversation signalled that the meeting hadn't begun. Damn. He wouldn't be able to slip in unnoticed.

"Mr. Ricci, how wonderful to see you." A squat, balding man in his middle fifties hovered by the door. "We've delayed the start of the meeting until you arrived." The convener's unctuous tone grated on Luc's nerves.

"Bene, signor. Let's begin. No grazie, I will stay here," Luc said, declining the man's gesture towards the far end of the room where a large oval table seated upwards of forty people. Those who had arrived early, had already taken their places. Luc preferred to remain on the outskirts, valuing the ability to slip away when boredom set in.

The man appeared affronted. Luc collected a glass of sparkling wine, saluted him with it, then wove his way to the window side of the room. The last rays of daylight edged around the monolithic office tower next door.

A tall woman, who bore a striking resemblance to the one with the coffee, occupied the prime spot by the window. She stood with perfect posture, leaning on the windowsill in a way only a keen observer would notice. Her eyelids hovered at half-mast as if she longed to close them and absorb the sun's final warmth but needed to appear engaged in the meeting. Loose auburn hair framed her face, one side tucked behind her ear, revealing a delicate profile—a tiny, rounded chin and a straight nose.

The slim fitting red dress, cinched with a broad belt in matching fabric, accentuated her narrow waist and well-shaped curves. Intrigued, Luc drifted closer.

The meeting droned on for an interminable three-quarters of an hour—sinking funds, window-washing schedules, carpet replacements and tenancy vacancy rates. Luc paid little attention, preferring instead to monitor the copper-haired woman as she gradually relaxed against the window.

As the meeting concluded, a drinks server passed by. Luc replaced his empty glass on the tray and retrieved two fresh flutes. With a subtle nudge of his elbow, he tapped the woman's arm.

"Scusi." Her eyes flashed open. "The meeting is finished. Would you care for a fresh glass?" He extended the second drink to her.

She spun to face him. The moment their eyes met, recognition hit him with a jolt. His heart gave an unexpected thump.

He'd found her.

"Ah bella. It is you." He aimed his most charming smile at her—the one that usually got him whatever he wanted. Not this time.

Drawing herself to her full height—nearly his equal on her spiky heels—she regarded him coolly. She pursed her lips, as though she had something cutting to say, then relaxed. Instead, she settled her hip against the windowsill. "You know what? Yes, you were careless and yes, you could have been more sincere in your apology for the inconvenience you caused. In the end, it doesn't matter."

"Your boss was not upset, I hope, about missing their coffee?"

"My job is not one where I fetch anyone coffee." She didn't roll her eyes, though the exasperation in her tone was enough. "The boss can get his own or go without. Do you expect others to run around wasting precious work time catering to your whims?"

"How do I answer your question without sounding like an egotist? I employ people whose task is to handle details leaving me free to focus on my role. It's not a waste of time. They're doing what I pay them to do."

"Right," she said, stroking the skin behind her ear with one long fingernail. "I, on the other hand, choose to gather a cup of coffee for my secretary along with my own when I return from lunch." She set her empty glass on the windowsill and took one from him. "This time, she went out to replace what was spilled over my clothes. When she got back, I was in my next meeting. A bonus for her—she got both coffees. I, on the other hand, missed out on my afternoon pick-me-up. Now, I'm dead on my feet."

He chuckled. "Let me make it up to you. Allow me to buy you dinner."

She peeked at him over the rim of her glass. "You haven't had enough of throwing things on me today?"

A bark of laughter escaped him, drawing curious glances from nearby guests. He leaned in, lowering his voice. "If you refuse me, you'll shatter the playboy reputation I'm working so hard to cultivate."

"If I accept, mine, as a perfectly sensible woman, will be destroyed." She smirked, tilting her head to one raised shoulder.

She intrigued him. There was a strength about her—an undeniable spark—that he found captivating.

"We have a dilemma." He drew one hand across the rasp of light stubble on his cheek. "I propose a compromise. I'll withdraw my invitation if we can instead sit at the same table, enjoying our own meals?"

"Hmm. A girl must eat, I guess. The restaurant here has a good reputation..." Her eyes twinkled under the gleam of the chandeliers.

The committee convener bustled over. "Mr. Ricci, was there anything in the discussions you would like me to address immediately? I'm at your service."

His lady-in-red withdrew from the human triangle. "Nothing, thank you. If you will excuse us, we have an appointment." He held one hand close to, though not touching, her erect back.

"We haven't met, have we? I'm Paul Wilson." The convener addressed her with the saccharin smile he'd applied to Luc.

"Tristan Sinclair," she said, extending her hand to take Wilson's. "It's lovely to meet you. I must go. Good night."

Luc tilted his chin in farewell to Wilson, then strode with Tristan until she bent to retrieve a large handbag from behind the door. Tucked into the top was the pink outfit she'd worn earlier in the day.

"May I have your suit cleaned?" he asked.

She glanced at him. "Thanks for the offer. I'll do it at home. Goodbye."

"Wait. You have a date with me, remember." He pivoted to find the subject of her gaze. "Wilson? Don't worry about him. Come."

"I don't think so, and I didn't promise you a damn thing—certainly not a date. Besides, this little black duck's not so good at being fawned over because of the company she keeps." She hitched the bag onto her shoulder.

He couldn't let her go without a fight.

"We're not keeping company. We'll be sitting at a table enjoying a meal. You'd be rescuing me from another lonely dinner." Consciously, he softened his gaze. She blushed. He'd won.

"You don't take no for an answer, do you?"

"When it is a matter of consent, I do," he said. "When I am haggling for something I want very much, I do not."

"Am I the something you want? I'm not for sale." She scowled at him along the length of her nose.

"Signorina, if you were for sale, you'd be all over me, no?" He chortled, waited a pulse beat, then another. When she didn't leave, he said, "The tagliatelle amatriciana here is close to how I had it as a child. Delizioso. And the scallopini... oh my."

"Haggling, huh? The food had better be as good as you promise, though, or I'll write a seriously bad review."

Her smile took his breath away. He'd wanted time to woo her, and the fates had granted his wish. He had one chance.

Chapter Three

"Signor Ricci. Signorina. Buona sera." The maître d's slight inclination of the head signalled deference to her companion. Though his demeanour carried an air of practiced grandeur, the gesture mirrored Paul Wilson's earlier servility, unsettling Tris further.

Few diners were seated at this early dinner hour, giving Tris the opportunity to take in the restaurant's understated opulence. A single glittering chandelier in the entryway scattered shards of rainbow light across the polished parquet floor, casting a warm glow over the room. The head waiter led them into the plush-carpeted dining area to a table already set with a pre-opened bottle of red wine, its cork resting on a small saucer beside it.

The maître d' pulled out a chair for Tristan, then, with a practised flick of his wrist, spread a crisp napkin across her lap before passing her a menu. "Some water, signorina? Still or sparkling?"

"Sparkling, thank you." A wave of discomfort rolled through her—a familiar reaction to displays of wealth and the grovelling attention that often accompanied them.

"Signor?"

"The same. A large bottle of San Pellegrino, please, Pietro," Ricci said.

The man inclined his head, preparing to step away.

"Un attimo, Pietro," Ricci said, halting him with an easy command. He turned to Tris, his fingers making a give-me motion. "Hand over your clothes."

She blinked. "Excuse me?"

"The hotel is quite efficient. They will handle it while we enjoy our meal." He leaned in slightly, lowering his voice to a coaxing whisper. "Don't fuss, bella. Give it to him, and it will be ready for you to wear again in no time."

Tris searched his expression for an ulterior motive. The worst had already happened—the suit was ruined, beyond saving without professional cleaning. With a reluctant sigh, she withdrew the roll of coffee-stained fabric and handed it over.

Ricci issued instructions in fluid Italian, and the maître d' accepted the bundle without a flicker of surprise, departing with seamless efficiency. As if such requests were perfectly normal in Ricci's world.

"I asked for it to be returned by the time we order dessert. Shall I pour you a glass of this ambrosial Barbaresco? We call it the queen of wines. I find it is softer than Barolo, the king, which has its place when I feel the need for a deep red."

"Why was the wine uncorked? Can you trust it?"

A fresh smile lit his eyes and his mouth. "I am predictable with my wine. The sommelier would have removed the cork at precisely five o'clock. If I were detained in the office, and chosen to eat at eight, the nose would have opened more, though it will be drinkable now."

"You drink a bottle of wine every night?"

"I open a bottle of wine—there is a difference. I enjoy a glass or two only. What happens to the remainder of the bottle, I neither know nor care. Try it. Let me know what you think."

Her years as an officer in the Navy taught her much about all kinds of alcoholic beverages including how to appreciate excellent wines. He poured the garnet-red liquid into her glass till it was one-third full.

She took the glass by the stem, giving it a lazy swirl before dipping her head to scent the nose.

"What did you find?" he asked.

"It opens slowly. Berry, aniseed…" She sipped, rolling the wine around her mouth, swallowed, and sighed. "Strawberry, roses, sort of pot pourri with lavender. Delightful. Thank you, Signor Ricci."

She scanned his features as she set the glass on the table. Short dark chestnut, lightly wavy hair sat above arched brows and those beautifully compelling, soft caramel eyes. His nose was straight and narrow, directing attention to a perfectly proportioned mouth, the slightly fuller bottom lip hinting at erotic pleasures. His cheekbones and blunt jaw combined to give the face a strong frame—a face of authority.

He frowned. "What?" she asked.

"Call me Luc," he said, pronouncing it like 'looch'.

"I might, if we'd been introduced. The only clue I have to your identity is Paul Wilson and the maître d' called you, Mr. Ricci or Signor Ricci."

His face lightened. "How very rude of me, Bella." He extended his hand. "I am Luciano Ricci of Naples, Italy. You are Tristan?"

"Tristan Sinclair of Melbourne, Australia. How do you do?" Static electricity arced between them as his hand touched hers. Her body jolted. "Hmm, let's not do that again," she said. His smile showed a knowing edge.

"You're cultivating a reputation as a playboy, huh?" she asked.

"It is what people expect of me," he shrugged.

The implied contradiction confused her. Maybe he worked like everyone else after all. "If you're not a playboy, what do you do for a living?"

A young female server delivered an antipasto platter, distracting Tris before Luc could respond. "Are you ready to order, or would you like more time?"

Tris skimmed the menu. "Is the tagliatelle as good as he claims?" she asked, casting a sideways glance at her companion.

"Certainly. Do you prefer mild, medium or spicy for the chili component?"

"Medium thanks, and the scallopini," Tris said.

The server stood poised, her hands behind her back, awaiting Luc's selection.

"I'll have the same," he said, handing over his menu.

"Salad?" she asked.

"We'll share an insalata mista, grazie." Luc said. The server smiled, collected Tris' menu, and strode away.

"How do they do that?" Tris asked. "Remember orders without writing them down."

"Trade secrets," he laughed, edging the platter towards her. "Everyone has their own strategy. If I took an order for the special, I'd tweak my thumb—right hand for primo, left for secondo."

"You waited tables? I find it hard to believe." She selected an artichoke heart, prosciutto and a spoonful of olives.

"In a family business, everyone did everything." He shifted the conversation to the earlier meeting. "Since you were asleep for most of it..."

"Was it obvious?"

"Only to me," he said, a teasing glint in his eye. "I kept watch in case I needed to catch you."

His smile was devastating. A surprising warmth spread through her belly, delight fluttering in her chest.

"If you must report on the meeting, the key points were..." He proceeded to list them with astonishing recall, filling in details she wouldn't have retained even if she'd been paying attention.

"Wow. No wonder you were good at restaurant orders," she said. "I wouldn't have remembered half of those."

"Because you were mellow, like a cat in the sun. It amazed me you didn't topple over," he said.

"We all have ways of managing our circumstances." Like how to catch two-minute power naps to survive a twenty-eight-hour military manoeuvre.

The server cleared the platter, replacing it with the pasta, as perfectly delicious as Luc promised.

Conversation didn't falter, ranging across countries and places of interest each had visited. The question of Luc's work didn't arise again though he seemed to travel a lot. He kept her entertained by his descriptions of various cities and attractions in his home country.

Her forays into the Mediterranean had been aboard naval ships, limiting her experience of places inland. Luc's commentary covered the length and breadth of the country, urging Tris to make the opportunity to spend more time there. She refrained from telling him she was travelling to Italy this weekend. Uncanny coincidences didn't sit well with her, no matter how much her body tingled every time his gaze lingered on her.

"Would you care for dessert?" he asked.

"No, thank you. I have an early start. I will collect my suit and be on my way."

"Coffee then? To replace the one I destroyed?"

"Not even coffee. If you call for the bill, I'd appreciate it."

The smile should have warned her. "I have addressed it."

"What do I owe you?" she asked, mentally gritting her teeth.

"Nothing. Thank you for the pleasure of your company."

"Have I mentioned I don't care for overbearing men who take over without at least lip service to asking what my wishes are?"

"It is but a meal, bella, an apology for my carelessness today. Please accept it as such. Next time, we will play by your rules. I will find your clothes."

She wasn't mollified, but short of demanding the server reverse the payment and split the bill, there was little she could do. Having made her views known, she would leave it there.

He raised his index finger from where his hand rested on the table-top and a server appeared promptly. The conversation again was in Italian with both men shooting glances in her direction. Luc drew his brows together, waving the server away. "There was some confusion. They have delivered your laundry to my suite along with my coat. Shall I send them to fetch it, or would you like to accompany me?"

"To see the exquisite paintings you do in your spare time?" Tris twisted her mouth to one side.

"Paintings? No, I don't paint or draw." His confusion appeared to be real.

Should she try to explain the expression? It might appear she expected him to be interested in her beyond sharing dinner. "You have a suite here?" she asked, to redirect the discussion.

"It is close to the office."

She couldn't afford a basic room for one night in this establishment, let alone an extended stay in a 'suite'. "Some family business, if you can afford the rates here," she said.

He shrugged. "Do you see me sitting in the boardroom in Rome? I am what you call the black sheep, no? I had a minor matter to handle in Melbourne. Tomorrow, I leave."

And that would be that. Her heart dropped but her brain twittered she'd had a close call. This man was way too tempting for her peace of mind. "I see. It would be quicker if I collected it and got on my way. Thank you for dinner." She picked up her bag.

He rounded the table, holding her chair as she got to her feet. His hand on her back sent a frisson of energy down her spine. She should shrug it off, but the magnetism of him was something she rarely encountered.

He hadn't addressed her question of his work, leaving his own description of himself as a playboy dangling in the air. She'd do well to bear in mind he wouldn't be hanging around for the long term.

They entered an empty lift, and the doors closed only to open immediately.

"Made it," a young woman said. She danced into the space with six others in tow. They wedged Tris to Luc's body, her back plastered to his front, her hands tightening on her bag pulling it to her midriff. His hand rested on her hip balancing her from the women's jostling. Shivers of desire ran through her. The fragrance of the man, the strength of his arms separating her from the other guests, and his height conspired against her.

Desire changed to near panic as the old evil, claustrophobia, crowded in on her. Too many people in the small space, not enough air to breathe. Shivers wracked her body.

The hand on her hip became insistent, rubbing up and down her side. "Turn around," he whispered in her ear. She did. "Close your eyes. It's just us here, bella." She complied, breathing him in, focussing on his scent, counting each fingernail as it dug into her palm where it clenched around the handle of her bag.

She shuffled to move from his arms when the others exited at a floor lower than Luc's and she could breathe once more. He held her fast between his arms, his cheek resting on her forehead while soft crooning rumbled from his chest.

Her heart stuttered at his continued nearness. Her body wanted to melt into his. She was in trouble.

* * *

The alert pinged, and the door opened on his floor. Luc guided her out, striding briskly to his suite and ushering her inside.

He spun her into his arms to comfort her. Hers edged around him.

"Do you often have those attacks? What causes them?" he asked, massaging her shoulders, her nose tucked into the base of his neck.

"Storms and close spaces. One from a traumatic event and the other from childhood discipline. No, they don't happen often," she said, bowing her spine away from him though not removing her arms. "Usually, I'm prepared. Tonight, you distracted me."

He stared into her green eyes.

"Probably because you're a playboy, right?" she smiled, the shaking in her body subsiding.

"Mmm. What can I say?" He lowered his arms to mirror the way hers lightly looped around his body.

"Ah," she said. "Thanks for rescuing me and hiding me from the others." She touched his cheek and nudged against his embrace.

"My pleasure," he said, holding her gaze, drawing her back.

He should have let her go but holding her like this was a gift. He'd been fascinated by her when she'd stood up to him, then he'd walked away. She'd distracted him for the rest of the afternoon. Finding her again, enjoying dinner with her, he wanted more of her, more time, more everything.

She halted her retreat, firming her arms around him.

Holding her gaze, he swept an errant strand of hair behind her ear, his thumb caressing the softness of her cheek.

"I've wanted to kiss you since we met in the doorway," he said. His attention snagged on the movement of her throat as she swallowed. "May I?" He studied her face while he lowered his head in incremental stages giving her the chance to pull away. Her eyes widened and she sighed into his mouth when he reached her.

He whispered his lips across hers. Silky, yielding, intoxicating. Her body eased into his. His mouth coaxed her lips apart and he darted his tongue in to savour the flavour of her, nuanced by the remnants of her wine. Her musky fragrance drifted from the crease at the base of her throat, erotic, demanding. His manhood rose against the softness of her belly as she hooked herself closer, her thighs pressed hard on his.

Changing the angle of their joining, the kiss went deeper, hotter, more insistent. He pulled back, she followed, not allowing him any distance. He brought his lips hard onto hers, sucking, tasting, plundering. God, he couldn't get enough. His hands ploughed through her hair, gripping her scalp.

With a gentle shove, she withdrew from him. Disappointment speared low in his gut.

She smoothed her hands over the front of his shirt and slid his fine wool jacket from his shoulders. He caught it and tossed it onto a nearby sofa. Then, sliding her hands behind his nape, she dragged his mouth back to hers, gorging on him with the same frantic honesty he'd relished with her. His heart swelled.

He lifted his head and took her face in his hands. "Tristan, if we don't stop now, there'll be no turning back."

Gripping his shoulders, she slanted her body towards him, then stepped away. Her face was flushed. Without meeting his gaze, she made a half-pivot away from him.

"You're right. Sorry. I haven't had enough to drink to blame the alcohol. It must be you who has me intoxicated," she said.

"If I have you intoxicated, you have me completely out of my mind." He caught her hand to bring her round to face him. "I've needed to kiss those lips since I met them in the wind."

"Huh. Me too. Now we have. If you'll get my suit, I'll leave," she said.

"You could stay." He'd beg if that's what it took to keep her.

"I don't do rich and famous."

Resting his forehead on hers, he said, "Our company is rich and famous. I'm just me. I would much rather you didn't go."

"I don't know the rules for a one-night stand," she said.

"We make each other happy. In the morning, we say goodbye."

"No strings, huh?" She raised her face, lifting her eyebrows.

"I wish this time it were not so."

"Flatterer." Her teeth scraped over her swollen bottom lip. "You said you leave tomorrow."

He kissed the mark her teeth had left. "I'll return," he whispered. "I promise."

"No promises. I don't believe in them." Her lips brushed his as she spoke, her breath warm and tinged with wine. He gathered her closer, pressing into the curve of her body.

Their kisses turned urgent, desperate. She flicked the buttons on his shirt, skimming her fingers across his bare chest, tracing the ridges of muscle.

He lowered the zip of her dress until he met the barrier of her belt. Without breaking their kiss, she undid the front buckle, letting it drop away. He slipped his hands through the open fabric, smoothing over the soft skin of her back, unhooking her bra, then pushing the dress to the floor.

Her naked breasts pressed against him, warm and yielding.

"Dio," he groaned. He'd dreamed of this in his afternoon fantasy and now here she was, offering him everything.

He tugged her gently towards the bedroom. She didn't resist.

* * *

Tris awoke to the sight of Luc, leaning on one elbow, observing her.

She couldn't remember the last time she'd awoken with another person beside her in bed. The warmth of his presence, the quiet intensity in his gaze—both unsettled her more than they should.

One hand lazily traversed the curve of her body, instantly rekindling the sensations of the night before. He leaned in and kissed her soundly.

"I must go to a meeting in half an hour. I couldn't leave until I said farewell." His hand skimmed her hip, his mouth lingering on hers. A deep breath expanded his chest where it brushed against her. "This cannot be goodbye. I must see you when I return."

His words sent a ripple through her, but she steadied herself. "One-night stand, we agreed. No strings. You leave today." She had clung to that thought throughout the night, even as her heart threatened to betray her resolve.

"I'll be back. Give me your contact details." He sat on the edge of the bed, watching her.

She pushed herself up on the pillows. "I don't think so," she said softly. "My heart couldn't stand waiting for a call that never came." She traced the heart-shaped mole on his collarbone with the tip of her finger, committing it to memory. "If we're meant to meet again, it'll happen. Maybe I'll go out for coffee some windy day and a coat with a mind of its own will fling the tray at me." She stretched her mouth into a smile to mask the ache in her chest.

He narrowed his eyelids. "I'm not worth the wait?" he asked.

She tightened her fingers on his shoulder. "We had an amazing night. I don't do rich and famous, remember?"

The look he gave her pierced straight to her soul. Then, without another word, he stood abruptly and strode to the bathroom.

Tris chewed the inside of her cheek, then exhaled slowly, and dragged herself from the bed to don one of the fluffy robes from the wardrobe. She wandered to the powder room near the main entry, needing a moment to compose herself. When she returned, he was already dressed—dark trousers, an open-necked shirt, the picture of effortless elegance.

His eyes smouldered as they swept over her bare legs and the robe cinched loosely at her waist. "If you change your mind about me, text me at this number," he said, handing her a business card which read 'Luc' printed above a number.

Before she could respond, he captured her mouth in one last, searing kiss—one that sent her emotions spinning as he had all through the night.

Oh God, could she really let him go?

His fingertips ghosted over her face as though memorising every detail, branding her with his touch.

When he finally pulled back, he held her gaze, unwavering. "We will meet again." With a final lingering gaze, he pivoted and strode out of the apartment.

Tris slumped on the foot of the bed, the plain white card clutched between her fingers. Was he serious?

She straightened her spine then eased to her feet.

Her freshly laundered outfit from yesterday hung in the wardrobe in a clear plastic bag. There wasn't a trace of coffee stains on her blouse, skirt, or jacket. The staff here knew their craft.

Thank God. The last thing she needed was to walk into work wearing last night's red dress.

Shaking out her clothes, she snatched the belt before it fell. The dress. She'd never be able to wear the frock again without remembering him—the connection, the way he made her feel.

Carefully, she rolled the fabric into a tight cylinder and tucked it into one of her fold-up shopping bags. Then, with deliberate finality, she buried it at the bottom of her tote, out of sight.

If only she could do the same with her memories of Luc.

The reality was blunt. The moment he'd left the apartment, he'd become part of her past.

Today, there were more pressing things on her agenda.

A few hours in the office, then home to pack for her flight.

First up: a meeting with her boss.

Chapter Four

John Trevethan rolled his chair away from his desk when Tris knocked on the open door.

"Tris. Come in. Have you decided what you're doing with your three weeks off, or are you using it as a swot-vac for the new job?"

"There'll be swotting. I've got to make sure I'm across all our divisions before the interview. On the other hand, a friend called yesterday and offered me an Adriatic cruise she can't make."

"Excellent. A break will do you good. You'll come back relaxed and ready to hit the ground running. I've invested a lot in you, my girl, and I want to see you succeed here."

"Thanks John, your support means a lot."

"As an old seafarer myself, I know the transition back to civvy street can take time." He leaned back in his chair crossing one leg over the other, his hands resting on his lean torso.

"It's been four years since I left the Navy," she reminded him.

"Yeah, yeah." He raised his hands in mock surrender. "All I'm saying is it's not always easy on your own."

Maybe he meant well, but a flicker of doubt crossed Tris' mind. If John didn't believe she could handle herself in the world, how could she trust him to back her taking charge of a significant chunk of the company? She pushed the thought aside.

"Do you have questions about the new role?" he asked.

Tristan canted her head, considering. "How open would the board and the CEO be to expanding the role into a four-line profit sheet, a 4BL—including company culture along with the social, environmental and financial elements of the bottom line?"

"This is a first step for us. Sure, we've been doing a lot of the social stuff anyway, looking after our people as far as we can. Why? Is there something about the culture of the organisation you don't like?" John asked. "If so, I wouldn't recommend bringing it up in the interview."

"There's still a pretty solid glass ceiling here—for women, First Nations people, and immigrants. I'd like to influence that mindset. Most of our cleaning staff are women and immigrants, and there should be a stronger career path for them." It was a battle she'd been fighting wherever she had influence.

"You're going to be the one to break through that ceiling," he said. "You can work on the human aspect within the social component of the role, but don't try to change the world overnight. Get into the job first." His tone was firm, pragmatic.

"As you saw at yesterday's meeting, plenty of others want this position. You need to be smarter and more strategic if you're going to win it. Focus on planet, people, and profits. Once you've got the job running smoothly, then come talk to me about culture. Or..." He raised a brow. "Are you already calling it 'patriarchy' to fit with people, profits, and planet?"

"You know me well," she said, keeping her tone light, though another flicker of doubt stirred in her chest. Something about John felt different today—off, somehow.

He smiled, then his expression turned serious. "My advice? Focus on the business and the brands that make up the company. Your priority has to be policies that ensure we choose the right products—ones that protect us from the environmental eco-warrior Nazis and part-time labour watchdogs while still delivering a multi-billion-dollar profit."

"Nazis is a strong word." She baulked. "We must consider the environmental impact our business has. We source products for catering, cleaning, laundry and facilities. Customers want to know we're as soft-footed on the carbon imprint as we can be."

"I call it as I see it," he said with a shrug. "If it were up to me, I wouldn't let the unions in, either. They just get in the way of business." His tone was sharper than usual, a near snarl crossing his face—out of character for him.

Tris ran two fingers across the bunched muscles on her forehead. "Where is all of this coming from? I've never seen you as an ultra-conservative before. Unions exist to protect workers from unscrupulous employers." She narrowed her gaze. "Wasn't Michael promoted to union boss?"

John grimaced. "Yeah, well. Unions go beyond their brief and union bosses make threats about ending personal relationships at the worst times."

Her stomach flipped. "Are you and Michael having trouble? After twenty-six years together?"

He let out a heavy breath. "Sometimes people you trust let you down when you least expect it." A shadow crossed his face. "He didn't turn up for the gallery thingy. Left me standing." Then as if shaking it off, he asked, "Did the meeting go all right?"

"Same old, same old. They'll start washing the windows next week." There was no way she would tell her boss how she spent last night.

"Noted." He rested his elbows on the desk. "Tell me about your cruise." His mood lightened, if only a little. "If it's a good one, it might be the tonic Michael and I need."

"It runs from Naples down to Sicily, over to Greece, north to Croatia and back through a few Italian ports before finishing in Venice. I'll stay on board for the return trip to Naples."

"Who's it with?" John asked.

"It's an Italian cruise line at the upper end of the market. There are nearly as many crew on board as there are guests. They're ECM—Eleganti Crociere nel Mediterraneo—pardon my Italian. Elegant Mediterranean Cruises," she translated. "All their cruise ships are called 'Dorata-something'. That's 'Golden-whatever'…"

"I've heard of them," John said, nodding. "We bid for some of their port-side services when they planned to expand into this region, but they seem to have it locked up. When do you leave?"

"Tonight. Melbourne to Dubai and on to Rome. I'll take a train to Naples the next day."

"Naples, huh? Make sure you visit Christmas Alley—Via San Gregorio Armeno. The whole street is lined with shops selling Christmas decorations and Nativity scenes. Take your time looking around before you buy anything—chances are the next shop will have something even better." He waved a dismissive hand. "Anyway, you're practically on holiday already. Take the rest of the day to get organized."

"I'll take you up on that and leave after lunch. There are a couple of things I want to finish first." She hesitated. "By the way, I'm changing my absence to leave without pay. I filed the paperwork with HR this morning. I'd rather hold onto my recreation leave, and who knows? I might end up working on the ship for a few days. It'd be good management experience."

John gave a nod of approval. "Fine by me. Whatever you do, stay safe, and come back here to land that job and kick ass." His lips quirked in a smirk. "Just don't do anything stupid like fall in love with a handsome Italian."

Tristan laughed as she headed for the door, but the light-hearted moment didn't fully shake the unease creeping into her thoughts. She'd had the chance to explain her real reasons for this trip but had held back. John was in an odd mood today. It wasn't like her to keep secrets, but something told her this wasn't the time to share the truth.

Just as she hadn't told Luc last night.

Neither man needed to know and neither would, unless something went terribly wrong. She'd cross that bridge if it ever appeared on her horizon.

* * *

There were advantages to a solitary lifestyle, Tristan thought, pulling the door shut behind her that evening. The airline chauffeur had arrived at the appointed time, knocked once, collected her luggage, and whisked her to the airport with silent efficiency.

At check-in, she bypassed the economy queues, heading straight to the business-class counter before breezing through Immigration. On a previous trip to Siena, she'd flown economy—never again. The endless shuffle through security and passport control had been enough to make her vow that, as soon as she could afford it, she'd always fly business. Tonight, her priority express card granted her an even smoother passage. Heaven.

In the lounge, she ordered a glass of sparkling wine and a small plate of cheese and crackers As the attendant handed them over, movement beyond the trellised partition caught her eye. A tall man inclined his head toward the check-in counter.

Tris froze.

It couldn't be Luc.

She strained to get a clearer look as he strolled toward the far end of the lounge, but the partition blocked her view. Her pulse pounded. She was being ridiculous. Wishful thinking, maybe? She'd made her choice—set her own rules. Luc was already in her past.

She took a deep sip of wine, willing her racing heart to slow.

Rich, privileged men weren't her style. It wasn't just the memory of her Navy colleague who'd broken her heart—she barely remembered his name. It was the entitled attitude of the wealthy that made her bristle. The way they used and discarded people without a second thought. A therapist would have a field day analysing why a girl who'd grown up in the welfare system held such a grudge.

Then again, wasn't she indulging in a little privilege herself?

She sipped her wine. Maybe. But she had a defence ready if anyone challenged her: she needed to be sharp when she landed. Long-haul economy seating left her body twisted into knots for days.

Sighing, she pulled her tablet from her carry-on, flipping it open. If she focused on catching up with world news, maybe—just maybe—she could stop thinking about dilemmas she couldn't control.

As soon as the airline display switched her flight status from 'open' to 'boarding,' Tris gathered her belongings and made her way to the gate. There was plenty of time, but she liked to be early—organized, settled, and ready to put her personal flight plan into action.

The business-class cabin had a 1-2-1 seating configuration: single window seats on either side and pairs in the centre. Her last-minute booking had landed her in the middle section.

A retractable privacy screen between the seats sat in its lowered position. She left it that way. Sleeping on planes could feel claustrophobic enough without an extra wall closing her in. Hopefully, her seatmate would feel the same—if not, she'd have to live with it or spend the night sitting up.

A steward approached with a welcoming smile, offering a glass of sparkling wine and a menu. "I'll return shortly to take your meal order," he said, before moving on.

Tris sank into her seat, took a sip of wine, and scanned the menu. She planned to have dinner later—syncing her meal with Dubai's time zone to help adjust. For now, some nuts with her drink and a movie would do.

She was weighing her options—Moroccan-spiced lamb or surf 'n' turf with beef fillet and king prawns—when a thud landed beside her.

A bag hit the seat.

She glanced over the divider, and her breath caught.

Honey-caramel eyes locked onto hers.

Luc's arms stilled mid-motion as he lifted his carry-on into the overhead compartment. A slow, knowing smile spread across his lips.

"Hello," he murmured. "Waiting for me?"

Tris carefully placed her glass on the shelf beside her and met his gaze head-on.

"It is you," she said.

His gaze dropped—lingering at her mouth.

"Yes," he said. "It's me."

"And you're here all the way to Dubai?" Her heart thumped.

"Nowhere to stop between here and there," he said, stowing his bag before dropping into his seat. Without hesitation, he took hold of her hand.

Tris froze. The heat of his palm sent a pulse of electricity through her skin, igniting memories—his body sliding against hers, the press of his mouth, the way he made her feel.

"Bella." His voice was low, teasing. The smile in those honey-caramel eyes curled through her stomach like a slow-burning flame.

She yanked her hand away, sitting back sharply. Control. She needed control. This man had a way of slipping past her defences, and if she wasn't careful, she might never recover.

"We said goodbye." Her voice came out steady, firmer than she felt.

Luc's smile deepened. "Have a pleasant flight," she added, retreating into the menu, flicking him a quick, dismissive glance.

"That's it?" He tilted his head, amusement flickering in his gaze. "You're—what do you Aussies call it? —blowing me off?"

She forced her expression blank, batting her lashes for effect. "Is it a novel experience for you?"

His smile faltered, just a fraction, before the steward arrived to take his drink order.

Tris used the moment to scroll through the entertainment system to focus on anything but him. A movie. A documentary. Hell, an in-flight safety video would do. But his presence pervaded her space—his scent, his warmth, the weight of his gaze lingering on her.

Her fingers jabbed at random buttons on the control. Then—warmth. His hand covered hers, strong and sure.

A sizzle shot through her body.

Luc leaned in slightly. "Relax." His voice was smooth, coaxing. "I can't jump your bones on the plane—even if we both wanted to. Let's just enjoy the flight, hmm?"

Her breath hitched.

Slowly, she met his gaze. Nodded.

But as her eyes flickered to his mouth—lingering for a fraction too long—she grabbed her wineglass and knocked back the rest in one gulp.

The steward returned, clearing the cabin for departure.

Tris grabbed the headset from the console beside her seat and slipped it on. Time to get back to her personal flight plan: snack with movie, dinner, sleep, snack, movie, breakfast, and—if there was time—one more movie before Dubai. She'd honed this routine over years of travel. It kept her organised, in control.

Determined to project the image of being fully engrossed, she selected a recently released James Bond action flick.

The safety briefing interrupted her, followed closely by take-off. She loved this part. The raw power of the engines, the force pressing her back into the seat as the plane thundered skyward—it always sent a thrill through her. Eyes closed, she let the sensation wash over her.

As the plane levelled out, she sighed, opened her eyes, and reached for her headset—only to catch Luc watching.

"Enjoy flying, do you?" His eyes twinkled with amusement.

"Oh, yeah." Tris grinned. "Always have, always will."

She flicked him a quick smile before turning back to her movie.

Just as she lost herself in the on-screen action, a light caress on her arm made her jump. She shot Luc a sharp look. He was watching her like she was the most entertaining thing on board.

"Yes?" She kept her voice neutral, flipping her headphones off.

Luc gestured toward the steward beside him. "Richard would like to know our meal preferences and when we'd like dinner."

She pressed her lips together so she didn't snap at him. 'We'? There was no 'we'.

Turning to the attendant, she said, "I'll have some nuts and the New Zealand Sauvignon Blanc for now. Then, the beef with the Coonawarra Cabernet in about two hours. Thanks."

She offered a polite smile, then refocused on her screen—only to grit her teeth when Luc added smoothly, "Dessert? Right. Sì, she'll have the pavlova, I'll have the cheese. Coffee for both of us. Thank you."

Hmph. He was making menu choices for her now?

Her head snapped toward him.

Luc just smiled. Smug. Unapologetic.

This was going to be a long flight.

Tris grunted under her breath and pressed play on her movie. She replaced her headphones, pointedly ignoring Luc as she focused on her movie. When her wine and nuts arrived, she blocked out everything but the sounds of the entertainment. By the time the credits rolled, her body demanded she uncoil herself and stretch her muscles.

She strolled the length of the cabin and back, taking her time before returning to her seat. As she did, she caught sight of a steward setting Luc's table for dinner. A moment later, another attendant adjusted her tray and lay out her own meal.

Luc raised his wineglass. "Alla tua buona salute," he said smoothly. "And a smooth flight."

Tris hesitated, then clinked her glass softly against his. She could be gracious.

Luc dined as though they were at a fine restaurant, not high above Australia—or wherever they were now. They had been in the air for nearly three hours, which meant they were likely over Western Australian airspace.

Fine. She'd play along. It could just as easily be a corporate function, and he was the stranger randomly seated next to her.

"Are you spending time in Dubai?" he asked.

"No. It's a transit stop. You?"

"Heading home to Italy for a couple of weeks."

Ah. The odds of meeting him again so soon were already astronomical, but now they were on the same flight, with adjoining seats? Too coincidental.

Her instincts prickled. Siena's phone call had put her on high alert. Yes, they had used the old phones, but if someone was watching Siena, it wouldn't take much to track the call. If her friend was under surveillance, then anywhere she frequented—including her apartment—could be compromised.

Tris forced a neutral expression. No need to let Luc see where her mind had gone.

"Did you watch a movie?" she asked, steering the conversation away from destinations and plans.

He nodded. "One of those action thrillers you skipped over. What are you watching next?"

"Next? I sleep."

Luc tsked. "Too soon. You can't sleep right after a meal. You'll have nightmares. My nonna told me so, and she was right about everything." His faux-serious expression nearly made her laugh.

"Oh? And what would your nonna suggest?"

"Watch something light. Let your body relax. Then you can sleep." He leaned in conspiratorially. "Preferably a comedy classic you've seen a million times—so you don't have to think, just enjoy."

His charm was impossible to ignore. Damn him.

The steward returned, replacing Tristan's empty appetizer plate with her main meal. Her mouth watered at the sight of a perfectly seared scotch fillet, crowned with three plump king prawns.

"If I ate like this every day, I'd have to run up the stairs to work instead of taking the lift."

Luc chuckled.

"You work in the building where we met, yes?" His eyes twinkled, and he lifted his brows slightly at 'met.'

Tris kept her expression neutral. "Obviously."

"What do you do?"

Her internal alarm bells rang louder. She took a slow sip of her wine before answering.

"Office work," she said lightly. "Nothing glamorous, but if someone doesn't do it, the wheels of business grind to a halt." It was strictly true. Her work was in an office—though her goal was to climb high enough to influence policy.

She tilted her head. "Do you work there too, or were you just visiting?"

Luc's smile didn't falter. "Sometimes, yes. Other times, they send me into the field."

Tris widened her eyes in feigned awe. "Sounds dangerous."

He grinned. "No, not dangerous. We're a travel firm. My job is to ensure customers get the experience they pay for."

Right. A travel firm based in the upper floors of a building that required security access—just to select the floor in the elevator. Hardly customer friendly.

She set her knife down with a snap. "How's your steak?" she asked, switching the conversation to a neutral, no-need-to-lie topic.

"Perfect," he said, cutting into the meat. "It's amazing what they can produce in those tiny galleys."

"Have you picked your next movie?"

Luc's lips quirked. "Groundhog Day. If it's on the list, I always watch it as my nonna movie."

"Nonna movie?"

"Yeah. The movie my grandmother would tell me to watch." He leaned back, a lazy smile playing at his lips. "I know it back to front. It still makes me laugh, and, if I fall asleep part way through, I already know how it ends."

Tris grinned. "I love that movie."

Luc's gaze warmed. "Yeah?"

"Yeah." She sipped her wine, remembering. "I once sat across from an older guy on a plane who was watching it. When we boarded, he was so serious, all stiff and proper. Once the movie started, he burst out laughing. Loudly. His poor wife kept trying to shush him, but every time, he laughed harder. In the end, she gave up and started laughing at him. They both had tears streaming down their cheeks."

Luc's smile deepened. "And that's why Groundhog Day is the perfect nonna movie."

Tris chuckled. Damn him. He was impossible to dislike.

"Right. We'll watch it together," she said.

The conversation about their favourite movies carried them through the rest of the meal. Tris received her pavlova and coffee without comment, opting to enjoy them despite Luc's high-handedness in ordering for her.

When the stewards cleared their trays, Luc walked her through synchronizing their video screens.

As the opening credits rolled, she wriggled into a comfortable position. She already knew what was coming, chuckling in anticipation before the jokes even landed. When she raised a hand to swipe away a tear of laughter, Luc caught it, pressing a pristine linen handkerchief into her palm.

A flicker of déjà vu struck—just like the coffee incident yesterday. Had it really been just yesterday? So much had happened since then.

She dried her eyes, barely getting a moment's respite before the next burst of hilarity. When she glanced at Luc, she found his gaze bouncing between the screen and her face, his shoulders jiggling with suppressed laughter.

When the credits rolled, she held out the handkerchief. "Here. Thanks."

"No, keep it," he said, his voice warm with amusement. "If you dream about the movie, you might need it."

She snorted softly. "You could be right."

Standing, she grabbed the light leisure suit she'd packed for sleeping. A brief pang of nostalgia hit—she still missed the days when airlines provided complimentary pyjamas. Collecting the toiletry bag from her seat pocket, she made her way to the bathroom to change.

By the time she returned, her seat had been transformed into a fully flat bed, the doona folded neatly back in welcome. Luc had been quicker than her, already settled under his own blanket, watching her approach with hooded eyes.

As she stepped closer, he pushed himself up on one elbow, beckoning her near.

Curious, she placed a knee on her bed and leaned toward him. "What is it?"

His hand slid to the back of her neck, pulling her a fraction closer—right as a pocket of turbulence jolted the plane. She lost her balance, toppling onto him, her breath catching as their lips hovered millimetres apart.

His smile was lazy, his voice low. "Mmm. Nice."

Her palms landed on his shoulders, her pulse hammering as she tried to push herself upright. She froze. His mouth was so close, his breath warm against her lips.

Just once more.

The thought formed before she could stop it.

Her lips brushed his—light, fleeting. But the hand cradling her neck stopped her retreat. He deepened the kiss, his tongue tracing her lips, teasing, coaxing her closer.

Her body responded before her mind could argue.

Dangerous.

And yet, she didn't pull away.

Lost in the kiss, she struggled to regain her senses. Her pulse thrummed, her breath uneven. Finally, she pushed against his shoulders, breaking the spell.

Her mind raced in sync with her heartbeat. Higher ground. She should reclaim it. Yet... she had never been so completely swept away by a kiss—never lost all notion of her surroundings simply because of the press of lips.

Leaning back, she studied his face, taking satisfaction in the slight daze lingering in his eyes. Good. He was just as affected as she was.

She huffed a laugh. "That was nice. Good night." With a deliberate twist, she rolled onto her bed, putting space between them.

Luc gave a soft chuckle, then trailed a single finger down her cheek. A shiver rippled through her.

"Buona notte, cara." His voice was deep, a slow caress in itself. He held her gaze a beat longer, something dark and unreadable flickering there, before retreating to his side of the divider.

He inserted his earplugs and pulled on his eye mask, shutting out the world.

Following his lead, she settled in, sliding in her own earplugs before layering them with soft classical music through her headphones. She double-checked that her seatbelt was fastened over the doona, then pulled her eye mask down, a warm glow in her chest as she sank into the plush bedding.

The kiss was incredible, and waking up beside him in the morning? That would be a bonus.

Chapter Five

"Forty-six hours, Mr. Griff." Tristan's tone was firm, unwavering. "If I don't have a physical passport in your name on my desk, you won't be leaving port with the ship."

The man standing before her scowled, his dark brown eyes flashing with frustration even as his shoulders hunched, as if bracing for impact.

"I've explained, Ms. Sinclair," he said, his voice edged with irritation. "They didn't transfer my passport from the previous ship. It's the same company. Can't you just use the information already on file until my passport comes through?"

He'd been repeating the same argument for the last fifteen minutes. Tristan folded her arms.

"The company has no record of a passport for Nico Griff. No birth certificate. No supporting documents. Nothing except your job application." She leaned forward, locking her gaze on his. "I will not clear you for this voyage without a valid passport. I understand your inclusion was last-minute because the accountant went on leave—that's irrelevant. I have to answer to immigration authorities at every port, and any irregularities put the entire company at risk. We depart at four-thirty Wednesday afternoon. If I don't have your passport by noon on Wednesday, you're not boarding."

She tracked the tension in his jaw, the way his hands curled into fists at his sides. What part of this didn't he understand? If he'd worked on other ECM ships, he should know the rules.

With a heavy sigh, Griff finally dropped into the chair he'd ignored until now, burying his face in his hands.

"I need this job," he said on a light groan. His fingers dug into his scalp before he looked up, his glare sharpening. "I was told the passport wouldn't be a problem because the owner himself demanded I be here. I don't have the cash to throw around getting an emergency passport."

Tristan canted her head, studying him. Something felt off. Her instincts hummed, a warning note vibrating beneath the surface. Was he trying to con her? There was an almost imperceptible smirk playing at the edges of his mouth, as if he were amused at her expense. This was not a frivolous matter.

Gripping the edge of her desk, she forced herself to stay calm. Maybe Siena's warnings about trusting no one were making her paranoid, but something in this scenario wasn't adding up.

She scrutinized him again. His eyes—dark brown—distracted her in a way that unsettled her. They weren't honey-caramel like Luc's, but they triggered a familiar sensation, a low hum in her stomach. Maybe it was because she and Luc had spent the entire night tangled together in Melbourne, reminding her body of everything it had been missing. Or maybe it was the cologne—the exact same scent. That had to be it.

The reaction was irrational. This man was no Luc.

He was tall—or he would be if he weren't perpetually hunched, as if trying to make himself smaller. A strawberry-coloured birthmark, about the size of a matchbox, extended from the side of his nose beneath his right eye. It wasn't particularly unsightly, but she suspected he was self-conscious about it. His hair was an unremarkable muddy brown. His beard and moustache framed his mouth in a vertical oval, giving him a slightly dated look.

She lay her hands flat on the desk and made her decision.

"I have the authority to advance you some cash, which we'll deduct from your salary," she said. "The ship needs an accountant to assist the financial controller, but I will not jeopardize the company's credibility to make that happen. If you don't have the required documents in time, your only other chance is to join us in Sicily. You'll have to make your own way there."

Griff held her gaze, unreadable.

She leaned forward slightly. "Time's a-wasting, Mr. Griff. If you want to be on the ship when we sail, you need to get moving on your passport."

He bounded upright. "You're right. I'll need euros up front."

His sudden shift in tone startled her. Gone was the hesitant, self-effacing man—replaced by someone far more self-assured. The amount he named was consistent with the cost of procuring an Italian passport.

Suppressing a flicker of unease, Tristan retrieved the cash box from the bottom drawer of her filing cabinet. She counted out the requested sum, completed the necessary paperwork, and sent him on his way.

The moment the door clicked shut behind him, she exhaled, long and slow. Half a day into the job, and she was already dealing with crew members who thought they could put one over on the newbie. They had another think coming.

This guy—Nico Griff—the bumbling accountant with the slumped posture and oddly unconvincing awkwardness intrigued her. His appearance seemed almost calculated to be off-putting, yet something about him drew her in. There was a magnetism to him, a faint echo of Luc's pull.

Was it just because he was Italian?

Her fingers drifted to the business card resting on her desk. Luc. She'd spent the flight to Dubai beside him in an odd coincidence—if she believed in those. He'd claimed to have snagged the last seat. That was possible since Siena said there were only two available when she'd booked Tristan's.

In Dubai, they'd parted ways when he'd hurried away to make his onward connection. Her flight had been later.

He hadn't mentioned his final destination. Neither had she.

He could be anywhere in the country.

One place he wouldn't be? Standing in her office, begging for funds to pay for an emergency passport.

Tristan inhaled a deep breath, then dropped the card into the drawer and slammed it shut. Luc was a one-night stand. Period. Time to get him out of her head.

* * *

A passport in no time.

The temporary purser was relentless. Determined. Luc loved it. Who would have thought the woman of his dreams would walk back into his life with such force?

When he'd arrived at the office and found her standing there, he'd barely contained the urge to grab her, to revel in the sheer luck of their paths crossing again. Instead, he'd forced himself to play the part—shuffling, hesitant, exuding just enough self-doubt to keep her from seeing through his disguise.

Torture.

Damn, it was hard to maintain the whipped-dog act when all he wanted to do was pull her close and celebrate. But now, a nagging thought crept in.

She hadn't mentioned working for ECM. On the plane, she'd been careful with her words, never letting on that she was heading to a job—on his family's cruise line, of all places. Had she known who Luc Ricci really was? Was their seating arrangement on the flight from Melbourne to Dubai truly a coincidence?

From Dubai, they'd gone in separate directions. Or so he'd thought. Now she was here.

Was she going to help or hinder his investigation?

She was already making his life difficult. Normally, short-term hires were laid-back, more interested in coasting through their contracts than getting tangled in regulations. Fewer hassles meant more time to enjoy themselves.

Tristan was different.

She was taking the role seriously—too earnestly. His gaze had flicked to the stack of management books on her desk. The Fourth Bottom Line. Making People Feel Valued. Management in the New Age. ECM's operational framework was already ironclad, so why would a temp need those? Was she angling for something beyond this single cruise assignment?

There was no denying she was gorgeous, with those ultra-kissable lips and that sharp, no-nonsense stare, but she was supposed to be temporary. He should have been able to get around her with the "paperwork hasn't come through yet" excuse his father had suggested. She didn't even flinch.

He'd slipped toward the end of their conversation—his frustration had bled through, his voice too steady, too strong. And she'd noticed.

He needed to be more careful.

Maybe—just maybe—he should be grateful she was so damn good at protecting the company, like a real crew purser should.

If he was going to sail with the ship, he needed a passport—now—in the name of Nico Griff.

Zio Guido was his only hope.

Except, dealing with Guido was always a dangerous game.

Luc slid into a cab at the dockside taxi rank and gave the driver the address. As the car pulled away, he leaned back, weighing the wisdom of what he was about to do.

His mother, Isabella, and Guido had grown up together in a rough quarter of Naples. They weren't related by blood, but they had survived together—watching each other's backs, dragging each other out of trouble, even saving each other's lives more than once.

Both were raised by single mothers after their fathers had died in separate, violent incidents. Somewhere along the way, they had formed an unbreakable pact, helping each other claw their way through childhood.

Then their paths had diverged.

Isabella married Ettore Ricci, believing him to be a humble stevedore. And Guido? He became a leader in the underground, black market world.

Their friendship had survived everything—almost everything.

Luc still remembered the moment it nearly fell apart.

He had been a teenager, working summer shifts on one of the company's cruise ships. Before a trip to Dubrovnik, Guido had casually asked him to deliver a package to a 'friend.' Luc agreed. The friend had handed him a small token in return—something Luc thought nothing of.

When the ship docked, Isabella was waiting for him.

He had been so proud of himself, eager to tell her he had a message to drop off to Guido.

She had turned to stone.

"Show me," she had demanded.

Confused, Luc had handed over the small shoebox-sized parcel. She took one look, then stormed into Guido's office.

Luc had followed, wide-eyed, just in time to see his mother slam the package onto Guido's desk.

"Here is your package, Guido."

Her voice was like ice, edged with fury. "This is the first and the last. I will not have you using my son. My son. As one of your mules. This is my boy, Guido—leave him be."

Luc had never seen her like that. Never seen Guido look so unsettled.

On the way home, she had given him the lecture of a lifetime.

"Don't do favours. Don't ask for favours. If you ever need something from Guido, you pay. Or you get paid. Like anyone else. No favours, Luc. It must always be business."

That had been more than a decade ago.

Now, here he was, about to break her rule. Again.

Over the years, he and Guido had done many transactions.

Most recently, Luc had paid for one of Guido's specialists to alter his appearance for the job on board the Dorata Laura. Now, he'd be purchasing a fake passport and identity as Nico Griff—all to satisfy the diligent, maddeningly gorgeous crew purser who refused to bend the rules. The favour he'd ask was to get it done at light-speed.

Back in Melbourne, Luc had pegged Tristan as a secretary. He was wrong.

A person couldn't just walk into the role of Human Relations Manager on an Eleganti Crociere nel Mediterraneo ship without the right qualifications—unless they were fake.

He could check.

Neither of them had discussed work during their time together. He had kept his silence to avoid outright lying. What was her excuse?

The taxi stopped in front of a towering set of aged wooden doors, nearly six meters high and set close to the gutter. A smaller, discreet entry was built into the left panel—a meter wide, two meters high. At any other time of day, he would have gone straight to Guido's office by the docks, but Guido always lunched at home, so here he was.

Luc pressed the bell beside the smaller door and lifted his face to the surveillance camera.

A soft click signalled the lock's release.

He ducked his head, stepped inside, and crossed the cobbled courtyard into the main house. The former palazzo had once belonged to an aristocratic family and rivalled the Ricci estate in both size and grandeur.

A uniformed maid led him through a set of gilded double doors into the dining room. Though a domestic setting, the space still exuded quiet opulence—intricately designed cream-and-gold flooring with lapis blue and carnelian accents, high-strung drapes in rich gold and cobalt softening the room with understated elegance.

At the far end, a familiar voice rang out.

"Luciano, my boy. It is good to see you."

Guido's arms enveloped him in a strong embrace.

"Come," he said, leading the way to the table.

The scent of freshly cooked orecchiette drifted through the air. Luc's stomach tightened in response.

A woman bustled into the room carrying a large bowl of pasta. She barely spared him a glance before frowning deeply.

Guido turned, grinning.

"It's Luciano, Mama," he said, as if reminding his wife of something unspoken.

"Luciano?" She craned her neck, peering at him.

"Sì. Umberto does good work, no? Not even you recognized him." Guido said to Luc, gesturing toward the bowl his wife carried. "She has a cook and a house full of servants, yet she still insists on preparing lunch."

"Luciano, you will eat with us," Margherete said, setting the bowl on the table. The well-rounded form of his honorary aunt bustled toward him, wrapping him in a fierce embrace.

"If you cooked it, Zia, how could I resist?" he said, as her head jiggled against his chest.

She lifted her face and studied him. "I don't think I like this new you at all. I prefer my perfect little boy." She released him with a sigh and returned to her seat.

"You're here for business or visiting?" Guido asked, gesturing for him to sit.

"Both. Business is a good excuse to see you."

Guido nodded. "Later."

As the meal wound to a close, the maid Luc had met earlier returned to clear the table. The three diners stood.

"I'll see you tonight, Mama. I won't be late." Guido kissed his wife on the cheek. Luciano gave her a hug, thanked her for the meal, and promised to visit again in a few weeks.

Guido guided Luc to the street through the access exit as a large black car pulled to a halt beside them. Opening the back door, Guido climbed in first, with Luc following. The ride to the docks was silent.

They pulled into a spot in front of a warehouse where two burly men lounged near the entrance.

Luc wasn't deceived by their apparent indolence. The men eyed him suspiciously until Guido waved them down. "Luciano," he said, tipping a thumb in his direction.

Slow grins spread across both men's faces as they relaxed back into their seats.

Inside, Guido closed the door to his opulent upstairs office and took a seat behind his oversized desk. "Now, what had you arriving at my home in disguise, scaring your zia half to death?"

"I need a passport and documents for Nico Griff by lunchtime Wednesday—sooner if possible. Otherwise, the crew purser won't let me sail."

"Interesting. Santino's received orders for a dozen or more pass-ports to be ready tomorrow."

Luc sat forward. "What nationality?"

"A mix—mostly Filipino."

"Are they connected to the Dorata Laura?"

Guido shrugged. "Why are you on this cruise? It's unusual for you to be on your own ships. I assumed your disguise was for another com-pany."

"There's something odd going on—maybe embezzlement, maybe just sloppy processes. Papa wants me to find out what. Have you heard anything?"

"Not yet. I'll let you know if I do. Let's go down the hall to Santino, see if he can fit you in for your passport."

As a teenager, Guido began his climb through the underworld. Early on, he'd rescued Santino from the streets—a once-prized forger cast aside by another crime boss when he lost the sight in one eye. Guido had never regretted pulling him into his fledgling organization.

Luc had known Santino most of his life and had relied on his skills more than once to secure the cover he needed for his jobs.

The forger glanced up from his work as Guido pushed open the door.

"Santino, my friend. Luciano needs a new passport."

"What country?"

"It could be Greek or Italian," Luc suggested. "Whichever is quicker and easier for you."

Santino scoffed. "Nothing about this work is quick or easy. Italian is more accessible. What name?"

"Nico Griff. He's an accountant, aged about—" Luc hesitated. "Well, how old do I look in this disguise?"

Santino peered at him. "Umberto did a fine job with the face. The birthmark draws the eye, so people won't linger too long on your features. Clever." He tilted his head. "The hair's a bit dry, though. You might want to use some oil." A smirk tugged at his lips. "I'll make you thirty-six, born in Sicily—explains the greasy hair, eh?" The old man chuckled.

"Can you have it by tomorrow?" Luc asked, ignoring the jab about their southern neighbours.

"For you? Sì. The others can wait."

"Grazie, old friend."

* * *

Luc arrived at the ship just before lunch the next day, his new passport in hand.

A sudden flash of sunlight reflecting off the windshield of a black limousine momentarily blinded him. The car had pulled up to the steps leading to the gangplank. As his vision cleared, he saw the ship's captain, Venn Argstrom, holding the front passenger door open. A grey-haired man stepped out, then turned to assist a woman of similar age. A younger man followed closely behind her.

Too late to avoid them, Luc committed to walking past.

"Mr. Griff, come over here and meet the owners of the ship," the captain called out cordially. "Mr. and Mrs. Ricci, I'd like you to meet our newest officer on board. Mr. Griff is an accountant and will be working in Mr. Diamond's department."

Luc met his father's gaze.

"Mr. Griff," Ettore Ricci said, extending his hand, a knowing twitch tightening his lips. "Welcome aboard. I'd like to catch up with you at some stage to go over a few things."

"Certainly, sir," Luc replied in a deferential tone. "At your convenience and with the Captain's approval." He cast a wary glance toward his superior.

"Of course, you can meet with Mr. Ricci whenever he chooses, Griff. It's his right to know how things are running," Argstrom said in his usual booming voice.

Ettore gave a slight nod to the Captain before turning back to Luc. "This is my wife, Isabelle." He took Isabelle's left hand, giving it a light squeeze.

Her eyes flicked briefly to her husband, but he kept his focus on the new accountant. Schooling her features into polite detachment, she extended her right hand. Her gaze skimmed over the strawberry birthmark on his face. Her eyes met his—and faltered.

"Lu..."

Luc's attention snapped to where Ettore's thumb pressed into her palm—an almost imperceptible signal to those unfamiliar with their silent communication.

His mother recovered quickly, smiling. "Lovely to meet you. Mr. Griff, was it?"

She rotated his hand in hers, lowering her gaze to the scar extending from the web between his thumb and forefinger. With a featherlight touch, she brushed her thumb over the mark, her expression softening as she looked back up at him.

He had earned the scar when he was seven, after insisting he could help prepare vegetables in the kitchen. The knife had slipped, slicing deep into his hand and along the edge of his thumb, leaving a pale, two-centimetre weal.

Luc applied a bit of extra pressure to his grip—an unspoken acknowledgment of his mother's recognition—before letting her hand go.

His father continued, "My son, Sebastian."

Sebastian took the accountant's hand perfunctorily, his attention barely reaching as far as the blotch on Luc's face.

"Griff," he said flatly, then dropped Luc's hand and turned away.

Luc caught the humour in his mother's eyes. She conceded, without a word, that her younger son had failed to recognize his own brother.

"Mr. and Mrs. Ricci are here to share the usual pre-cruise lunch with us, Griff. Are you able to join us?" the captain asked.

Luc hunched his shoulders. "I'm sorry, sir, I can't. I have a meeting with the crew purser—already arranged. She needs my passport and documents before I'm cleared to sail." He flicked a sidelong glance at his father, the unspoken I-told-you-so passing between them.

His father raised an eyebrow but said nothing.

"Thank you for the invitation, though," Luc added, stammering slightly to reinforce the air of uncertainty he was cultivating.

"All right, off you go then," the captain said.

Luc kept his head ducked as he peered up at his father. "It was good to meet you, sir." He gave a jerky flick of his hand—a half-wave—before turning and scurrying up the gangplank.

"Strange fellow," Argstrom remarked behind him, "but he comes highly recommended. This way, if you please. Be careful of the step, Signora Ricci."

Luc descended to the third-level offices, reflecting on the silent communication between his parents. Thirty-three years of marriage had refined it to an art, their ability to anticipate each other's thoughts and reactions near effortless. He had no doubt that once they were out of the public eye, his father would be subjected to a thorough interrogation. His mother would demand to know why—and in full detail—how her firstborn was in Naples, aboard one of their ships, and had not come home to see her.

He chuckled to himself—then pulled up short as he reached the office floor, shifting back into character. He had to remember: he was Nico. Bumbling, self-conscious, competent Nico.

And it was Nico who arrived at Tristan's office door, where two nameplates marked her dual roles: Crew Purser and Human Relations Manager. The latter was her official title, but it was the former that most of the staff recognized.

He knocked.

"Come in."

Tristan looked up as he entered. "Oh, it's you, Mr. Griff. Do you have your passport?"

He handed it over. She added it to the neat stack of similarly pristine documents on her desk. He glanced at the pile, recalling Guido's comment about Santino's backlog of passport requests.

"Are they all crew passports?" he asked.

"Yes, new crew joining for this voyage."

"There'll be a training session for them, then. Will I need to attend since I'm transferring from another ship?"

"Yes, you will. So will I." She tapped the pile with a manicured nail. "Emily is running the briefing at oh-six-hundred tomorrow in the bar area. Judging by this, it'll be a full house. Make sure you're on time, Mr. Griff."

He gave a clumsy nod, exaggerating the bumbling shuffle as he exited.

The awkward performance he projected on the outside did nothing to quiet the restless spark of energy in his chest whenever she was near.

The Tristan in the office was composed, controlled, in command.

In ten days, the cruise would be over. When the moment came, he'd take his time unravelling that professional persona, peeling away the layers to rediscover the woman he'd known in Melbourne—the willing, enthusiastic, playful lover with whom he could spend the rest of his life.

Chapter Six

The bar area, in the early morning, still carried the lingering odour of spilled alcohol. Tris wouldn't call it a stench, but it certainly wasn't the aroma she wanted to start her day with. She rubbed the tip of her wrinkled nose with a forefinger.

The bar wouldn't open until passengers boarded later in the day. Located away from any major thoroughfares, it served as a convenient space for staff training.

Nico leaned his hip against the bar, chatting awkwardly with Emily. Only the three of them had arrived for the safety briefing. They waited fifteen minutes past the appointed time. No one else showed.

Curious.

Tardiness wasn't tolerated in the cruise industry. Safety depended on punctuality.

"Emily, put out a call for those who aren't here, please," Tris said. "None of us has time to stand around waiting for laggards."

Emily stepped behind the bar and used the below-decks public address system to carry out Tris' directive.

Another fifteen minutes passed. No one came.

It was clear now—this briefing wasn't happening.

Since Emily oversaw onboard safety, she took it upon herself to contact the supervisors of the absent crew members.

"Heads will roll if there isn't a damn good explanation," Emily muttered. "The company takes safety seriously. I won't tolerate crew ignoring it. Last time this happened, Peter Davies volunteered to run a special night briefing for new hires and reported back. He's not here this time. All new crew must go through me." She dragged a hand over her head.

"Look, from what I gather, you're both seasoned crew. I'll email you the online version. When you complete the briefing, it will automatically report back. Please do it today. Do you have any questions now? No? Good." Emily stormed off, leaving Tristan and Nico in the bar.

Tristan clenched her teeth. "We have passengers arriving this afternoon. We can't be training staff and passengers at the same time. The crew needs to be in place, ready to demonstrate competence and knowledge of the ship."

Nico hesitated. "I was wondering... were these the same crew members who had their passports delivered yesterday? I mean, are they new crew, or are they transfers, like me? If they've worked on other ships, they might not have thought the directive applied to them. Not all cruise lines insist experienced crew attend these briefings."

Tristan studied him. Should she trust him? He was new on board—like her—so he couldn't be involved in whatever was going on with Siena.

"Let's find out," she said.

They took the stairs down to the office area on level three. Tristan unlocked a filing cabinet and pulled out a thick folder.

"If I'd already filed these, we wouldn't be able to test your theory—whatever it is," she said. "Do you have the list of crew scheduled for the briefing?"

Nico nodded.

"Okay, who's first?"

"Jelvin Rodriguez. Philippines."

Tristan flipped through the passports. "Here he is. Looks brand new."

"What does he look like?" Nico asked.

"I hate to say this, but he's the stereotypical Filipino—coffee complexion, dark hair and eyes, roundish face. No outstanding features I can see," Tristan said.

"Where does he work?"

"Um, give me a sec." She pulled up the employment file on her computer. "He's part of the cleaning crew. I'll check with his supervisor to confirm he's on the ship."

Nico scratched his forehead. "Out of curiosity, how many Filipino crew do we have on staff?"

Tristan raised an eyebrow. "Why?"

"Humour me." He offered a closed-lipped smile, canting his head slightly. Was he trying to be charming? Because if he was, it wasn't working. He just looked...off—like a gangly puppy still figuring out its legs.

Huh. This guy was no puppy.

She ran a search for crew members who had listed the Philippines as their nationality. As the results loaded, she glanced at Nico—and caught a glimpse of something different. His expression had hardened, a sharp contrast to the self-conscious accountant he usually projected.

Intriguing.

She turned back to the screen. "Sixty-nine." The muscles in her brow tightened.

"What is it?" Nico asked.

She tapped the monitor. "It could just be the quality of the photos, but our Jelvin seems to be triplets. Look. His photo looks nearly identical to Bayani Andrada's and Piolo Mendoza's. Same face, different shirts."

Nico leaned over her shoulder to examine the screen.

Her body reacted before her mind caught up. Without the awkwardness of his bumbling persona in front of her, her senses knew him. His scent, his presence—everything screamed familiarity. She could feel his arms, his lips.

No. Stop it. This man is not Luc Ricci.

Then his hand brushed her shoulder, snapping her out of it. She flinched.

"Sorry. Did I hurt you?" Nico's voice, thin and uncertain, dragged her fully back to reality.

"No, sorry," she said. "My mind wandered for a second. You startled me."

The photographs of the three men were virtually identical.

"What's the point?" Nico muttered, retreating to the other side of the desk.

Tristan exhaled quietly, relieved. Not seeing him was more distracting than having him stand in front of her.

"Where do the doppelgängers work?" he asked.

"Doppelgängers—good word. Except these guys are triples, not doubles," she said, scrolling through the files. "They're all service crew. Who else do you have?"

One by one, they cross-checked the names. Every crew member who had failed to report for the safety briefing matched a brand-new passport—and had at least one duplicate image onboard.

"What's the point?" Nico repeated, frustration creeping into his voice.

"Could it be to draw two salaries?"

"If that were the case, they'd know their alternate identities and would have responded to the call for the briefing. They'd also have to be working double or triple shifts to cover for themselves." He pressed his middle finger against his brow.

"So what does someone else get out of it?" Tristan asked.

"I don't know." He pushed off the desk. "I'll check where their payments are going."

She followed him next door to his office.

"Okay," he murmured, eyes scanning the screen. "Bayani Andrada's salary is being deposited into a Philippine bank account. Piolo Mendoza's... is going through an Italian institution. Hmmm. Jelvin Rodriguez—" He paused as his computer lagged. "Come on, don't slow down now... Ah. Jelvin's salary is also going to the same Italian bank. Let's check the others."

Tristan tapped her fingers against the desk, thinking aloud. "We need to confirm who's actually on board and who's just a name on the payroll. The real crew members versus the ghosts—the fakes, the duplicates, the doppelgängers."

She reached for her phone. "I'll text Emily to arrange individual meetings with the cleaning, catering, and laundry crews as they come off shift tomorrow. We should have a full rotation ready to interview by 06:30, 14:30, and 22:30. It's going to be a long day."

"There'll be too many for you to handle alone," Nico pointed out. "And the crew won't want to hang around—they'll want food and sleep. I'll take half."

"Okay," Tristan said. "I'll have Emily split the list—half will come to me, the other half to you. We'll need a set of non-threatening questions, something casual. We'll say we're verifying contact details and payment options due to a computer glitch." She met Nico's gaze. "Which, technically, we are."

"And if they don't show?"

She shrugged. "Then we stop their payments."

Nico hesitated. "Isn't that a bit harsh?"

"This is a ship," she countered. "There's nowhere else for them to be. They're not off visiting Granny or stuck in traffic. If they're crew, they show up. If they don't, they're ghosts." Her voice was firm. "Something isn't right here, and as HR manager, it's my job to fix it. I'm not authorizing salaries for people who don't exist."

Nico drew his brows together. "We're supposed to help with the passenger tour to Taormina tomorrow."

Tristan dragged her teeth over her bottom lip, recalculating. "Then we start today. We'll interview the day and evening shifts as they finish. I'll stay late tonight. We'll catch the overnight crew in the morning before we leave. There are fewer of them anyway." She levelled her gaze at him. "Can you handle this afternoon?"

He flicked a quick thumbs-up.

"Good." Tristan turned away, already in motion. "I'll get Emily to coordinate with the supervisors. Our first 'customers' should be here by 14:30."

* * *

Nico's gaze tracked Tristan as she left his office. He clenched his fist in silent victory. Yes! And, it had nothing to do with uncovering the mystery on board.

Despite his disguise, despite everything, her body still responded to him. Her head might fight it, but deep down, she wasn't immune. That sent his ego soaring.

Being this close to her had his own body reacting—too much. He'd barely kept himself in check, using the back of her chair as a barrier. If she'd noticed... Damn it, get a grip, man. He needed to stay in character. She couldn't know who he was. Not yet.

He forced himself back to the task at hand, but then—damn it again—Tristan reappeared in his doorway, holding a sheet of paper.

She'd scraped her beautiful, long auburn hair, into an upturned ponytail. Like her, the hair would not be constrained and loose strands had escaped the tie. His fingers twitched with the memory of running through those locks, of her body arching beneath him. The crisp white uniform did nothing to hide the curves he knew by heart—her breasts, her slim waist, the smooth flare of her hips.

Hell. This woman got to him.

He caught his lips widening and forced the smile away. Stay in character. Keep it awkward, bumbling.

"Can I help you?" His voice came out too sharp.

Tristan flinched. Just for a second. But it was enough. Suspicion flickered in her eyes.

Careful, Ricci.

"No," she said coolly. "I'm sure you've thought of your own strategy for dealing with the crew." She spun on her heel and stormed out.

Nico swore under his breath and followed. "Tristan, I'm sorry. My head and heart were in different places, and my brain... well, it wasn't even present." Shit. That sounded ridiculous. He scrambled for an excuse. "I—uh—got an unsettling email. Caught me off guard."

She sat behind her desk, watching him. Silent. Waiting.

For what, he wasn't sure.

Nico recognized the tactic. Silence was one of the best tools in an interrogation—whether for an explanation or a confession. Most people rushed to fill the void, either revealing the truth or digging themselves in deeper.

He did neither. He waited.

Tristan tilted her head, lips pressed tight. Her eyes held his, unblinking.

The tension shifted. This wasn't a confrontation anymore—it was a test of wills.

Slowly, the muscles in her face relaxed. A small victory.

She narrowed her gaze, then thrust the sheet of paper at him, dismissing him with a flick of her hand before refocusing on her computer screen.

Nico scanned the interview prompts. "We should confirm their identities first," he said, keeping his tone neutral. "Start with, 'What's your full name and date of birth?' That way, we know exactly who's in front of us."

"Thank you for your suggestion. You can go now." Her voice was clipped, her focus locked on the screen. "I'll email the list when I'm done."

Dismissed.

He didn't move.

She looked up, fixing him with a sharp glare.

"Don't huff, Tristan," he said, lowering his voice. "It doesn't suit you."

A beat of silence. Then, softer, "I'm sorry about before."

He dipped his chin in acknowledgment, then turned and shuffled out the door.

* * *

Tristan refocused on developing the proforma, dismissing the brief power play with Nico. She had no idea what had prompted it. Did the man have a personality disorder? Sweetness and light one moment, a barking Rottweiler the next.

Shaking off the thought, she structured the interview sheet. The top half contained the questions, while the bottom held the correct answers from staff files. By folding the sheet, she could conceal the reference information, ensuring only the interviewee's responses were visible. Once they left, she'd quickly cross-check their answers. Any discrepancies would be flagged for immediate follow-up.

The list wasn't long. Nico's suggestion—full name and date of birth—came first, followed by:

What nationality is your passport?

When did you start working for Eleganti Crociere nel Mediterraneo?

What was the name of your first ECM ship?

What was your position then?

What is your position now?

Into which bank do we pay your salary?

The questions were neutral enough to avoid suspicion while providing crucial identity verification.

She printed a test copy using the details of the three Filipino crew members. When their identical photos appeared on the page, it jolted her.

Good grief. Had it really been only an hour since she'd uncovered this? It felt like days.

Satisfied the document was as refined as time allowed, Tristan emailed it to Nico with concise instructions on how to use it. She had barely finished compiling the list of expected crew when the first interviewee arrived at her door, forcing her to shuffle through the sheets to find the correct one.

The woman's drooping shoulders and slack expression telegraphed exhaustion.

"You just came off shift?" Tristan asked.

"Yes, ma'am, and I'm ready for my bed. There seems to be so much more to do than usual."

"I won't keep you long. There's been a glitch between shore-based records and those on board. We just need to verify a few details." She smiled, running quickly through the questions. The woman answered without hesitation.

"Thank you, Marta." Tristan stood and extended her hand. "I appreciate you coming in, and more than that, I appreciate the work you're doing. The company depends on you. Sleep well."

"Thank you, ma'am," Marta murmured before shuffling out.

Her interview set the tone for the rest. A small queue had formed outside her door, so she kept the meetings brisk. None of the crew she interviewed showed any signs of hesitation or deception, leaving her confident they were exactly who they claimed to be.

Several had not shown up.

Her stomach rumbled loudly, a sharp reminder that she hadn't eaten since breakfast. No time for food now. Overhead speakers crackled to life, calling the crew to their muster stations for the passenger safety briefing.

Tristan hurried to Deck Five, weaving through passengers carting life jackets as they assembled. Every guest was required to attend the safety demonstration once the general alarm sounded—seven short blasts followed by one long one.

Forty minutes later, she was finally free to leave. A quick freshen-up, some food, and then the obligatory officer's presence at the welcome party for the well-heeled guests. After that, she'd be back in her office, ready to interview the next batch of crew this evening.

At least the afternoon's focus had kept her mind off the strange man next door.

Chapter Seven

Stripping off in her cabin, Tristan stepped into the shower, letting the hot water pound against her tense shoulders. She kept her shower cap in place—no time to deal with a hairdryer if she wanted a quiet meal before mingling with guests and tackling the regular work she'd put aside because of the crew interviews. This whole adventure on Siena's behalf was pushing her into situations she wouldn't have chosen for herself.

When she'd boarded the ship early Monday morning, she had identified herself to the attendant before heading to her assigned cabin on Deck Three. As a junior officer, she hadn't expected much, so discovering she'd been given a single room was a welcome surprise. Private space was a rare luxury on a ship, especially a smaller vessel with a full staff. Not that she'd be spending much time here.

Walking past the other cabins, she'd noticed most doors had two or three names listed. Only one other room had a single occupant—Nico Griff. At the time, she had wondered who he was and what position he held. Now she knew.

The man was a contradiction. His sharp, assessing eyes didn't match his hunched posture and bumbling demeanour. He was a puzzle, and she had enough of those already.

A door slammed somewhere nearby, jolting her from her thoughts. She sighed, reluctantly shutting off the water.

After towelling off, she slipped into clean underwear, gave herself a generous spritz of deodorant, and pulled on the same uniform from earlier. With a quick glance in the closet mirror, she straightened her belt buckle and took a steadying breath.

What had Siena been thinking, putting her in this position?

She stepped over the small door ledge and into the corridor—slamming straight into a solid wall of muscle.

Sparks shot through her, familiar Luc-type energy.

"Oh, sorry," she gasped, stumbling back, her hands instinctively smoothing down her sides.

Not Luc. Nico.

"Heading to dinner?" Nico's voice rumbled through her, sending a frisson of energy straight to her chest.

"Yep. Starving," she said, tamping down the butterflies in her gut.

His smile was almost her undoing. There it was again—that contradiction. Who was this guy? And why did he make her feel like a teenager on her first date?

He leaned back against the wall, gesturing for her to walk ahead.

They arrived at the mess at the same time as two of the cruise's gentlemen hosts.

"Fresh meat!" one of them declared, and before she could react, they each took an arm and whisked her toward a table.

Bewildered, Tristan hesitated—partly amused, partly horrified. Should she assert her position as an officer? Before she could decide, one pulled out her chair while the other helped her into it with exaggerated courtesy. Then, as if choreographed, they settled into the seats on either side of her.

She turned her gaze from one to the other, trying to suppress a grin.

"Oh, how dreadfully rude of us," the silver-haired man said, his English accent crisp and polished. "We haven't been introduced. I am Nicholas." He gestured toward his companion. "And this is James."

James extended a hand, his smile warm. "A very great pleasure to meet you, madam." His lilting accent was difficult to place—Scottish, perhaps, or Irish.

Tristan shook his hand. "Good evening, gentlemen. I'm Tristan Sinclair, the human relations manager. And... fresh meat?"

Nicholas waggled his eyebrows mischievously. "We're always on the lookout for new victims to practice our teaching techniques on." He cocked his head. "So, you're the HR manager? Wonderful." His eyes sparkled. "Tell me, lovely Tristan, do you dance?"

"I'm not on board to dance, I'm afraid," she said lightly.

"But when given the opportunity...?"

She chuckled. "I'm more of a 'throw-my-body-around-in-any-direction-I-please' kind of dancer."

"With your innate grace, I'm sure we could have you quickstepping and foxtrotting proficiently before we reach Venice. What do you think, James?"

"Definitely," James agreed with a twinkle in his eye. "With a good Scottish name like Tristan Sinclair, you'll be a natural, lass."

"We'll make it a date," Nicholas announced. "Seven-thirty every morning for forty-five minutes, and we'll see how we go."

She leaned back, raising a sceptical brow. "I have work to do."

Nicholas waved away her protest. "Oh, my dear child, even on a ship, they don't expect you in your office before nine."

The conversation paused as the waiter arrived to take their orders.

Once the menus were out of the way, Nicholas picked up where he'd left off. "We're teaching Emily too. It's such good fun. A pity about Siena—she was coming along well. Do you know her?"

"I'm standing in for her, I believe," Tristan replied, choosing her words carefully as Nico slid into the seat opposite.

"We can tell you she's lovely, engaging, and oh so gentle with souls like us—who are neither fish nor fowl as far as the crew purser is concerned."

"What do you mean?" she asked.

"We're not employees, but we're not guests either," James explained, his gravelly Scottish accent becoming more distinct as he spoke. "As Gentlemen Hosts, we pay a small fee to be on board. In return, we act as volunteers, keeping the real paying customers happy. Siena understood that contradiction. She made us feel like part of the team. That's not always the case."

"Why do you do it, then?"

"For me, I get to see the world," James said. "My flat in Edinburgh stays booked through short-term rentals at a better rate than if I leased it permanently. And if I ever want to go home early, it's waiting for me."

Tristan's gaze flicked between them, inviting both to elaborate. "And when you're not doing this?"

Nicholas was the first to answer. "I'm a professor of physics at a certain university in London. It's a job I quite enjoy—moulding young minds, igniting the Newtonian spark. But the cruises? They give me a complete break for a couple of months each year. Here, I dance, chat, and harmlessly flirt with hundreds of ladies—without taking any of them home or paying their bills."

"What about you, James?"

The Scot tilted his chin. "I wear a few different hats across various businesses, but the most reliable one is private finance. I help people achieve their dreams when they need a little financial boost."

"We call him Shylock," Nicholas teased with a growling chuckle.

James smirked but didn't protest. "Like old Nick here, I enjoy socializing with the lovely ladies on board. I lost my Mary six years ago. I'm not looking to replace her, but I do appreciate good company."

"None of your ladies has tempted you to change your mind?" Tristan asked.

"Ach no. None could hold a candle to my Mary." His expression softened briefly before he added, "Some try to be persuasive, of course, but we've been trained to handle that. If things get tricky, I signal one of the other hosts, and we help each other out. We all like what we do, and none of us wants to jeopardize our position."

As their meals arrived, Tristan flicked a glance across the table at Nico. He hadn't contributed to the conversation, but he was paying attention. The moment her eyes met his, he shifted his focus back to Nicholas, who continued explaining their role.

"We make sure no lady on board ever feels left out or lonely," Nicholas said. "For some, this is their first time venturing out into the world after losing a husband, or something similar. It's important they feel included—but not overwhelmed. We host tables at dinner, dance with them, join them on shore excursions, but we never—ever—sleep with them or make any one woman feel more special than the others."

"That must be a fine balance," Tristan mused. "Especially if you have needy women around."

"It is," Nicholas agreed. "But like Jimmy said, we're not about to risk our job—or our reputation—on someone we might never see again after a ten-day cruise. Our actions reflect on all the hosts. It's just not worth it." He pressed his lips into a grim line.

"Random question," Tristan said. "If you're hosting a dinner table, why are you eating now?"

The hosts exchanged a knowing smile.

"Because we won't actually get to eat," James explained. "We'll be at the table, but our job is to engage everyone. For the first few nights especially, that means doing most of the talking."

Tristan groaned. "Now I feel guilty for making you talk all through your meal."

Nicholas offered a mock-malevolent smile. "We've signed you up for dance classes in the morning. Consider it revenge."

"It'll have to wait until Friday, I'm afraid. I have crew meetings from six tomorrow. Then Nico and I are heading to Taormina with one of the shore groups."

"Friday, then. We use the bar area to practice—no one's in there in the mornings. We'll see you then."

With a nod to both Tristan and Nico, the hosts left.

Tristan turned to Nico. "What did they mean when they said they pay for the privilege to be here?"

He was more experienced with other ships and might have a better sense of what the men had meant.

"The bottom line?" Nico said. "They're self-employed. They pay the cruise line a daily rate—roughly the cost of breakfast—which covers shared passenger accommodations with another host and access to the same facilities as the guests. In return, the cruise line gets cheap labour and happy clients. Win-win. They work long hours—shore excursions during the day, then entertaining guests late into the night."

"Something you'd like to do?" Tristan teased.

Nico hunched his shoulders. "I'll stick with numbers, thanks. Are you really going to learn to dance with them?"

"This whole experience is something I never expected. So why not?" She set her cutlery neatly on her plate. "Do you dance?"

"A little."

"You should come along for practice."

"I'll think about it," Nico said, though his expression suggested he'd do anything to avoid stepping foot on a dance floor.

Tristan smirked. "It's dancing, not an execution."

He gestured toward her glass. "More wine?"

The tilt of his lips might have been a smile. His dark eyes shone in the light, igniting a warmth in her chest. She didn't need wine to heighten her senses around him. When he smiled like that, it reminded her too much of Luc.

"No, thanks. One is enough. I have a long night ahead. I'll take a coffee."

"Dessert?"

"Not tonight."

Nico signalled for the waiter and ordered their drinks.

They drank their coffee in companionable silence, then strolled through the mess hall and into the bar area to mingle with the guests, unsure what curly questions might come their way.

Chapter Eight

Tristan and Nico returned to their offices in time to meet with the evening shift crew. Neither made it to their cabins until well past midnight. By a quarter to six the next morning, they were both back at their desks, ready for the next round of interviews.

The morning followed a familiar pattern—crew members arrived tired but direct in their responses. Again, there were names on the list who didn't show. By nine o'clock, the number of missing interviewees had grown significantly.

Tristan strolled into Nico's office, where he was tracking salary disbursements. Together, they sifted through the records, searching for links.

"Okay, this is what we've got," Nico said, tapping his thumb on the desk. "The crew we've seen have their salaries paid into accounts in their home countries. It's trickier for those who haven't appeared." He shifted the screen toward her. "Their salaries are all being deposited into one of two accounts at a bank in Naples. At first glance, it wouldn't seem suspicious, but, when you lay it out like this, the pattern becomes clear."

Tristan studied the screen. "You're right. The coincidences are too big to ignore. These people don't exist, but the company is paying them." She rapped her knuckles on the desk. "Someone is running a scam, and the crew on board are suffering for it."

Her phone rang in the other room. She ignored it, holding Nico's gaze. A second later, Nico's phone lit up. He put it on speaker.

"Good morning," a cheery voice greeted them. "This is Shelley, reminding you to be ready to board the tenders in five minutes. Do you know where I can find Tristan? She's not answering her phone."

"Ah, yeah. We're just wrapping up a meeting," Nico replied smoothly. "I'll let her know. We'll see you soon." He hung up.

"Damn. I forgot all about Shelley." Tristan scrubbed a hand over her face.

Nico's expression darkened. "I think we should keep this to ourselves until we know exactly what's going on and who's behind it."

There was something different in his tone—an edge of quiet authority replacing his usual restraint. Tristan narrowed her gaze.

A slight blush rose on his neck.

"We'd better get down to Shelley," she said, letting it slide for now. "I'll duck into my office and change into jeans and a T-shirt to blend in with the other tourists."

"I'll see you outside in two minutes?" he asked, his usual hesitation returning.

"Okay," she said, and dashed through the door.

They reached the departure area moments before the first guests arrived. Shelley directed them to the second lifeboat-turned-tender, ready to ferry passengers to the dock at Giardini Naxos.

Nico took Tristan's hand to steady her as she climbed over the side, ducking her head to enter beneath the solid canopy of the craft. A familiar zing sizzled up her arm at his touch.

The only other person who had ever affected her like this was Luc. Was she suddenly susceptible to the touch of any man? She'd have to do some research on that. She mentally smirked at her own wayward thoughts. It might have shown on her face given the lift of Luc's eyebrow in her direction.

Two tour groups, of fifteen guests each, filled the tender, along with Nico, Tristan, and two entertainment staff—the professional ballroom dancers. Even at rest, the dancers seemed governed by some internal choreography, their movements fluid, their posture effortlessly poised. Years of training had imprinted elegance into their very being.

Tristan envied them.

With more than thirty people on board, the tender wasn't overly crowded, but Tristan still sought out the seat beneath the hatchway so she could see out and avoid feeling closed in. The crossing was smooth, taking less than fifteen minutes.

Onshore, Nico and Tristan introduced themselves to Carlotta, the middle-aged tour guide, as the assigned crew members for the group. Carlotta gave them a quick double thumbs-up before taking her place on the internal steps of the bus.

With a warm smile, she raised a laminated white card from the dashboard, identifying the bus as serving guests from the ECM line. The name of their ship, Dorata Laura, was printed in bold.

Theirs was Taormina tour number three: Tao 3.

"You must find a purple bus, then check—ECM, Laura, Tao3. Okay? It is important," Carlotta emphasized, scanning the group. "Today, there are several ships in port, even our own Dorata Isabella on her way to Naples. Many buses, many tours. You might easily be confused, so please check carefully. ECM, Laura, Tao3."

She lifted a green circular paddle with a large white number three. "This is my guide paddle. Remember it. Now, let's get underway."

Settling into a jump seat near the driver, she launched into her spiel, pointing out the peculiarities of Giardini Naxos, a village steeped in history dating back seven hundred and fifty years before Christ.

"Our first stop is the village of Castelmola, perched high on the hill overlooking Taormina and the bay of Giardini Naxos, where our ship is moored," she explained. "This medieval town was founded to protect the people of Giardini Naxos from repeated invasions. In fact, when Dionysius the Tyrant arrived in 403 BC, he found the villagers had fled to escape subjugation. Enraged, he ordered the entire town to be destroyed. I think they were wise to get out of his way, no?"

A few guests chuckled.

"We will have forty minutes to explore Castelmola. The town is compact, built in tiers around a castle designed to shield its people. You may climb to see the castle ruins, visit the Duomo with me, or wander through the narrow streets in search of a café. I highly recommend sampling the local almond wine—it is very popular.

Her gaze swept the group. "Now, listen carefully. The bus cannot wait where it drops us off. Piazza Sant' Antonio is small, and we are not allowed to park there. You must return five minutes before the bus is due, so we can board efficiently."

As the guests disembarked, Tristan turned to Carlotta. "What do you need from us?"

Carlotta waved a hand. "Go for a walk, have a coffee. Plenty of little cafés here. Just keep an eye on the time and stay near your phone. Make sure you can hear me if anything happens. It never does, but just in case..."

With a quick nod, she raised her paddle and led the group toward the Duomo, her voice carrying over the cobbled streets.

Tristan stood beside Nico, on the lookout for stragglers until the group disappeared around a bend.

"Wow, look at this view," she murmured, leaning over the piazza railing to take in the stunning panorama. Far below, the sea stretched out in glistening blues. Their ship—a sleek contrast to the colossal floating cities anchored nearby—bobbed gently on the water.

Nico pointed toward Taormina, nestled below them to the left. "That's our next stop."

A hush had settled over the town, broken only by the occasional gust of wind and the distant murmur of tour groups.

Tristan exhaled in awe. "How on earth did they get everything up here to build this place? We must be at least five hundred meters above the sea, and these hills are steep."

"It would have been a challenge," Nico mused, shifting his weight as he rested his arms on the railing. "When your home and family are threatened, what else do you do?"

The sun glinted off the dark hairs dusting his strong forearms. As he leaned forward, his polo stretched across his broad shoulders, tapering down to his slim waist. His toned legs were framed by expensive-looking designer jeans. Interesting. He'd given the impression he was broke, needing this job. So who was he really? The jeans could be knock-offs... but they looked real enough. Tristan kept the thought to herself.

She pulled out her phone, panning the camera from left to right, capturing the winding roads leading down to Taormina and the coastline stretching beyond. The last few shots included Nico—unaware, relaxed.

They turned as one and wandered deeper into the alleyways.

Tristan paused in front of a street stall, puzzled by a display of keychains—each adorned with tiny, brightly painted wooden penises. Baskets overflowed with them, in all sizes and shades, though red seemed to be the local favourite. Some were decorated with flowers and rhinestones, others bore animal engravings, while a few were left plain. Must be some cultural significance, she thought. They were everywhere.

The town was waking up slowly, with only a few cafés open. As they strolled down a narrow street, the familiar hiss of steam from a coffee machine filled the air.

"I hear coffee," Tristan said.

Nico quirked an eyebrow. "You can hear coffee?"

"Absolutely." She followed the sound, stepping into a small bar and heading straight for the counter. "Caffè?" she asked in her limited Italian.

"Sì," the barista answered with a smile.

"Due cappuccini, per favore."

"In cups or mugs?" he asked in English, amusement dancing in his eyes.

Tristan grinned. "Mugs, please."

"Take a seat. I'll bring them over."

She turned to find Nico already settled in a small booth by the window, a knowing smirk playing at his lips.

"You could have let me order," he said. "I happen to speak Italian very well, have done since I was a baby."

Slapping a palm to her forehead, she groaned. "Urgh. I didn't even think. I'm just used to doing things myself."

"Sometimes," he said, his gaze steady, unreadable, "others can help."

Something in his tone made her pause, but before she could analyse it, her attention drifted to the cozy, dimly lit space around them. Heavy wooden furniture filled the café, the low lighting coming from scattered lamps.

Then she froze.

The lamp stand on their table was unmistakably shaped like a penis.

Her gaze darted to the ashtray. Another one. The painting on the wall? Ditto. Everywhere she looked, phallic imagery stared back at her.

Heat flared in her cheeks.

What is it with this town and penises?

She wasn't a prude, but she had never seen anything quite like this. There was nowhere to look.

Tristan darted a glance at Nico, whose shoulders shook with silent laughter.

"You knew?" she accused.

"I'd heard of this place," he admitted, eyes twinkling. "I'd never seen it for myself."

"The coffee had better be good."

"But it is, signorina," a deep, teasing voice cut in.

The waiter, all smirk and charm, placed two steaming mugs in front of them. Tristan's face warmed even more.

Nico chuckled—a rich, unexpected sound that sent a ripple of warmth through her. Her stomach did a somersault. That laugh. It had turned her inside out before. But where?

Images flashed through her mind—watching Groundhog Day on a plane, the hum of an engine, quiet laughter in the dark. No. This man was not Luc. Her heart was playing tricks on her. Maybe Nico was just another quintessential Italian male, no matter how hard he tried to mask it with his stooped posture and greasy hair.

Tristan hesitated before picking up her mug, checking the handle—half-expecting it to be shaped like everything else in the café. Satisfied, she took a sip. Ah, ambrosia. Rich, hot, dark, and fragrant. A quiet moan of pleasure escaped her lips.

The shift in Nico was immediate. His laughter faded, his posture stiffened. He cupped his hands around his mug, eyes darkening as he watched her.

The air between them tightened.

Tristan dropped her gaze, focusing intently on her coffee. They sat in loaded silence, sipping their drinks, neither acknowledging the sudden tension.

When her cup was empty, she checked her watch. "We should get back."

At the counter, the barista was waiting, smirk still in place.

"The coffee, signorina," he drawled. "It was to your taste?"

"Yes, thank you. It was wonderful." She twisted her lips, glancing around. "The rest was... unexpected."

The knowing gleam in his eyes deepened. "You were very brave, signorina."

Before she could respond, he produced two small glasses and poured a pale golden liquid. Leaning forward, he slid them across the counter, his gaze locked entirely on her.

"This will help you recover from the shock."

Nico stood at her shoulder, ignored.

Tristan hesitated, then took a cautious sip. The almond wine was smooth, sweet, with the warmth of a good liqueur. "It's lovely. No wonder it's famous."

"As is our caffetteria," the barista said smoothly. "You must come again. Bring some friends." He winked. "Do not warn them, eh?"

She chuckled.

Nico's voice cut in. "I'd like to buy a bottle."

The barista finally turned his attention to Nico, breaking the strange little game he'd been playing.

As they stepped outside, the man called after them, "Come again, signorina. I will be waiting to serve you."

"Not bloody likely," Nico muttered.

Tristan blinked. "Sorry? Did you say something?"

"Just going over things to be done." His tone was light, too casual. "If we hurry, we can visit a souvenir shop. My mama collects magnets—for the fridge. She likes to track where I've been."

He lifted his shoulders in a slight shrug, then let them settle into their usual slouched position.

Interesting. Maybe there were depths to this man beyond being an eccentric accountant.

The souvenir shop had more than just the infamous keychains on display.

Tristan picked up a deck of cards featuring images of the town, thumbing through the glossy pictures. She would have loved to buy one of the risqué keyrings—just for the sheer absurdity of it—but with Nico standing nearby, she decided against it.

Back at the palazzo, they found their bus driver locked in a heated argument with a traffic warden, a stout woman, radiating authority. She brandished her ticket book in warning while the driver barked back in frustration.

Tristan and Nico exchanged glances before slipping onto the bus unnoticed.

"What's he saying?" she murmured.

Nico chuckled. "He's reminding her how much the town relies on tourists and that she should be grateful he even brings his bus up these 'rickety roads.'"

Satisfied he'd had the last word, the driver slammed the door shut and pulled away.

In the rearview mirror, he caught Tristan's eye and waved her forward. "Carlotta is late. Call her and tell her to meet us at the alternative location."

Tristan returned to her seat and dialled Carlotta, suppressing a smile. She suspected Samson had no interest in facing the traffic warden again—not even for their tour guide.

The bus rumbled along the winding roads, pausing at turnouts to allow oncoming cars to pass. Eventually, they rounded a bend where Carlotta waited with a small group of guests. Once the last of them boarded, the journey to Taormina resumed.

Tristan slid into the vacant seat behind the guide. "Everything okay? Samson couldn't wait—traffic warden trouble."

Carlotta glanced over Tristan's shoulder, as if ensuring no one was eavesdropping. "In this job, you learn that there are always those who ignore the set time. That's why we have a backup plan. If you're late, you walk down the hill to the next stop." She chuckled. "Perhaps I should have warned them. Might have kept them punctual, eh?"

Tristan nodded.

"Did you enjoy the town?" Carlotta asked.

"I did," Tristan replied. "It's quaint—and impressive how they navigate such narrow passageways." A beat of hesitation. "Carlotta, can you explain the town's fixation with penises?"

Carlotta blinked. "With what?"

Tristan searched for a clearer way to phrase it. "You know, the male organ? The dangly bit men have, and we don't?" She gestured vaguely. "We had coffee in—"

Understanding dawned across Carlotta's face. "Ah. That café?" She threw back her head and laughed, then reached into her handbag, pulling out a large red phallus.

"I have been asked about these," she said, holding it high. "Can you see what I have?"

A mischievous cackle erupted from a grey-haired woman in the row behind them. "Oh yes. I bought three."

"For those wondering about their significance…" Carlotta paused theatrically. "There is none. It's a gimmick. A café owner decided to have some fun, and the word spread. Now people come to Castelmola to see for themselves. The souvenir shops joined in, adding their own flair—more colours, more sparkle." She wagged a playful finger. "Did they tell you the red ones are the most virile?"

Laughter rippled through the bus.

"They are not, sadly." Carlotta grinned. "But it's good fun. Now, on to Taormina. No more penises, but plenty of history." She gestured through the window. "To our left, you'll see the rocky path the Saracens once used to travel between Castelmola and Taormina."

Just like that, she was back on script.

Tristan slid into her seat beside Nico.

"For you," he said, handing her a small brown paper sack. "A memento of our visit. Unless… you don't think it's appropriate?" He hunched his shoulders slightly, as if bracing for rejection.

She peeked inside. A beautifully decorated, mid-sized red phallus, encrusted with white and green diamantes, glinted back at her.

A rogue chuckle escaped her lips. "Without context, maybe not. But I was too shy to buy one for myself." She canted her head. "Now, every time I open the secret compartment in my purse, I'll remember that café."

Their gazes locked.

The warmth that rushed through her was unmistakable—the same inexplicable zing she'd felt before. That Luc-like familiarity. But they were different men.

She dipped her chin, breaking eye contact before the moment stretched too long.

"Thank you," she murmured, tucking the bag safely into her purse. A small, unexpected glow of appreciation settled in her chest as the bus rolled on.

Chapter Nine

Tristan brought up the rear with Nico as their group of sightseers followed Carlotta through the streets of Taormina. The guide exuded pride as she recounted the town's rich history and its significance to Italy's story.

Holding her green paddle high, she led the group along Corso Umberto, where shop displays and café chairs spilled onto the thoroughfare, past the baroque fountain in Cathedral Square, and up the narrow streets to the ancient Greek Theatre. Her monologue rarely paused, except to check that everyone was keeping up. Some of the older guests, however, were struggling with the steady incline.

"If you keep going, we can rest a little further along," Carlotta called.

A few muttered reluctant agreement and pressed on, while others decided they'd had enough and veered into the nearest café. Carlotta sighed. "What a pity," she said. "Now they will not see it. Just another three hundred meters, and there is a place to rest."

At last, the group reached the entrance of the Teatro Greco. Carlotta distributed their tickets before leading them up a steeper incline into the open-air, tiered colosseum. "You see?" she said, gesturing to the stone seating. "Now you can rest while I explain the history of this magnificent place."

With the group settled and Carlotta in full lecture mode, Tristan retraced their path to check on those who had chosen not to continue. Nico fell into step beside her as they reached the ticket office. By their count, five passengers were missing. Their search was complicated by the presence of several other ECM tour groups, each following different coloured paddles.

They stopped at the first café they came across but found no sign of their group. As they stepped back onto the bustling street, a voice called to them from farther down.

"Hey, you two. Are you heading back to the bus?"

Tristan turned to see the elderly woman who had proudly announced her souvenir purchases from Castelmola.

"More or less," she replied.

"Good. Can you help me with these guys? They're pooped. I couldn't just leave them," the woman said. "I'm Betty, by the way."

"Hi, Betty. I'm Tris, and this is Nico," Tristan said. "I can wait with these guests if you'd like Nico to take you up to the theatre."

"No thanks. I've seen it before and no doubt I'll see it again." Betty turned to the woman beside her. "Come on, Marianne. On your feet." She coaxed her friend up with a firm but kind touch. "Are you alright, Olaf?"

The older man nodded.

"Good. We're meeting back at the post office, right? That's what the guide arranged? We'll head there," Betty said.

Nico offered his arm to Olaf while Betty guided Marianne down the street. Tris trailed behind, checking the coffee shops and souvenir stalls along the way. She finally located the other missing couple in a small café near the post office, leisurely sharing a pizza and a glass of wine. Behind them, a tiny black kitten mewed plaintively from a banquette, ignored by both the café owner and the patrons.

Tris pulled out her phone and sent a quick message to Carlotta, letting her know the rest of the group had been found. She was slipping her phone back into her bag when it rang.

"Matthew, hi," she answered, recognizing the number for their direct boss on board. His voice held an apologetic note.

"Sorry to bother you, Tris. I've been trying to get hold of Nico."

"One moment, I'll pass the phone to him."

Nico's conversation was brief. "Yes? Understood. Certainly. No, no trouble at all. Goodbye."

He returned the phone, frowning. "I've been asked to authorize a consignment of wine and spirits from a local trader. Matthew doesn't have time to handle it, and apparently, Davis usually does it."

"I'll come with you," Tris said. "Our guests are happy here. How come we're dealing with a merchant in Taormina? Isn't everything arranged ahead of time in Naples?"

"The company's always sourced regional provisions when possible," Nico explained. "As long as the quality meets standards, they prefer to support local economies for the same reason we bring tourists to smaller ports. Some places wouldn't survive without the extra income."

Tris nodded, turning the information over in her mind. He certainly knew his facts. Had he read that in company policy, or was he just that well-informed?

They found the trader tucked down a side street they hadn't yet explored. A low, narrow doorway led into a cavernous space, dimly lit and more warehouse than storefront. Behind the counter, a wiry man leaned on his elbows, watching them with a neutral expression.

Nico approached him. "I'm here to authorize the ECM shipment."

The merchant nodded toward a small stack of cartons. "There's your lot. Invoice is ready. Sign here."

Nico hesitated. "I'll check the contents."

The merchant's eyes narrowed. "Why? Mr. Davis always trusts me."

"Yes, sir, but I'm new on the job, and I have to do things by the book for now." Nico hunched his shoulders, projecting a nervous deference.

The man sniffed, as if detecting an unpleasant odour over the lingering scent of old wine. "Alright, alright. Suit yourself. I'm not going to stand around while you do it. Call me when you're done." He strolled away, disappearing through a doorway.

Nico grabbed the invoice and methodically lifted each heavy carton to check its contents. Tris silently admired the way his muscles shifted and tensed with the effort. She'd noticed it back in Castelmola too. His physique—strong, controlled—seemed at odds with the self-effacing, bumbling persona he projected.

"Yes, it's all here," he said, glancing over the final box. "Though it's a bit on the expensive side." He muttered the last part under his breath as he stepped behind the counter, following the direction the merchant had gone.

The man stuck his head back around the door. "Everything as it should be?" he asked, a trace of sarcasm in his tone.

Nico gave a curt nod. "The invoice matches the goods."

"Then sign here, and your people can pick it up whenever they like."

Nico scrawled his signature on the paperwork, then tapped the invoice. "Out of curiosity, these prices seem high."

The merchant shrugged. "Not when you add it all up. You don't have a dolly with you, so where do you want me to put Ms. McFarlane's stock?"

Nico stilled. "Ms. McFarlane's?"

Tris frowned. "Where is it?"

The man jerked his thumb toward a smaller pile in the corner—three cartons of wine and a couple of separate bottles.

Tris eyed the boxes. "Can you confirm they're separate from the main order? We'll have it collected with the rest. I'll make sure it gets to her."

"Mr. Davis usually takes them with him," the trader said. "So they don't get mixed up."

"Where's the invoice for those?" Nico interjected.

The man sneered. "Ah, friend. You are green, eh? There's no invoice for that lot. It's all included." He tapped the side of his nose.

Nico's frown deepened. "Right," he said slowly. "I'll let the ship know to collect the goods."

They stepped out of the dimly lit shop, the heavy scent of aging wine giving way to the warm breeze outside. As they strolled back toward the post office meeting point, Nico cast a sideways glance at Tristan.

"Do you know this McFarlane person?"

"She's the purser I'm covering for. Injured on the last cruise—won't be back until after dry dock." Tris kept her tone even. Siena's warnings echoed in her mind.

Trust no one.

It had been half a joke, Siena parroting their favourite '90s cult TV show. But Tris had sensed her unease—something was off, and Siena had been wary, even afraid.

"She likes her wine," Nico mused. "Good stuff. Premier restaurant stock."

"I wouldn't know," Tristan said. That was a lie. Siena barely touched wine. She was a beer girl, always had been. Stockpiling expensive vintages? That didn't add up.

They arrived at the café to find their group still seated, their numbers swelled by other passengers who had abandoned the trek to the Greek Theatre. Betty, ever the self-appointed leader, held court at the centre of the gathering.

"Come have a drink, kids," she drawled, her glass lifting in an unsteady salute.

"We appreciate the offer, ma'am," Nico said, flashing an 'aw shucks' grin. "We'll stick to water. The boss frowns on drinking on the job."

Betty hooted with laughter.

Tristan was relieved no one had caught them sampling the almond wine in Castelmola.

"Ah, sit down anyway," Betty waved them over, her hand moving in an exaggerated arc.

Tris leaned against a vacant banquette, watching the older woman through narrowed eyes. "You okay, Betty?"

"Sure," she slurred. "Might've had a glass too many, but in this heat, ya gots to, y'know?"

The conversation stuttered as Betty squinted at Nico, closing one eye as if trying to focus.

"Ya know?" she mused. "You can get those growths taken off these days. Bit of surgery, maybe. I don't think laser would work—it's too big. Ya know? You could be quite handsome if you got rid of it."

A heavy silence fell over the group. All eyes flicked to the bright pink birthmark on Nico's face.

Nico met Betty's gaze, his expression unwavering. "It's who I am, ma'am. If I got rid of it, my mother wouldn't recognize me." He smiled, polite but firm.

Tristan pushed off the banquette. "You're right, Betty—it is hot." She glanced at Nico. "I need something colder than water. There's a gelateria across the street. Do we have time for an ice cream?"

Without waiting for a response, she looped her arm through his and steered him toward the shop.

Nico let her lead him away, amusement flickering in his eyes. "I thought you agreed with Betty," he said.

Tris shot him a sideways glance. "It's your business."

They reached the gelateria, and she turned her attention to the display case. "Rum and raisin. Yum. Would that count as drinking on the job, Nico?"

A rich laugh spilled from him, warm and unguarded. As always, it sent a strange, electric flutter through her—an unsettling mix of nerves and exhilaration. A Luc feeling.

She forced her focus back to the selection of flavours.

A server asked Nico for their order. "Double rum and raisin, and a double limoncello," he said, his voice firm, authoritative.

Tristan flicked a glance at him.

He shrugged.

With their cones in hand, they paused under the overhang, savouring the cool, sweet relief of gelato. Tristan wiped her fingers with the paper napkin that had wrapped her ice cream, brushing off the last traces of stickiness. She had no desire to return to Betty and her merry band, so she scanned the narrow street for an excuse to linger.

The green paddle appeared, bobbing toward them. Perfect.

She crossed to the group. "Carlotta's coming. Let's head to the post office so she can find us easily."

A flurry of movement followed—the restaurateur sorting bills, and the passengers hastily gathering their belongings before shuffling toward the designated meeting point.

Betty required extra assistance boarding the bus. "Let me help you onto the tender, Betty," Nico offered. Without hesitation, he scooped up the petite woman and carried her onto the craft.

The return trip to the ship was, thankfully, uneventful. As soon as they checked back in with security, the passengers dispersed, vanishing into the vastness of the vessel.

Tristan exhaled. It had been a long day—starting with crew interviews, followed by playing tourist. And the afternoon wasn't over yet.

Back in her office, she slipped off her jacket, draping it over the back of her chair before powering up her computer. Her mind was elsewhere—on the man she had just left.

What was it about Nico? His appearance wasn't conventionally attractive, nor was his slow, almost whiny-mournful way of speaking. Yet... there were moments when something else surfaced. A quiet confidence. A sharper edge. The barest touch between them sent jolts through her, as though her body recognized him before her mind could catch up.

Then there was the gift.

She retrieved it from her bag, turning it over in her palm. Objectively, it was inappropriate—arguably even provocative. In another context, it might have been considered borderline harassment. But here? It was something else entirely.

He had noticed her hesitation at the shop. Had known she wanted a souvenir but hadn't bought one. So he did it for her.

Sweet.

She burrowed through her bag, tucking the keyring into the secret compartment next to the black phone.

Shaking off thoughts of Nico, she focused on the growing pile of tasks before her. Hours passed unnoticed until the ship's engines rumbled to life beneath her feet.

The digital clock in the corner of her screen startled her.

Lordy, she was due at dinner in less than half an hour.

She had to move.

Chapter Ten

As a ship's officer—even a temporary one—Tristan was required to help host the Captain's Welcome Dinner, a formal affair demanding full dress uniform.

Her assigned table included two couples from the premier suites. Co-hosting with her was her boss, Ricardo Catalan, the Hotel Manager. He had climbed the ranks within ECM, starting as a cleaner before working his way through nearly every hospitality role on board—kitchen hand, server, junior steward, restaurant manager, human resources, purser—until he now held the highest hotel position on the ship. He answered only to the Captain, though even the Captain often deferred to him on hotel operations.

Catalan had already made his feelings about the event clear.

"The last thing I need after a full day is three hours of playing nice with overprivileged patrons," he'd grumbled. "But if we can get them to post positive reviews, it might help offset the recent negative ratings. We need to stop the slide."

He cast a pointed look at her. "I trust you'll hold up your end of the social chit-chat, young lady. We're hosting the VIP guests from the Royal Suites. The Captain has the Venetian aristocrats—I'm glad he got them."

"What do we know about our guests?" Tris asked.

Catalan glanced at his notes. "Two Australian university professors—you can handle them. Then there's an elderly English couple who are regulars on our cruises. I've never hosted them, but I'll keep them entertained."

Tristan smoothed her skirt, adjusted her epaulettes for symmetry, and straightened the swallow-winged tie at her throat. Growing up in the welfare system was a far cry from the trappings of a moneyed background, but Tris's Navy years had taught her how to navigate all levels of society. She had mastered the art of small talk, developing a script that needed only minor tweaks for a cruise-ship audience.

"Where are you from? Has the cruise lived up to your expectations? What do you do for work? What drew you to it? Do you have children? Are they grown? What do they do?"

When the well ran dry, she could always fall back on travel stories. And if Catalan—stoic and businesslike in meetings—seemed uncomfortable, she had a plan for him too. She'd steer him into discussing career opportunities in the cruise industry, the benefits of the diversity of the crew, and the camaraderie on board.

Satisfied with her mental preparations, she stepped out of her cabin—nearly tripping over a box of wine.

Across the narrow corridor, two crewmen were unloading cartons into the vacant cabin opposite hers.

"Party?" she teased.

The men straightened at the sight of her uniform, though one grinned in return.

"No, ma'am," he said in a thick Geordie accent. "Not much chance of that. Mr. Davis would have our guts for garters if we helped ourselves to more than our share."

"I thought this was Ms. McFarlane's wine," she remarked.

"Doesn't much matter whose name's on the label," he replied. "It all ends up here, and Mr. Davis sorts it."

Her gaze flicked to the door. "Who's assigned to this cabin? I haven't seen anyone in there."

"It's empty, ma'am. There were a few no-shows this time. There's always a vacant cabin or two down this end."

"There were some separate bottles, too. Did they make it?" Tristan asked.

"No, ma'am. Those are for us—our pay for doin' the job, like," one of the crewmen replied with a casual shrug.

Before she could respond, Nico stepped out of his cabin. His gaze narrowed as he took in the scene.

Tristan squinted at him. "Good evening. You scrub up well."

His hair still looked too slick, but the fresh shave and crisp uniform gave him an air of authority. His navy jacket fit like a glove, highlighting the lean strength beneath. She dragged her attention away from his frame to focus on what he was saying.

"Hmm. What's going on here?" he asked the crewmen.

"Don't put them through the third degree again. I already did," she said, stepping around a wine carton to move ahead of him down the narrow corridor. "Let them get on with their work."

"Was that the wine addressed to McFarlane?"

"Yep, but the crew made it sound like Peter Davis is the one who really controls it. They said it didn't matter who it was addressed to—Davis deals with it. Whatever that means." She shook her head. "He's an accountant. What's he doing handling wine?"

Nico frowned. "Interesting."

"Did you see the names on the cabins?" she asked. "I didn't think about it earlier, but I can check later."

"I haven't," he admitted. "I figured the crew was on shift whenever I was here. You can go a whole cruise without seeing some people."

"The way the crewman talked, it sounds like there are always no-shows in this section. Almost as if someone already knows exactly who won't show up." She paused. "Sorry. Thinking aloud. Bad habit."

He gave her a measured look but said nothing.

"Who's your co-host tonight?" she asked instead.

"I'm with Shelley. I won't have to say much." He smirked.

"Don't be so sure," she teased. "She'll probably ask you about to-day's excursions so guests can compare notes or get inspired for next time." She fluttered her eyelashes at him playfully.

He groaned, shoulders sagging. "Great."

"Maybe not," she said with a shrug. "Forewarned is forearmed. Oh, and ask Shelley if Nicholas and James have subjected her to their dancing lessons yet. That way, I'll know what to expect tomorrow."

"I'll find out what I can." His slow smile was unexpectedly disarming—one of those rare moments when his charm broke through his usual reserve.

If Luc had smiled at her like that, her knees might have given out.

She studied Nico for a second longer. She liked him, she decided. She'd like him better if he straightened his shoulders and carried himself with confidence. But, since she wasn't planning on marrying the man, she'd deal with him as he was.

"Any idea who you're entertaining tonight?" she asked.

"No clue. If it's not too unkind, am I allowed to hope it's not Betty?"

"You'll cope. I liked what you said earlier about not changing too much—your mother wouldn't recognize you." She canted her head. "You still have your mother?"

"Yes, and she worries if I do anything too strange. What about you?" he asked.

She glanced away, then spotted their destination. "Ah, here we are. Good evening, Milosz. I'm at Mr. Catalan's table."

Milosz, ever efficient, nodded. "Indeed, Ms. Sinclair. You're the first to arrive." He turned to a waiting hostess. "Milena, please escort Ms. Sinclair to table thirty-five." Flipping a page, he glanced at Nico. "And you, Mr. Griff... yes, table twelve. Radoslaw will escort you. Ms. Smithson is your co-host. Enjoy your evening."

Tristan wove her way through the elegantly set tables, their white linens pristine, silverware gleaming under the chandeliers. French drapes over the fake windows softened the illusion of enclosure, back-lit to create a glow of artificial light.

An Australian couple in their mid-fifties arrived at her table, the woman in a cream-colored sheath dress, her husband in a dinner suit.

"We're university professors," they told her in response to her query. "Taking the cruise to celebrate our thirtieth wedding anniversary."

Tristan smiled warmly. "That sounds like a wonderful reason to celebrate. Congratulations."

"You're Australian?" the woman asked, eyes bright with curiosity. "There must be a couple of hundred people on board this ship, and you're the only other Australian we've met. Isn't she, Jack?"

Jack nodded. "Not many of us about."

Tristan smiled. "There are a few Aussies among the crew, but yes, we're definitely outnumbered."

Their conversation was interrupted by the arrival of the second couple. Older than the Australians, they carried themselves with a relaxed ease. Once introductions were exchanged, Shirley, the Australian, leaned forward conspiratorially.

"We've been commenting on the range of nationalities on this cruise—among both the crew and the guests. Tell me, do the Brits still count themselves as Europeans these days?"

Tristan caught the twinkle in Shirley's eye. She was baiting the table, and sure enough, the discussion quickly escalated. The English couple had strong opinions—and not in favour of England's European ties.

Shirley held up a finger, clearly ready to lob another verbal grenade, but Tristan smoothly intervened. "What do you do, Mr. Smith?"

"Call me Arthur, Miss," he said with a hearty nod. "Joanie and I had a hardware business in Hertfordshire. We sold it seven years ago when it got too much for us. We've taken a cruise every year since—mostly with ECM. Always good, eh, Joanie?"

"Aye," Joanie agreed. "Never had cause to complain. Well, until now."

"It's wonderful to have you with us," Tristan said warmly. "It appears something has delayed Mr. Catalan, but we shouldn't wait for him. Let's go ahead and order. He'll catch up when he arrives. As our Hotel Manager, the only part of the ship he doesn't oversee is the deck, so you can imagine how many things might demand his attention. My apologies on his behalf."

She signalled for Milena, the ever-efficient server, who approached swiftly. Her presence steered the guests toward their menus.

For a few moments, silence reigned as they made their selections. Milena refilled wine and water glasses as she took their orders.

Shirley frowned. "Aren't you going to write it down?"

Milena gave a polite smile. "No, ma'am. That's not the way we work. If I get it wrong, you can let me know."

Shirley looked sceptical but rattled off her choices.

Please, Milena, get it right, Tristan pleaded silently.

Once the orders were dispatched, conversation resumed. Tristan guided the English couple into reminiscing about their previous cruises—the best, the worst, and how this one compared.

Arthur sighed. "If I'm honest, the service hasn't been as great as earlier cruises. The cleaning feels rushed, and the staff don't have time to chat like they used to. It's not as personal."

"Aye," Joanie agreed. "We've had worse experiences with other lines, but ECM was always the standout. Something's changed, and it's not good, is it, Arthur?"

Tristan nodded. "Thank you for your honesty. I'll pass your feedback along. What is it that keeps bringing you back to ECM?"

The shift to a more positive topic helped steer the discussion onto safer ground, just as the first course arrived—along with the Hotel Manager.

"My apologies for being late," Ricardo Catalan said as he pulled out his chair. "Please go on with your meals while I organize something for myself."

Tristan beckoned Milena over.

"Whatever you think, Milena," Ricardo said, rubbing his temples as if still preoccupied with other matters.

"Certainly, sir. I'll be quick."

True to her word, she returned in moments with a bowl of chowder and crusty bread—before the rest of the table had made it a quarter of the way through their course.

Ricardo still seemed distracted, so Tristan smoothly took the lead, introducing each guest again, summarizing their backgrounds and interests.

At the mention of the hardware business, Ricardo's attention sharpened. "My grandfather had a hardware shop," he said. "When I was a boy, he'd spend hours teaching me about tools—how to use them, how to store them. He had sayings for everything. There are no bad tools, only poor operators. Or, you can judge a man by the way he treats his tools—a worthy man handles them with respect."

Arthur let out a satisfied grunt. "Aye. Your granddad was spot on, I'd say."

A sense of ease settled over the table as Ricardo engaged with Arthur, their shared appreciation for craftsmanship forging an unexpected connection.

As the main course wound down, Ricardo's pager beeped. He glanced at the screen, then immediately excused himself. "Enjoy the rest of your evening," he said, rising. "And please don't hesitate to email me if you have any concerns or suggestions."

Shortly after dessert and coffee, the English couple stood to leave. Tristan stood too. Following Ricardo's lead, she said, "If there's anything I can do to make your experience better, please let me know."

Arthur nodded. "You've been a delight, Miss Sinclair."

The Australians, however, remained seated. Tristan settled back in her chair, not quite ready to leave either. Shirley studied her with sharp, assessing eyes.

"I like you," she announced. "It takes an intelligent woman to do what you did tonight."

Tristan arched a brow. "Play hostess? Women have been doing that for millennia."

Shirley chuckled. "Not always with your grace and wit, my girl. Where did you go to university? Somewhere in Australia?"

"Yes. My first degree was at ADFA."

"The Defence Force Academy?" Shirley's eyes gleamed with interest. "Navy, I'm guessing?"

"Correct."

Shirley held her gaze for a moment longer, as if piecing together a puzzle. Then she nodded. "Right. Well, there's a show in the theatre tonight we want to catch. Thank you for hosting us. I hope we'll see more of you in the coming days. Good night."

Tristan watched them go, then absently traced the stem of her wineglass, waiting until they were clear of the area. Finally, she rose, thanked Milena and Milosz, and made her way to her office.

A light glowed beneath Nico's office door. She knocked twice.

"Come in," his voice called.

She stepped inside, raising her brows as she leaned against the doorframe. "What are you doing here at this hour?"

He smirked. "Probably the same thing as you—trying to make sense of what's happening on this ship." He rubbed his temple. "And catching up on everything I didn't get to today because of our doppelgängers."

"How did you go?"

He took a deep breath. "I can't figure out the motive. The wine stored in our corridor might be a clue, but I haven't cracked it yet. And my actual workload? Not even close to done." He shook his head. "I'll be here for a while."

"Me too," she said simply, then left him to it.

* * *

Nico's gaze followed her until she disappeared from sight. He exhaled sharply, forcing his attention back to the screen, willing his heartbeat to steady. Never in his life had he met a woman like Tristan Sinclair—one who could send his pulse skyrocketing without even touching him. Just her presence was enough.

The sooner he could shed this ridiculous identity, the better.

He worked for another eighty minutes, but the warmth of the office, the steady hum of the engines, and the ship's gentle roll lulled his body into fatigue. His head drooped over the keyboard. A sharp knock at the door jolted him awake.

"Yes?"

"It's nearly midnight. The rest can wait. I'm going to bed," Tristan said from the doorway.

"I'll come with you," Nico replied, powering down his computer.

She chuckled. "I don't think so."

"What?" He glanced at her, still half in work mode.

"I don't think you'll be coming to bed with me," she clarified, amusement dancing in her voice. "Good night."

Several retorts flashed through his mind, but they were Luc comments—not to be aired. Instead, he grabbed his jacket. "I'll walk you to your cabin."

They strolled in easy silence, passing the officers' mess, crossing the open lift lobby, and heading down the corridor toward their rooms. Then, the ship pitched suddenly, sending the weary Tristan off balance. She stumbled straight into him.

Nico's arms wrapped around her instinctively, steadying her. Her soft curves pressed against his chest, her breath warm against his neck.

She moaned quietly, resting her head on his shoulder for the briefest moment. Then, in the softest whisper, "Luc."

The single word sent a jolt through him.

As if suddenly aware, she straightened. "Sorry. Can't even blame my wobbly boots."

"Wobbly boots?" he echoed, his voice husky.

"Aussie expression." She waved a hand. "I'll explain when I can think. Thanks for catching me. Good night."

She unlocked her door and slipped inside, leaving him standing there, pulse hammering.

He hadn't wanted to let her go.

She might not know the truth yet, but her heart did. In that brief moment, she had known him. If he had his way, one day soon, she wouldn't have to question it.

For now, though, he had to keep up the charade.

The time would come.

And when it did, he'd make damn sure he was there to catch her—not just in the hallway in her 'wobbly boots,' but always.

Chapter Eleven

Tristan was in her office by six the next morning as the ship eased alongside the port of Corfu. She had stripped out of her uniform the night before, fallen into bed, and slept straight through.

A long, reviving shower had her ready to face the day. By convention, day three meant casual attire in the office, but, with staff interviews continuing, she opted for her uniform—adding a layer of authority, even if it meant enduring the dreaded dance lesson in it.

She interviewed five more crew members. When no one else appeared, she checked the corridor. Empty.

Sighing, she grabbed her untouched coffee, now cold, and made her way past Nico's office. His voice carried through the door—he was in a meeting.

In the mess, she filled a plate with bacon, eggs, and toast. Breakfast was the only meal the ship didn't serve à la carte, and today, she was grateful for it. She needed ten minutes without thinking, without talking.

She was cradling her coffee when Nico slid his tray onto the table across from her. She didn't speak, recognizing his need for quiet as much as her own.

Slipping out of her seat, she went to refill her coffee. His tray lacked its usual black brew, so she poured one for him, too.

"Thanks," he muttered, without looking up. He exhaled. "I don't know how teachers do it."

"Hmm?"

"This—nonstop talking, one-on-one meetings, trying to keep track of who's who. Teachers do it all day with a couple dozen people demanding their full attention. And they have to teach them something." He shook his head. "I'll stick to numbers." A tired half-smile tugged at his lips. "At least they don't talk back."

"Numbers can be cruel, though," she said.

"Not as cruel as people."

Tristan let that slide, checking her watch. "I've got a dance lesson soon. Nicholas and James said it'd be forty-five minutes."

"I'll come, too. Maybe if I get my body moving, my brain will follow."

They sat in companionable silence for a few more minutes, finishing their coffee. When they finally pushed their chairs back at the same time, she glanced at him.

"Okay, Nico. Smile."

He frowned. "Smile?"

"Yes. You look worried. Only you and I need to know anything's amiss. So, smile. We're going to a dance lesson, and we're going to have fun."

"I guess." He forced his mouth into something vaguely resembling a grin.

Tristan burst out laughing. "Maybe not."

His expression softened into something far more natural, and for the first time that morning, he looked less burdened.

They arrived in the bar to be greeted by James.

"Here you are, lovely Tristan. And you've brought your own partner—how wonderful." He clapped his hands together. "Nicholas and I were concerned, you see. Both Shelley and Emily are coming, and we didn't want anyone left out. Do you dance, young man?"

Nico's shoulders lifted slightly, as if retreating. "A little."

"Well, that's something to build on. Come along. Let's see what you've got before the ladies arrive. A waltz to begin—one, two, three, one, two, three—you know?"

Nico gave a short nod, almost reluctant.

Tristan stepped into his arms, resting her left hand on his shoulder, her right slipping into his. The moment their bodies connected, an electric buzz whipped through her.

James started the music. "Here we go, and…"

Nico guided her effortlessly across the floor.

Tristan barely recognized herself. She had always considered herself hopeless at dancing, yet here she was—gliding, turning, moving as though she belonged in his arms. His confidence steered her, their steps in perfect synchronization. And their closeness…

Each turn pressed her body to his, her thigh momentarily slipping between his legs. Was that—?

Heat shot up her neck. She glanced at his face. He was staring past her, his jaw clenched, throat working as he swallowed. But he didn't pull away. If anything, his hold tightened, his fingers pressed into the small of her back as they moved together, locked in a rhythm that felt stolen from a dream.

The music swelled. If they were in a movie, this would be the part where the whole world faded away, leaving only them.

She sighed, allowing herself to follow wherever he led.

As the song came to an end, James let out an exaggerated huff. "You are a fraud, young man. And you, Tristan. There's nothing to improve there."

Tristan lingered in the warmth of Nico's arms. "I'm a hopeless dancer," she murmured. "That was all him. He took control."

James beamed. "As a man should. Not many women surrender so easily on the first go on the dancefloor. You two—" he waved a dramatic hand "—are a match made in heaven."

Tristan opened her mouth to protest, but before she could, James brightened.

"Ah, here are Emily and Shelley. Right, let's move on to the fox-trot."

As Nicholas called out the steps, Nico led her seamlessly through each movement. Every turn, every shift, every brush of their bodies sent a new wave of awareness through her.

He wasn't just good. He was too good. She wasn't sure whether that was thrilling—or dangerous.

Time sped past until James called a halt. "Rightio, folks, that's all for this morning. Same time, same place tomorrow." He stretched his arms. "Nick and I need some breakfast before we take a group through Corfu Town."

"Yes," Shelley added. "Nico, Tristan, you're with the group visiting the Paleokastritsa Monastery. Make sure to cover your shoulders and legs." She shot them a knowing look. "I've given you the short run to-day—you'll be back onboard for lunch. You're not allergic to cats, are you?"

"No, why?" Tristan asked.

"They're everywhere at the monastery," Shelley said. "Check before you sit down. I'll see you by the buses in forty-five minutes."

Calling their thanks to James and Nicholas, Nico and Tristan returned to their offices.

"I need to tackle some of my actual work," Tristan said. "Can we pick up the mystery after the excursion?"

"Sounds good. Even thirty minutes on my real job will be a mira-cle," Nico agreed.

An hour later, they stood on dry land, helping passengers board the bus for the steep climb to the headland. A full group of forty tourists had signed up for the monastery visit, Betty among them. She looked no worse for wear after her adventures in Taormina the previous day.

Once the passengers were seated, Tristan and Nico climbed aboard. The only available seats were at the very back, where a five-seater banquette was already partially occupied. A rather large man took up the middle seat.

Tristan squeezed past him into the corner, leaving Nico to wedge himself into the remaining space—nearly on top of her. Without a word, he slid an arm around her shoulders, easing the pressure of being crammed together.

The downside? Every movement of the bus sent his body jostling against hers. After their morning dance lesson, her senses were already on high alert. Usually, being penned into a small space made her anxious. As if sensing it, Nico directed her attention to the passing scenery, keeping her engaged.

The bus climbed higher, and Cristana, the tour guide, paused her commentary. Betty seized the lull.

"Last time I did this trip to the monastery," she began, loud enough for everyone to hear, "we went to a taverna for lunch. The food was nice, but they had this couple doing Greek dances. The girl hardly smiled, and the bloke—oh, he was all Opa! this and Opa! that. I swear, every time he kicked his leg, I could see clear up to his crotch. And he kept getting closer to me! Trying to shock me, he was. All too much for my poor old heart. I decided to skip it this time."

A ripple of laughter spread through the bus.

Cristana picked up her spiel before Betty could add more.

"The monastery is built on two levels. At the top, you'll find the church, dedicated to the Virgin Mary. Shoulders and legs must be covered. If you haven't dressed appropriately, coverings are available to rent.

"There is also a well on the upper level," she continued. "They say if you toss in a coin, you are destined to return."

"Must it be a Greek coin?" Betty asked.

Cristana smiled. "No, no. Any coin will work—if you truly believe in the magic."

She glanced out the front windshield as the bus slowed. A red light ahead forced them to stop.

"Hmm," she murmured, pursing her lips. "The road to the monastery is very narrow. Two vehicles cannot pass at the same time. We must wait for the one coming down before we continue."

At last, the bus rumbled into the monastery car park. A young man stood guard over a pile of scarves and skirts, ready to be rented by those whose attire didn't meet monastic standards. Thanks to Shelley's briefing, the ECM passengers had come prepared.

Betty, her small frame surprisingly sturdy, helped the same woman from yesterday up the incline. "Come on, Marianne," she urged. "You'll love it. Olaf can spend half an hour staring at the icons in the museum, and you can do whatever Catholics do when they go to church. It's a beautiful building—eighteenth century, I think."

Marianne murmured something Tristan didn't catch.

"Me? No, I'll pop into the shop, see what they've got," Betty said. It's a pity there's no café, but I'll pick up some of that cumquat stuff and sit quietly among the cats—my kind of bliss." She paused. "I threw a Greek coin in the fountain last time, and look—I'm back. Must've worked. I'll try a dime this time."

Her voice trailed off as she wandered toward the entrance.

Nico and Tristan strolled behind the passengers, taking in the serene surroundings. The scent of olive trees and incense drifted through the air.

Tristan caught her foot on an uneven cobblestone and stumbled. Nico's hand shot out, steadying her. Instead of letting go, he simply held on.

A familiar jolt of energy shot through her—Luc-like, unmistakable. She didn't pull away.

They explored the church together, moving in quiet synchronicity. When they reached the fountain, Nico pressed a coin into her palm. Tristan glanced up, questioning.

He only shrugged, his fingers still wrapped around hers.

Without breaking eye contact, she tossed the coin into the water.

They moved on to the lower level, where the museum housed Byzantine icons and relics steeped in history. Eventually, they climbed back to the upper courtyard, where Cristana was gathering the group.

Beyond her, Betty dozed under a shady tree, a half-empty bottle of cumquat liqueur at her side, two cats curled up against her.

Nico and Tristan exchanged a knowing smile.

Nico released Tristan's hand to tap Betty's shoulder.

The elderly woman blinked up at them, bleary but content. She turned to Tristan. "Did you try the cumquat stuff? So-o-o relaxing." She stretched into a luxurious yawn.

"Would you like me to carry your bag, Betty?" Tristan asked.

Betty sighed happily. "That'd be lovely, Button. And if your young man can help me up, I might even make it back to the bus before I fall asleep again."

As the group ambled toward the car park, Betty leaned heavily on Nico's arm.

The large man from their ride up stood by the bus door, watching them approach. "I'll let you guys go first so you don't have to climb over me," he offered.

Tristan smiled in thanks as Nico helped Betty into her seat. She tucked the woman's bag beside her, careful not to crowd her legs.

With Betty settled, Tristan moved ahead of Nico to the rear of the bus.

A flicker of anticipation of being wedged against him again for the ride back curled in her stomach.

She slid into her seat, unable to fight the small quiver in her chest.

Chapter Twelve

As the last two guests exited the back row of the bus, Nico slid across the banquette, allowing Tristan to step ahead of him into the aisle. The bus jolted, slamming their bodies together. Heat surged through him, tightening his muscles as memories of their night together spiralled through his mind.

Control yourself.

He needed a moment—just a few seconds—to rein himself in. He couldn't afford to let Luc take over, not yet. No matter the temptation, he had to stay in character until this was resolved.

Bracing his hands on the seatbacks in front of him, he pushed himself to his feet, falling into step behind her.

Near the door, Cristana stood beside Betty, supporting her. "She says she's feeling 'woozy,'" Cristana explained.

Tristan crouched slightly to look Betty in the eye. "Got your wobbly boots on, Betty? I know what that feels like. Can we help you?"

The woman blinked, her expression blank.

Nico glanced at Tris, raising a brow. "Wobbly boots?"

She winked.

With a small smirk, he took Betty's arm and retrieved her bag from the guide. "I've got her," he said. A few minutes out of his day was no great inconvenience. Besides, he couldn't ignore the possibility that she might fall or hurt herself.

He helped her up the gangplank and onto the ship. Tristan pivoted toward the office stairs, and he gave her a quick wave before leading Betty to her cabin.

A senior steward, clipboard in hand, closed the door to an adjacent room as they arrived.

"Wait here a moment," Nico told the steward before stepping inside with Betty. He settled her in front of the television and handed her the glass of water she'd requested.

Ushering the steward into the corridor, Nico lowered his voice and glanced at her name tag. "Sonia, can you check in on her every half hour?"

Sonia let out an exasperated sigh, her expression tight with frustration.

"What is it?" he asked, slipping into Luc's voice.

Her shoulders rose with another heavy breath. "We're stretched too thin. It's not your fault, or hers, but we don't have time for babysitting."

"I'm not asking you to neglect your other duties. I'm telling you to check in on an important client every thirty minutes. It's the kind of service Eleganti Crociere is known for."

Her brows drew together. "Used to be," she muttered.

His gaze sharpened. "What's changed?"

"I'm supposed to have eight team members, including myself. I have six. Doesn't sound like much, but when you're dealing with fussy or demanding passengers, it adds up fast. We're drowning. Nobody listens. They claim the numbers are there, but the staff aren't." She clutched the clipboard to her chest. "It's probably the bloody owners cutting costs and pocketing the extra, all while we break our backs trying to do the job."

Her voice wavered with suppressed frustration. "My team used to get consistent five-star ratings for our service. We've slipped to three.

Three. Not because we're bad at our jobs, but because we can't keep up. It's not fair. I'm not staying here if they keep treating us like this. Dry dock is coming up. I'll figure out my options then."

She looked close to angry tears.

Nico listened, his mind racing through possible solutions. "I'll look into it," he said.

She let out a short, cynical laugh. "Yeah, right."

"Sonia." His voice held steady authority. She paused, her shoulders sagging. "I said I'd look into it, and I will. Do you know the names of the missing staff? If it's not breaching confidences or anything?"

Her mouth twisted. "You can't breach confidences of people who don't exist." Her gaze flicked to his attire, a frown forming. "Who are you? You're not in uniform."

He held out the card hanging from his lanyard. "Nico from admin. Second Officer, Finance."

She studied the ID, then narrowed her eyes. "Finance doesn't handle this."

"Not directly, but we work closely with HR. I'll speak with the crew purser to make sure this reaches the right people."

She hesitated before exhaling, her earlier fight dimming. "Any officer's voice is better than no voice." She ran a hand through her hair. "Fine. I'll get you the names."

They made their way to a small cabin marked Stewards.

Sonia grabbed a folder from the shelf above the desk, flipping through its pages before pulling out a staff list. "Here you go. The ones highlighted in yellow—I haven't seen them. It's not just my detail. Every senior is missing one or two crew. If you want, I can ask them to email their lists to you."

Nico nodded, handing her one of his freshly printed 'Nico' business cards. "That'd be great. Thanks—oh, and don't forget to keep an eye on Betty," he added with a small smile before leaving.

His mind churned. This wasn't just an HR mishap. The ship had serious staffing issues, and if ECM didn't fix them soon, they'd lose experienced workers like Sonia. A downward spiral of poor service would drive customers elsewhere. In a tight cruise market, that was a death sentence.

He found Tristan in her office.

"You were gone a while. Is Betty alright?" she asked.

"Yes, she'll be fine. One of the senior stewards is keeping an eye on her. But we have a bigger problem." He placed the staff list on her desk. "Let's grab a working lunch and figure out how to track down these missing people. I've got two more names here."

Tristan frowned, picking up the list. "I don't recognize these names. Would their passports already be in the system?"

"Lunch first," he said, stepping back to let her pass through the door.

She grabbed a yellow legal pad and a couple of pens before striding into the corridor.

They chose a secluded table, away from foot traffic, and placed their orders. Most of the staff had already eaten, which worked in their favour—fewer distractions.

As they waited for their meals, Nico recounted his conversation with Sonia, including her claim that the owners were cutting costs at the crew's expense.

Tristan shook her head. "It doesn't add up. They're losing big time. Don't get me wrong—I'm not one to defend the ruling classes, but fair's fair. If the ratings are dropping as much as Sonia says, the company's getting a double whammy."

Nico studied her, amused. Not one to defend the ruling classes, huh? How would she feel when she found out exactly who he was? His family had been part of the elite for centuries.

If he had his way, she'd be part of it too—when she married him.

He'd already admitted to himself that he wanted her forever. The question was, when would he get the chance to make her see it?

Not now.

For now, they had a mystery to solve.

Nico kept his expression solemn, though inside, he smiled.

"Any ideas?" he asked.

Tristan exhaled, drumming her fingers on the table. "We already uncovered one batch of doppelgängers. This new set takes things to another level—unless they're the same ones we already flagged. If they're different and still in the system, the scam is deeper than I thought. It must've been running for a while." She leaned forward. "There should be 220 staff on board and 270 passengers. That's an excellent staff-to-guest ratio. No wonder the line had five-star ratings—until now. So, what changed?"

"If this is orchestrated, someone senior with access to personnel files and payroll has to be pulling the strings," Nico said. "A scheme like this would take time—at least months, if not longer. Have there been changes in senior staff recently?"

"I'll check. The people with access would be in finance, HR, or hotel management. It's a pretty select group," she mused.

"Someone like McFarlane? She's fairly new, isn't she?" he asked casually.

Tristan flinched. "Why her, of all people?"

Nico lifted a shoulder. "Just a name that came to mind. But fair point—the culprit doesn't have to be onboard. That widens the suspect pool."

She rubbed the tip of her nose. "The fastest way to confirm if your missing crew are doppelgängers is by printing proof-sized photos of every staff member registered on this trip. That's how we caught the triplets. If we find more duplicates, we track down the real employees, eliminate the extras from payroll, and close the gaps."

"What about identifying no-shows who are still getting paid?" Nico pressed.

Tristan ran a thumb over her bottom lip—not in irritation, he guessed, but deep thought. "I could send a blanket email to all section heads asking them to report missing crew, but that would tip off whoever's behind this."

She tapped her pen on her notepad, then met his gaze. "We need another way."

"You've thought this through more than I realized," Nico said. "Do you agree this is bigger than just a bit of skimming?"

"It's looking that way. As far as having thought things through—honestly? It's easier to springboard ideas when I have someone to bounce them off. Solving things alone can be a headache."

He hadn't even registered finishing lunch until she shoved her empty plate aside.

"Time's a-wasting, Mr. Griff. We'd best get started."

The phrase sparked something in him—a thrill, a memory of his first encounter with her as the no-nonsense crew purser who still managed to shake his soul.

"You said that to me the other day—'time's a-wasting.' Where's it from?"

She shrugged. "No idea. I've always used it."

She pushed her chair back, impatience radiating off her. That was the Tristan he'd fallen for—the woman who got things done, who knew exactly what she wanted.

As they strolled toward the office area, she glanced at him. "Have you got time to play Watson to my Sherlock Holmes?"

"No. And I'm guessing neither do you," he said. "But for the sake of the crew working double loads, it's my priority. You're a temporary employee. You don't have to let it consume you," he added.

She shot him a look, then nodded. "You know what? You're right. I have other priorities—both for the job and for myself. I'll give this an hour, then move on to other things. Maybe stepping away will give me a fresh perspective."

A fresh perspective might make all the difference in getting things wrapped up, Nico reckoned.

The sooner this whole charade was over, the sooner he could stop pretending to be Nico and start loving her the way he desperately wanted to.

Chapter Thirteen

Tris left him at his office door and continued to her own, her mind whirring. Mentioning Siena, directly, had caught her off guard. Why had he zeroed in on her friend? Had Tris given too much away? A low-level anxiety settled in her gut. She and Siena had already explored countless scenarios and suspects—different from what she and Nico had discussed. He didn't need to know that. Not yet. Not until she had solid ground beneath any theories she might form.

She turned to her next task: compiling images of every crew member listed for the cruise. Even as she assembled the file, patterns emerged. Duplicate photos. Some faces appearing two, even three times, assigned to different roles. Did they really think they could get away with using images of staff already on board?

Her stomach tightened when she spotted one in particular—Siena. A carbon copy of her, slotted into catering.

Grabbing a handful of pens, she marked the duplicates in different colours. When she ran out of colours, she switched to symbols—circles, hash marks, triangles, ampersands—anything to differentiate them. By the time she was done, the sheet was a chaotic mess of ink, but the pattern was undeniable.

Fifteen percent of the crew didn't exist.

She was still collating the fakes when Nico strode into her office.

"I have more lists from the stewards," he said, setting them down.

"Great. We can cross-check these with the no-shows and eliminate some of the duplicates," she said, pushing the proof sheet toward him. "At least fifteen percent of the hotel crew are ghosts. No wonder everyone's exhausted." She rubbed her temples. "I'll be seeing these faces in my sleep tonight—trying to sort out who's real and who isn't. See if you can spot any I missed."

"No, you were very thorough," Nico admitted, rolling his shoulders. "Though I couldn't verify your selections because half the faces are buried under squiggles."

"They're right. Trust me," Tris said. "Read out the names from your list. I'll mark them in red on the chart. Then I can figure out which one isn't Siena McFarlane."

"She had a doppelgänger too?"

"Yep. Take a look." She swung her screen around.

He groaned. "What a mess."

"My table of data?" She raised an eyebrow. "I thought it was pretty good myself."

"Your table is clear and concise. I'd be hard-pressed to do better myself," he admitted. "I meant the staffing. No wonder people are at breaking point."

"The missing people are all casuals in the hotel section—cleaning, catering, laundry, hospitality," she explained. "None of those require specialized skills, just basic competencies. It's a sloppy loophole, and whoever's behind this is exploiting it."

Nico sat across from her, his brow furrowed. "To avoid making a mistake—and to spare ourselves some major embarrassment—is there any way to verify the rooms assigned to these people?"

"Cabin allocation technically falls under the Crew Purser's responsibilities," she said, tapping her pen against her lips. "But with Siena McFarlane on sick leave, someone else must've handled it. That's worth looking into."

She held his gaze. "The Crew Purser is required to check hygiene standards of crew cabins. It's usually done later in a cruise, but I'm new, so no one will question it if I do an early spot check. I'll send a ship-wide email letting the crew know I may be inspecting rooms in the next twenty-four hours. That way, when I start snooping around, no one will think twice about it."

Nico let out a dramatic groan and raked a hand through his thick, greasy hair—then wiped it down his trousers with a grimace.

The outburst was so uncharacteristic, Tris burst out laughing. "A bit dramatic, don't you think?"

His chest vibrated as if he were holding back laughter of his own. The shared amusement loosened the tension in her shoulders.

"Right, that's enough for tonight," she declared. "I'm leaving this until the morning. You need a break too. Go have a drink. I'll see you later."

She grabbed two hefty management textbooks that had been gathering dust on the corner of her desk since she came aboard.

"What are you planning to do?" Nico asked.

"Me? I'm going to take these bad boys to a shady spot on the outside deck, let the wind blow through my hair, and bone up on 'Management in the Twenty-First Century.'"

"Want some company?"

She hesitated, then tipped up one shoulder. "If you're quiet."

A flicker of amusement crossed his face. "I'll try."

They stopped by the crew bar to grab long, cold drinks, then ambled toward the outside deck.

Nico hauled a deck chair into the shade for her, then another for himself. With luck, they'd picked a spot where the shadow of the deck above would lengthen, sparing them the hassle of moving later.

They settled in, resting their drinks on the arms of their chairs. Tris dropped her textbooks beside her with a thud.

"Tell me about your family," Nico said.

She lowered her chin, sucking from her straw as she eyed him over the rim of her glass. "I came out here to study."

"I think you need a mental break before diving into those books. Relax your brain for a few minutes, or you won't absorb a thing." He gave her a teasing smile. "Like sorbet between the main course and dessert."

"Interesting analogy," she mused. Then, after a pause, "I have no family that I know of."

"I can't imagine that," he said, frowning. "How did that happen?"

She stiffened. That was a topic she avoided. "Just is," she said flatly. "You?"

"I'm Italian. Family is everything to me," he said without hesitation. "Mama and Papa keep track of me wherever I go, and I love knowing they're always there for me. I have a brother who's passionate about art—he'd rather spend his days working with artists than doing his actual job as a hotel receptionist." He chuckled. "My sisters couldn't be more different. One is a hard-nosed businesswoman—well, she will be when she graduates. She's determined to make her mark. The other is studying to be a doctor. She's the gentle one, always reminding us about our social obligations." His voice softened. "I love them all."

The warmth in his words made something inside her ache. That kind of connection—unshakable, unconditional—felt like a distant dream. If only she could find someone to love like that, to build a life and family with. Luc had been the closest she'd come to wanting that, but who knew if she'd ever see him again? Maybe in Melbourne, when she started her new job...

"It sounds like you have a wonderful family." She tilted her head slightly, signalling the conversation was over. "Thanks for the sorbet."

He gave a small nod, accepting the shift. "Why management?" he asked, nodding toward the textbooks.

"I mentioned I'm applying for a job back home in Australia, right? I want to have every possible scenario and answer at my fingertips before I walk into that interview. This job is important—it's the culmi-nation of years of biting my tongue when, inside, I was screaming for change." Her fingers tapped absently on the book's cover. "I want to be the change. A new way of thinking. Prioritizing people and their well-being. Improving job satisfaction."

"You'll get that from your books?"

"How do I explain?" She exhaled, searching for the words. "I have my own ideas, my own vision. The books give me the framework—the ammunition—to make it happen."

It was tempting, so tempting, to keep talking to Nico like this—when he was open, easy, like Luc had been. But neither man was in her future. The job was.

Setting her drink down, she flipped open the first textbook.

"Now, hush," she said, focusing on the words in front of her rather than the glittering smile he'd just sent her way—the one that sent ex-citement rippling through her system.

Chapter Fourteen

Nico leaned forward, resting his elbows on Tris' desk.

He'd enjoyed the past hour on the deck, watching her study. The way she furrowed her brow, the occasional disgusted humph—it all gave him insight into her ambition and drive. She wasn't just determined; she was relentless.

When she finally set the second textbook aside, he asked, "Anything worth sharing?"

"The business world needs me," she declared. "These books are full of yesterday's news."

He chuckled as she scrambled to her feet, collecting her books and empty glass.

"What's your plan, then? How will you convince them you know better?" he asked, following her lead.

"I'll make a list—document the standard answers and then my alternatives. I'll win." She gave him a confident smirk. "Quick dinner for me, then back to it. You?"

"I'll join you."

Returning to the office snapped them back to reality—the job at hand.

"We need to get replacement staff on board fast," Nico said. "How much have you told Catalan?"

"Nothing yet. He's concerned about falling standards, but I wasn't about to go to him with a half-baked theory and end up with egg on our faces."

He frowned. "You Australians—why would you put egg on your face?"

She burst out laughing. "Did I actually say that?" Shaking her head, she scratched a spot behind her ear. "Keep track of my colloquialisms, mate. I'll give you a tutorial when this is over."

Rounding the desk, her smile slipped, and she linked her hands in thought. "Let's think this through."

Using the knuckle of her index finger, she massaged her forehead, tracing a slow line from the bridge of her nose to her hairline and back again.

"There are two dozen staff missing," Tris said, scanning the data. "They have assigned cabins, they're on full pay—but they're not working. All from the hotel section, so we're down about twenty percent of that team. What's our top priority?"

"Getting the ship fully staffed," Nico said without hesitation. "Nothing else matters if the ship isn't running properly."

"We also need to figure out who's behind this and where the money is going," she reminded him.

"That's secondary. The investigation can keep going in the background, but if we don't get the crew situation under control, we'll lose more staff. Twenty-four short could turn into a full-blown crisis if people burn out and quit. Remember what Sonia told me?"

Tris exhaled sharply. "Yeah. The passengers are noticing, too—including the couple from the premier suite." She rested a finger against her cheek "The real problem is, where do we find ship-ready staff while we're in transit? And how? My instinct says we keep this away from the onshore team until we know who's orchestrating it all," she said.

Nico shrugged. "We pull staff from other ships."

"That makes sense, but we can't strip them bare either. Where are they?"

"Got a spare piece of paper?" he asked. As she handed him one, he began writing. "Laura—our ship. Isabella—departing Naples for Spain today. Donatella—Morocco. Paola—Rhine. Margherete—Atlantic. Giulietta—Trieste dry dock." He tapped the pen against the page. "These are the cruise ships. I didn't include freighters—their crews wouldn't have the service skills we need."

Tris frowned at the list. "How do you know all this off the top of your head?"

Nico hesitated for half a second before offering a casual shrug. "It's a hobby. I like to keep track in case I want to hop on a ship somewhere I haven't been before." He kept his gaze on the list. "The Giulietta is our best bet. She's in dry dock now, and since we go into dry dock when we return to Naples, she's not sailing for another week. That means they have staff onboard who've already finished their jobs and don't have much to do. They're still getting paid, but with no passengers, there are no tips—so they'll probably be eager for a transfer."

Tris folded her arms. "Okay, but how do we make it happen? We have to get the hotel manager to realize he's been duped, prove it to him, convince him to request extra staff, get approval for a transfer, and then arrange their transport. That's a hell of a lot. We don't even know if Ricardo Catalan is part of the con."

"They're all valid concerns," Nico admitted. "But we don't need Catalan. I've been around the company longer than you think—despite your doubts." His lips quirked slightly. "I know people. I can reach out to someone who can speak directly to the General Manager. We keep it simple—we're short-staffed and need reinforcements. No need to complicate it."

"Does this mean going behind Ricardo's back? And the captain's?" Tris asked.

"If we're not careful, it might look that way," Nico admitted. "The trick is to get the GM to initiate the investigation himself. If he demands a report within thirty minutes, it'll force action."

Tris scoffed. "Arrogant prick. How does he expect anyone to pull together a decent report in half an hour?"

"Because he already has the numbers," Nico said smoothly.

She huffed, but let it go. "Well, we need to get moving—fast. You talk to your contact. I'll get the list ready for room checks and stop the payments."

"Leave the payments alone," he cautioned. "We still need the trail."

As he stood, he accidentally dislodged one of her management textbooks. He caught it mid-air, glancing at the cover. Does My Workplace Contribute to My Happiness? He canted his head. "Interesting choice."

"It's the foundation of what I want to implement in my new job," she said. "A quadruple bottom line—profits, people, planet, and purpose. Business should serve humanity, not just shareholders."

"Sounds like a solid concept," he said. "Maybe you should stick around and put it in place here. If McFarlane is responsible for what's happening, there's going to be an opening." He arched a brow. "Right now, happiness isn't exactly radiating from the ECM team. It's on us to fix it."

Without waiting for a response, he strode into his own office, shutting the door. Digging out his private mobile, he dialled a number that wouldn't appear on the ship's logs.

The call was answered on the second ring.

"What news do you have, son?"

Luc leaned against the desk. "We've uncovered missing staff—twenty-four on full pay but not working. We're confirming room assignments now. You should demand a rapid report to force it into the open."

"It's not the HR manager?" Ettore asked.

"Tristan only joined because the last HR manager is on leave with a busted knee," Luc said. "McFarlane isn't off the hook yet—we haven't even started tracing the money. Can you charter a jet to bring the Giulietta crew from Trieste to Kotor?" Luc asked. "It'll take too long if they go through Berlin or Rome."

"I'll handle it," Ettore said. "I'll also contact the Laura's captain and hotel manager for a report. I'll frame it as a routine staff redistribution—we don't want anyone realizing we're onto them yet. Will you be able to sort out accommodations in time? You're an accountant, but can you go through housekeeping without tipping off Catalan?"

"Yes. I spoke to a senior steward yesterday—I can work with her. If I run into issues, I'll let you know."

"Good. The captain may have to delay departure to wait for the crew, but it's only a short hop to Dubrovnik. He can make up time and still have passengers ready for their tours in the morning." Ettore paused, then added, "Does your friend know who you are?"

"Not yet, Papa," Luc said, chuckling. "What did Mama say?"

His father sighed. "She's been in this business a long time. Plus, she knows you'd be with her if you could—so, it must be serious. She'll forgive us both."

Luc huffed a laugh and ended the call.

Back in Tristan's office, he leaned against the door frame. "It's in motion. My contact will see what he can do. For now, we wait on Catalan."

Tristan stood abruptly. "I want to check cabins."

"Do it in the morning," Luc advised. "Let our plans settle overnight."

* * *

Tristan sat on the edge of her bed, her head in her hands. So much had happened. They'd uncovered the scale of the crew scam, yet they still had no idea who was behind it, why it was happening, or exactly how much money was being siphoned—and where it was going.

She exhaled sharply and flopped onto her back, staring at the ceiling as if the answers might be hidden somewhere between the light fixture and the window. No luck.

Then there was the wine scam. Another tangled mess. The trader claimed the wine was for Siena, but the crew members said it was for Peter Davis. The stash was being kept in the cabin directly opposite Nico's—Davis's usual room. Conveniently, it was also near her own, which would normally be Siena's.

That put both Siena and Davis squarely in the frame for embezzlement. But were they working together, or did they have separate agendas? And was the wine connected to the crew scam, or was it just another layer of corruption? Nico seemed convinced Siena was the culprit. Tris refused to believe it.

How had things spiralled so badly? Where were the checks and balances? Who had enough power to manipulate the system and keep it hidden? Ricardo Catalan was clearly pulling his hair out over the ship's declining standards, so why wasn't he digging deeper? Or was someone he trusted leading him astray?

Then there was Nico Griff.

Second-officer accountants weren't supposed to have a direct line to someone who had the ear of the cruise line's owner. Yet, somehow, Nico did. He was charming in his own way, drawing her into his orbit despite their opposing views on Siena. But there were other things—small things—that didn't quite add up. The tilt of his chin. The way his forefinger rested against his lower lip. Those were pure Luc.

And yet... the bumbling awkwardness? That wasn't Luc at all.

Another mystery. She'd unravel it later—when it was the last secret left to uncover.

Chapter Fifteen

Tristan and Nico arrived at the officers' mess for an early breakfast but hadn't even taken a seat when Tristan's pager buzzed. A message flashed on the screen: Contact the hotel manager immediately.

She glanced at Nico and gave a slight nod—it had begun. Without another word, she turned and hurried to the exit, taking the stairs two at a time up to Level Four, where the hotel manager's office and suite were located.

"Good morning, Mr. Catalan. You called for me?"

"Yes, Ms. Sinclair. Please, come in. Take a seat." Catalan leaned forward, his fingers drumming against the polished wood of his desk. "Ms. Sinclair—Tristan—I have received a call from Signor Ricci."

"Ricci?" Tristan tapped her closed lips.

Catalan's eyes narrowed. "Do you know him?"

"I met a Luciano Ricci in Australia," she said, dropping her hand into her lap.

"Oh." Catalan visibly relaxed. "No, this is Signor Ettore Ricci—the General Manager and owner. There may have been a son named Luciano, but I believe they're estranged. Something about the boy squandering his father's money on a playboy lifestyle." He scoffed.

Tristan kept her expression neutral. Gossip mags loved that kind of story—take a grain of truth, stretch it, twist it, and sell it. But there was always a seed of fact there somewhere.

"Signor Ricci is concerned about declining approval ratings," Catalan continued. "I hadn't bothered you with it since you're only here for this one cruise. But now, he believes there's a conspiracy to make it seem as if we have more staff than we actually do."

"I've had some concerns too, because the supervisors have complained they don't have full rosters, but we have a full complement on the books. In fact, I have scheduled a meeting in your diary to seek your advice later this afternoon."

Catalan narrowed his gaze on her. "That will be too late. Signor Ricci wants a full report right away."

Tristan tilted her head. "When does he expect it?"

Catalan's mouth pressed into a thin line. "Half an hour."

"Half an hour?" she repeated, feigning disbelief.

"From ten minutes ago, in fact."

"How am I supposed to put together a report that quickly?"

"I'm sure you'll think of something." His tone was dismissive. "You know the personnel files better than anyone. I need your report here in fifteen minutes so I can analyse it before speaking with Signor Ricci." He waved a hand. "That will be all."

"Understood, sir." Tristan rose and left the office, her mind racing. *Fifteen minutes. How do I make it look rushed but convincing?*

Then it hit her—the photos.

She hurried back to her office, where Nico was already waiting.

"I have fifteen minutes to prepare a report that convinces Catalan—and Ricci—that there's a real issue on board," she told him. "I'll use the photos. The evidence is clear enough, and it won't look like we spent two days collecting data and interviewing staff."

Nico nodded. "It's the cleanest solution."

She grabbed the document from the desk, only to scowl. "Damn. We've scribbled all over this one. I'll have to print a fresh copy and mark it up again."

"It won't take long," Nico assured her. "If you print the same sheet, I'll read it out: Green circle, yellow triangle, purple square. We'll have it done in no time. Then, a five-line report saying we've identified multiple duplicate photos, confirming at least twenty-four crew spaces without active staff. Report's done. Catalan's impressed. We move forward."

"Thanks, Nico. You're spot on." Tristan pulled up the photo sheet on her screen and sent it to the printer. Then, she shot him a curious glance. "Why do you hide your intelligence? You're no fool."

He shrugged, offering nothing in return.

She waited, raising an eyebrow. Still, silence. Finally, she let it slide and grabbed the freshly printed sheet.

"Right. Here we go. Starting from the top left-hand corner, what do we have?"

As Nico compared the new sheet against their marked-up version from the previous afternoon, Tristan focused on drafting the report. She broke down the vacancies by department, making it clear how many staff were missing from each area.

When she finished, she handed the printed copy to Nico.

"Mmm. Good." He scanned the sheet. "But the photos alone don't show which departments the vacancies are in. We only figured that out from our meetings."

"Damn. What if we use a best-guess range—one above or below the real number?"

"Better," he agreed. "We don't want to be too specific, but we also can't afford to get five extra kitchen hands when what we actually need are laundry staff."

"What if we end up with more crew than we need? Can we accommodate them?"

"Yes. We won't get twice the number, so at worst, we'd have to convert some double rooms into triples. It'd only be for a few days." He smirked. "Now hurry up and fix your report. Someone recently taught me the phrase 'time's a-wasting,' Ms. Sinclair."

Tristan rolled her eyes, made the necessary adjustments, and tucked the report and photo sheet into a plastic file. Then, she headed back up to Deck Four.

Ricardo Catalan was waiting for her in the outer office. Or at least, it felt like it when he pounced the moment she appeared.

"Well? What did you find?"

Tristan handed the credit back to him. "You were right, Mr. Catalan. Shall we go into your office so I can explain in detail?"

She wasn't about to lay out the full scope of the mess in front of his secretary—not when she had no idea if the woman could be trusted.

Catalan led the way into his office.

Tristan held onto the folder as she spoke. "Mr. Catalan, what I've found will have serious consequences for morale on board. It is imperative that this is not discussed with anyone outside senior officers or administrators."

"You are telling me how to conduct myself, Ms. Sinclair?" Catalan frowned down his nose.

"No, sir. I'm reminding myself," Tristan replied smoothly. "The consequences could be explosive, and we don't need this being bandied about the lower decks."

He studied her wryly. "Am I at least allowed to speak to Signor Ricci and Mr. Argstrom, Ms. Sinclair?"

Tristan masked her amusement, aiming for humility. "Yes, sir. I'm sorry, sir." She took a breath. "What I've found is that somewhere between twenty-two and thirty staff are missing from departments within the hotel."

"Just within the hotel?" He blanched. "That's twenty percent of the staff."

"Yes, sir." She handed him the photo sheet. "As you can see, I've identified duplicate photos—each with an individual name. That means there are crew slots with no one actively doing the work. My report includes estimates of how many staff we need to bring the ship back to full complement."

The phone rang.

"That will be Signor Ricci now," Catalan said, reaching for the receiver.

"I'll wait outside," Tristan offered.

"No!" His voice shot up an octave. "I need you to explain the numbers."

"Certainly, sir."

Catalan picked up the phone. "Catalan here. Good morning, Signor Ricci. Yes, sir. By our estimates, we're missing between twenty-two and thirty hotel staff. Yes, sir. I'll have Ms. Sinclair explain. She's our current human relations manager."

He held out the receiver.

"Good morning, Signor Ricci. This is Tristan Sinclair."

"Ah, Tristana." Ricci's voice was rich with familiarity. "I have been fully briefed, but for Mr. Catalan's benefit, perhaps you can explain how you identified the missing staff?"

"Of course, sir." Tristan kept her tone professional. "I ran the photographs of all staff on board. There were no duplicates among the deck crew, but quite a number in the hotel section. From those clusters, Mr. Griff and I estimated where staff are missing."

A pause. Then, Ricci chuckled.

"I once knew a Mr. Griff," he mused. "A lovely man, but awkward. He died."

Tristan's grip tightened on the phone.

"I know the accurate figures, Tristana, and have already acted accordingly. Thank you for your help. You can tell Mr. Catalan that I've requested you email me the report." A beat. "I look forward to meeting you soon. Now, please hand the phone back to Mr. Catalan."

"Yes, sir. Thank you, sir." Tristan did as she was bid, returning the phone to her boss. The call ended.

"You didn't explain the numbers," Catalan noted.

"No, sir. Signor Ricci forestalled me. He asked me to email the report instead. He said you would have his contact details."

"Er, right." A mollified Catalan reached into his desk drawer, pulled out a business card, and handed it to her.

"Thank you, sir. Would you still like me to keep our appointment this afternoon?"

"No, that won't be necessary. That is all."

Tristan didn't wait for a second dismissal. She hurried to her office, her mind whirling.

If she'd thought a week sailing the Adriatic would be a relaxing escape from corporate politics, she'd been sorely mistaken. Different setting, different stakes—but still politics and intrigue.

Nico was waiting when she returned. "How did it go?"

"It was weird." Tristan perched on the edge of her desk. "I took the report to Catalan, and he had me explain the figures to Ricci, but before I could, Ricci just... cut me off. He said he'd already been fully briefed. And he kept calling me Tristana."

Nico smirked. "Tristana, eh?"

"I didn't correct him. He's the big boss, after all."

"The phone call was odd," she said moving around the desk to position herself in front of her computer. "He said I should email the report, but if he already knows everything, does he actually want it? I figured it'd be best to send it but keep the content minimal."

"Mm-hmm," Nico murmured.

"You think I should send it?"

"Safest option," he said.

"Okay. Then, I'll put together a clean list of the phantom crew. You'll need it to cross-check account numbers. If we're going to uncover who was behind this scam, the most logical course of action is to follow the money. Then there's the wine. Where does that fit in?"

She kept talking the whole time she prepared to send the email. Copying the address from the card Catalan gave her, she dispatched the report.

"Done."

She slumped in her seat and crossed her arms. "Then, when I mentioned you, Ricci said he once knew a Mr. Griff—but that the man was dead. The whole conversation was strange. If he's that eccentric, no wonder his son doesn't come home."

Nico's expression didn't change, but something shifted in his eyes. "What do you mean?"

"Catalan asked if I knew Signor Ricci. I told him I'd met a Luciano Ricci, but he said this was Ettore. Then he made some comment about the son being a sponging playboy. I mean, if you're heir to a multi-million-dollar empire, wouldn't you be learning the business instead of wasting your life? Selfish bastard."

"Did you know this Luciano well?" Nico asked.

"No," she said. "We'd only just met. I thought I wanted to know him better, but you never can tell, huh?" She shrugged.

"It might not be the same man," Nico pointed out. "It's a multi-billion-euro business, by the way. Maybe Catalan was talking about a younger son."

"Hmph. Doesn't matter. He's history."

"You'd dismiss someone based on gossip?"

"Look," Tristan exhaled sharply. "The guy I met said he was pretending to be a playboy for his own reasons. Maybe it wasn't an act after all. I don't like deception." She hesitated. "Besides, it's not like I'll ever see him again."

Nico's gaze bored into hers for several moments, his expression unreadable. A flicker of something—disappointment? —passed through his eyes before he shook his head. "Well," he said, shifting gears, "the crew from the Giulietta are packing their bags. They'll be joining us by this evening before we depart Kotor."

Tristan frowned. "That fast?"

"Signor Ricci knows how to run a business," Nico said, deliberately steering the conversation away from her scepticism about his father's character—and his own. "He's chartered a jet to bring them down."

The news lifted Tristan's mood. "Good. How many did we get?"

"Thirty."

"Thirty?" Her eyes widened. "Where the hell are we going to put them all?" Then she waved the question away. "Never mind. I'll check the cabins."

She reached into her desk, unlocked the bottom drawer, and retrieved the master key. "Coming?"

Chapter Sixteen

Nico made his way to Deck Seven, heading toward the stewards' office where he'd last seen Sonia, the senior steward. He spotted her in the corridor, walking toward him with a weary expression.

She groaned. "Yes?"

"Sonia, I have good news and bad news..."

She folded her arms. "Bad news first."

Nico rubbed a thumb over his chin. "I have a list of cabins to be checked and certified as ready for new occupants. There shouldn't be much to do, but a senior steward has to sign off on them."

She sucked in a deep breath, holding it like she was resisting the urge to launch into a tirade. Finally, she let it out in a slow, controlled exhale. "And the good news?"

"The cabins will be filled—with extra staff."

She blinked. "What?"

"If all goes to plan, you'll have a full team by the end of the day."

Her sceptical look returned. "No way. You can't just pluck trained crew out of thin air."

"You can if you ask for volunteers from a ship in dry dock. When the Giulietta's crew were offered a chance to join the Laura for the rest of the week, we were bombarded with responses. We asked for twenty-four—we got thirty."

Sonia's lips parted in surprise. "Really?"

"Really," he confirmed, handing her the list. "But we need those cabins cleared and certified ASAP. Think your teams can manage?"

In answer, she threw her arms around him, pressing a grateful kiss to his cheek. "Yes. Thank you. Thank you."

Nico disentangled himself with a chuckle. "Head office had no idea how bad things had gotten. Hopefully, this makes life easier for you."

Sonia nodded briskly, already scanning the list as she turned away.

Nico continued down the stairs to Tristan's office.

"Sonia's on it," he announced as he entered.

Tristan leaned back in her chair with a smirk. "Well, there goes our peaceful corridor. So... where are they putting the wine from the 'cellar' across the way?"

"I didn't include that cabin in the certification list," Nico said. "We need to figure out what's going on in there before anyone else starts wondering why there's a stockpile of wine. I did add the one next to it, though. Otherwise, we'd come up short."

Tristan frowned. "It hasn't been cleaned in ages, so it clearly hasn't been used. Do you think it was just overflow storage when they ran out of space in the cellar?"

"That's my guess," he agreed. "They'll have to manage with what they've got."

He leaned against her desk. "I ran into Shelley—she's looking for volunteers for the shore tours. I told her I'd check with you."

Tristan groaned. "Not today. I need to make progress on those accounts and write up the wine delivery report while it's still fresh in my mind."

"She's got three options: a two-hour walking tour of the old town, a four-hour trip into the hills and the old capital, or the eight-hour full tour with a degustation lunch. We could help her out with the walking tour."

Tristan rubbed the back of her neck and sighed. "I suppose we should be good team players. Fine. I'll do the walking tour. Besides, I've spent too much time sitting lately."

Nico grinned. "I'll let her know. Then we'll grab the breakfast we missed. The walking tour doesn't leave until the long-distance buses are gone, so we can squeeze in some account work first."

They made their way to the mess, loaded their trays, and took a seat at an empty table.

"This whole drama is eating up too much time," Tristan muttered. "We need to wrap it up."

"I agree, but all we can do for now is track the account numbers. Once we have them, I can get a trusted contact onshore to run a check."

Tristan arched an eyebrow. "Another secret squirrel with the General Manager's ear?"

Nico canted his head. "I told you—I know a lot of people. It didn't bother you before. It worked, didn't it? We got the staff we needed."

She didn't answer.

"You okay?" he asked.

"I'm fine. Can I just finish my breakfast in peace?"

"Ah," he said knowingly. "You haven't had your coffee yet." He leaned back away from the food. "Go ahead. I shall sit here, silent as a mouse. You won't even know I'm here. I'll simply observe—the way the light shifts on the ceiling as the ship rolls with the soft swell, the beauty of the sea beyond the window, and the play of the sun on the tips of the ripples making it appear the water is scattered with diamonds. No, I will be fine." He glanced at her.

Tristan choked on a laugh. "You're an idiot, you know that?"

He flashed a full smile.

Her laughter died. "Don't do that."

"What?"

"That smile." She sighed. "It reminds me of someone I'm trying very hard to forget."

"The playboy?" he guessed.

"Yes," Tristan said firmly. "We had fun on the flight. Did I tell you we happened to be on the same flight from Melbourne to Dubai? We laughed at an old movie together. It was nice, you know? Now it's rotten. He's rotten. I cannot abide deception."

"How did he deceive you?" Nico asked.

"Men. You just don't get it." She sighed. "He pretended to be something he wasn't. Gave the impression he was a hardworking business type because he was at a meeting with other execs—when in reality, he's just a lay-about, happy to live off his father."

"Did he actually mislead you, though?" Nico pressed.

Tristan's eyes narrowed. "Whose side are you on?"

"I am a man, as you noticed a moment ago," he said dryly. "Someone has to argue the plaintiff's position." He spread his hands in mock surrender.

"Oh, so now we're playing lawyer?" she quipped.

He nudged her coffee cup toward her. Then, wisely, he turned back to his own meal. Sometimes discretion was the better part of valour. Shakespeare said that, didn't he?

When they finished, they left the mess together.

"I'll buzz you when I have something," Tristan said, peeling off toward her office as Nico headed to his.

A short while later, she called him in.

"Okay..." She handed him a sheet of paper. "This is the list of names tied to those accounts. We need to track where the money's going. You know the saying, 'follow the money'?"

"I do," Nico said. "But I prefer 'cherchez la femme.' There's usually a woman in the mix somewhere."

"Either way, we need those account numbers to see if they leave a trail," she said. "When will we have the list of new staff? I have to process them. Are they bringing their own passports and visas, or is there an officer with them?"

"A senior staff member from catering is among them. She jumped at the chance to come because she wants to see how things run on the Laura," Nico explained. "You don't need to process them tonight. Their payrolls are still tied to the Giulietta. And none of them will be going ashore tomorrow—they'll be too busy settling in."

"I'll work with Emily on safety training in the morning," she said.

"You do take on more work than necessary." He shook his head. "These aren't newbies like the doppelgangers would've been. They're all experienced—both in their roles and in working on an ECM ship. All Emily has to do is an orientation, so they know where the muster stations are. Check with her, but I bet she'll tell you to butt out."

Tristan exhaled. "Fine. I'm going to my cabin to change. There'd better not be any dramas on the tour."

Nico laughed. "You sound like a petulant child." His tone softened. "It's been a long couple of days. I'll meet you on the gangway in fifteen minutes."

"Okay."

After tidying her desk and locking away confidential documents, Tristan left her problems in the office too, and closed the door with a snap. She was free—for a few hours, at least.

Chapter Seventeen

The walking tour was a welcome tonic for Tristan's soul. As she strolled with the guests through the medieval Old Town of Kotor, the weight of the ship's troubles momentarily lifted. Sun-warmed stone, the scent of fresh bread wafting from a bakery, the echo of footsteps on cobbled streets—this was the escape she had needed.

Nico, however, was not so easily dismissed. He walked beside her, his presence familiar, his laughter rich and unguarded. It was an echo of Luc's—the same effortless joy in shared moments. A wisp of sadness curled through her, an ache for what might have been. She forced it away, unwilling to dwell on a fantasy that had already unravelled.

The two hours passed way too soon.

Back on board, reality returned. Though she worked tirelessly all afternoon, she had little to show for it. Frustration settled between her shoulders like a weighted vest. With exhaustion gnawing at her, she retreated to her cabin, craving a few minutes of solitude.

Sitting on the edge of her bunk, she closed her eyes to think—and woke an hour later to loud banging in the corridor.

Disoriented, she sat up sharply, listening. The muffled hum of voices—some cheerful, one raised in irritation—filtered through the door.

Frowning, she cracked it open and peered out.

At the far end of the corridor, duffel bags stencilled with Giulietta were piled haphazardly, their owners sifting through them. Nearby, the same men who had delivered the wine the day before were at it again—four more cartons, plus a couple of separate bottles that looked like cognac or some other liqueur. Her pulse ticked up.

She needed a photo. Stepping into the hallway, she raised her phone, gesturing toward the Giulietta crew as if snapping casual shots of their arrival. The corridor was too narrow for anyone to be entirely out of frame, and she hoped the wine handlers wouldn't think twice.

They didn't.

She adjusted the angle just enough—keeping the near setting clear, the stacked cartons and the men moving them in focus. The Giulietta crew certainly wouldn't be nominating her for Photographer of the Year, their faces were conveniently blurred.

Two of the new crew arrived with their gear, stopping at the door directly opposite Tristan's. One of them swiped his key card, frowning when it didn't register straight away. He tried again.

From further down the corridor, the wine handler with the Geordie accent called over, his tone sharp. "Oi—ye can't go in there. It's private."

The crew member looked up, unimpressed. "It is to us, mate. This is the one we've been allocated."

Geordie's expression darkened as the door beeped and swung open. He took a step closer, eyes widening as he took in the state of the room. Turning to his colleague, he muttered in a dire tone, "They've allocated it."

His companion's face twisted in horror. The Giulietta crew member huffed a laugh. "Told you so. Looks like you've got a tough gig there, mate. Come down to the party later—I'll buy you a beer. One Englishman to another, eh?"

Geordie didn't acknowledge him. His grip tightened on the dolly handle as he turned to the other door—the one Nico had dubbed the cellar. He hesitated, waiting just long enough for the new crew to disappear into their room before unlocking it.

The door opened, and his colleague wheeled in the dolly stacked with wine cartons. Tristan retreated, slipping back into her cabin as quietly as possible. Had they noticed her watching? She exhaled slowly, pressing her back against the door for a moment before shaking it off.

A shower was in order.

The hot water washed over her, rinsing away the tension, leaving her refreshed. She dressed in casual jeans and a fitted camisole with a soft blouse over the top. She tied the blouse's front panels into a loose knot, rolled up the sleeves, then stepped into strappy low-heeled sandals before giving herself the once-over.

Casual but put-together. Just what she needed.

Her first stop was the officers' mess. As the steward approached to show her to a table, she glanced around.

"Is Mr. Griff still here?" she asked.

"Yes, ma'am. Would you like to be seated there?"

"Yes, please."

* * *

Nico tracked Tristan's progress across the room, battling the instinctive Luc reaction to her. She exuded an effortless confidence—relaxed, self-assured, and undeniably attractive. He forced himself to adopt his Nico demeanour—less polished, more awkward—as a server guided her to the seat beside him.

"Sorry I'm late," she said, settling in. "I fell asleep, then got caught up in some interesting action in the corridor."

He raised a brow but didn't press. Two other officers lingered at the table, sipping coffee, their meals already finished.

"Are you heading to the welcome party for the Giulietta crew?" Tristan asked.

"Is there a party?" one of them asked, intrigued.

"Seems like it. Deck two. One of the Giulietta guys mentioned buying someone a drink there. I figured I'd check it out after I eat."

The officers exchanged glances. "Sounds like a plan." With a nod of farewell, they rose and headed toward the lifts.

"Smooth," Nico said, approving.

"Thanks." Tristan accepted the compliment with a smile.

He leaned in slightly. "So, what happened in the corridor?"

Her tone was casual. "An interesting little scene between the cellar attendants and the Giulietta crew assigned to the dungeon."

"Dungeon?"

"The room next to the cellar—dark, dusty, mysterious." She sipped her water. "Well, was mysterious. Not anymore. It's been cleaned up like any normal crew cabin. Geordie wasn't pleased when he saw it."

Nico considered that. "Interesting."

A server arrived, and Tristan ordered, selecting something from all six courses.

Nico raised an eyebrow. "That's ambitious."

"Hmm. Maybe." She screwed her lips to one side, then turned to the server. "Scratch the pasta. I'll have everything else."

"You, sir?" the server asked.

"A half-serve of the soup, the cheese, and the panna cotta," Nico replied.

"Excellent, sir. Won't be long."

A second server arrived, presenting bottles of red and white wine.

"Would you care for some wine, ma'am?"

"Yes, thanks. I'll start with white."

He poured her glass, then moved to top off Nico's red.

Tristan raised her glass. "Salude."

"Salude." Their glasses clinked lightly.

She took a sip, then hummed in appreciation. "Mmm, this is nice. Is this the wine you signed off on in Taormina?"

Nico nodded.

"No wonder they wanted some in the cellar." She swirled the liquid in her glass. "Who handled the sign-off yesterday, since we were up with the cats at the monastery?"

"Matthew did it himself. He likes to go on shore in Corfu, apparently," Nico said.

"Did he mention anything untoward with the order?"

"No. Maybe it was all above board this time."

Her gaze sharpened. "There was another cellar delivery tonight—same as before. Four cartons. And some additional spirits."

Nico set his glass down. "That's... good to know."

Their soup arrived. Tristan's stomach welcomed the light vegetable broth, and she finished quickly, setting down her spoon before the server whisked her bowl away.

Her next courses followed in a steady rhythm—duck breast salad, rack of lamb with vegetables, a cheese plate, and finally, a selection of gelati. Conversation was sparse as she focused on her meal, while Nico—pretending not to—focused on her.

When the server placed her coffee in front of her, Nico leaned back. "Did you have enough to eat?"

Tristan smirked. "I probably could've managed the pasta, too, but I'm not starving anymore."

"Are you going to the welcome party?" he asked.

"For a bit. You?"

"I'll stop by," he admitted. "I'm not good with parties, especially if there's dancing." He hunched his shoulders in exaggerated discomfort.

"You were brilliant on the dance floor with Nicholas and James."

"Ballroom is different. You follow the steps—no improvising." He sighed. "One of my dates once said I dance like a flamingo on drugs."

Tristan burst out laughing. "Now that, I'd love to see."

He groaned. "Ready?"

They took the stairs down to Deck Two, where the party was in full swing. The music pulsed, voices overlapped, and the room buzzed with energy.

Somewhere in the crowd, a voice called out, "Darlin'!"

Tristan glanced toward the source. Nico did the same, his gut clenching unexpectedly. He didn't like the easy familiarity in the man's tone.

The guy raised a hand, pointing down in a beckoning gesture.

Nico felt an irrational urge to steer Tristan in the opposite direction, but before he could react, she grabbed his arm and pulled him forward.

"Lemme buy you a drink, darlin'," the man said with a grin. "As an 'Isn't it great to know you' salute, eh?"

Not happening.

Nico stepped in smoothly. "Let us buy you one instead. A 'thank you for answering the call' and a 'welcome aboard.' What'll you have?"

The man's grin widened. "That's a nice thing to do. I'll have a brown ale, if you don't mind."

"Right. And you?" Nico turned to Tristan.

She leaned in close, cupping a hand around his ear. It was the only way he could hear her over the noise. "Cola. Short glass. Ice."

As she withdrew, one of her nails snagged in his hair. He caught her hand before it could tug at his hairpiece, holding it just a second too long before releasing her.

By the time he returned with the drinks, the guy had shifted closer to Tristan, his hand hovering near her shoulder.

Nico didn't hesitate. He positioned himself neatly between them, forcing the other man to take a step back. "Your drink. Thanks for coming," he said, he made his tone as hearty as Nico could manage.

Tristan sipped her cola as if it were laced with something stronger. When she finished, she smiled brightly. "Well, that's it for me. Good night, everyone."

Nico took her hand, guiding her through the crowd. He didn't want to let go, but as soon as they were clear, he dropped it. They climbed the stairs side by side, walking in silence down the corridor toward their rooms. At her door, she turned to him with a soft smile.

"Thanks, Nico. For the drink, for being in the right place at the right time, and for getting me out of there." She patted his shoulder, lingering just a second longer than necessary.

"Good night." Her touch burned through his shirt.

He wanted to kiss her like he had in Melbourne. He wanted to pull her close, feel her warmth against him, hold her like he needed to. Instead, he swallowed the urge, and said, "Buona notte." Only when her door clicked shut did he finally retreat to his own cabin—alone.

Chapter Eighteen

Tristan slumped against the door the moment it clicked shut behind her. What was it with this reaction to Nico? He was awkward, yet opinionated beyond his pay grade. He carried himself like the vulture from the Road Runner cartoons. He definitely wore a hairpiece—an act of vanity she detested in a man. His voice was low and wimpy most of the time, unless something riled him. And that horrible beard...

The birthmark didn't bother her. But the rest? If she ever wrote a list of traits she hated in a man, those would be at the top.

They were choices he'd made—bad ones, in her opinion. He was intelligent. Why would he disguise it?

Despite all of that, whenever they touched, her body refused to let him go.

Tonight, when he had taken her hand, her senses were too consumed by him to focus on where she was walking or how much she'd wanted to escape the claustrophobic party.

Then there was his scent.

She closed her eyes, resting her head against the door, trying to capture it. He smelled like Luc.

Through the wall, she heard him moving around his cabin.

The corridor was soundproofed well—only loud noises, like an alarm or the commotion earlier, could be heard from outside. But the walls between cabins? They were another matter. If she wanted to, she could track his every movement.

But she didn't.

The unspoken rule she'd learned in the Navy was simple: ignore your neighbour. Privacy was a luxury in cramped quarters, one you had to give to others.

She did that now, switching off her awareness of him and stepping away from the door.

The accidental nap she'd taken earlier had refreshed her, leaving her wide awake.

Moving to her tiny desk, she retrieved her laptop from where she kept it—leaning upright against the wall beneath the desk. She pulled her phone from her pocket and plugged in the cable to transfer her photos.

As usual, an alert popped up: Erase after importing?

She hesitated.

If her phone went missing—by accident or by design—she didn't want anyone accessing the photos. On the other hand, Geordie knew she'd taken them. If it worried him enough, he might come looking. If he found nothing at all, he'd keep searching.

She scrolled through her shots from the afternoon. The images from the cellar and the dungeon she emailed to herself and erased them from her phone. They wouldn't sit in her gallery, but she could still access them if needed.

Then, she pulled up the ones from the corridor.

Two were clear: Geordie and his mate, their faces blurry but recognizable. The third had been taken accidentally as she moved the phone. It showed the corridor, a few indistinct figures, and the brownish shapes of wine cartons. No one was identifiable.

Even on the larger computer screen, the image was vague.

She emailed all three to herself and erased the good copies from her phone, leaving only the blurry one behind.

She continued scrolling. Photos from Taormina. The Greek Theatre. She downloaded them and erased them from her phone. Next, Castelmola.

She chuckled at the images of baskets full of bright red penises. Erase.

The breathtaking view from Piazza Sant'Antonio—download and erase.

Then, a different set of images.

A man's head obstructing the shot as she panned across the landscape.

She nearly dismissed it—until she noticed the slight turn of his profile.

Her breath caught.

"Luc!"

No.

She would have known if Luc was there. He hadn't been.

Tristan's fingers trembled as she moved to the next photo.

And there, his identity became unmistakable.

Nico.

The wind had caught the collar of his polo shirt, flipping it back.

Exposing a mark on his left collarbone.

Her heart slammed against her ribs.

She magnified the image.

In real life, it was about a centimetre tall—a small, heart-shaped mole.

On her screen, it was five centimetres across.

Incontrovertible.

Either Nico was Luciano's exact body double...Or Nico was Luc.

Shock roiled through her.

Her senses hadn't been playing tricks after all—the similarities between the two men weren't coincidences. They were the same damn person.

Her suspicions had been well-founded.

Questions crashed into her like waves in a storm.

Why was he on the ship?

Why was he in disguise?

Was he spying on someone? On something? On—her?

"Far out," she muttered, gripping the edge of the desk. "I gave him everything."

Siena had warned her. Don't trust anyone, and she'd gone and done exactly that.

Luc—Nico—had to have information he hadn't shared. There was no other reason for him to be here. How the hell had he even managed to get hired as the ship's accountant?

Her mind spun.

It's a wonder he didn't drop dead when I demanded a passport.

Then, he'd actually gotten one—fast.

Fake. It had to be.

He was the one who pointed out that the other passports didn't belong to real people.

Her breath came sharp and shallow.

Who the hell was he?

Was he really Luciano Ricci, the estranged son of the shipping tycoon? If so, was he here to rip off his father's company? Was he the one behind the missing money?

Too many questions.

No bloody answers.

A notification popped up on her laptop screen:

Download and erase?

Yes.

Her fingers hovered over the keys.

Download and erase.

She inhaled deeply, trying to calm the rage bubbling under her skin.

Then, in a deliberately sweet, simpering voice, she rehearsed:

"Oh, Nico, my phone had a meltdown. Power surge. Had to do a hard reset. Lost nearly everything—my photos, my books, my music. At least I can download the books and music from my cloud accounts, but the photos? Gone. Cactus. So sorry, A-hole."

Her teeth clenched.

She hit delete.

Then again. And again.

With a sharp snap, she slammed the laptop shut and shoved it away.

* * *

Muffled mumblings drifted through the wall from Tristan's cabin. Though the words were indiscernible, Nico's gut twisted with jealousy.

If that Englishman is in there...

He strained to listen. No male voice. Just hers. She could be on the phone, or maybe she was just closer to the wall, making it harder to hear the other person.

He killed the music he'd been playing.

This is a breach of protocol.

Didn't matter.

Justified or not, he needed to know she was okay.

Before he could overthink it, he was out of his room, slamming the door behind him. A heartbeat later, his fist was raised to knock—no plan, no excuse, just sheer instinct—

The door swung open before he could touch it.

Tristan stood in the doorway, face taut with anger.

"Yes?"

She was still dressed as before, but her entire demeanour was off.

"Er, um—"

Her posture shifted. Something in her eyes sharpened.

"I've got some bad news for you, Nico." She emphasized his name strangely, her voice smooth but edged with something he couldn't place.

A cold weight settled in his stomach.

"The power surge we had about half an hour ago fried my phone," she continued. "I had it plugged in when it happened. Had to do a hard reset. Not sure how much damage there is. I'll show you."

She unplugged the device from its charger and powered it up.

Standing close—too close—beside him, she tapped her music app.

"Damn. No music."

Next, her reading app.

"My books are gone, too. Oh dear."

She scraped her top teeth over her bottom lip, clicking into her photo gallery.

"Oh good, there are photos."

She scrolled through them. A few random ones remained—some with him, one blurry shot from the corridor—but nothing else.

A perfectly measured gasp. "What? Oh no. I don't have any of the dungeon and cellar photos."

She lifted her gaze to his, distress written all over her features.

His gut clenched.

"Nothing?" he asked.

She grimaced, shaking her head. Her shoulders sagged in defeat.

Nico's immediate instinct was to comfort her. He pulled her into his arms, holding her close.

This. This was why he came over. Just to touch her. Just to breathe her in.

If the photos were gone, they would deal with it. But something about this didn't sit right.

And then—

A drunken laugh slashed through the moment.

"Hey, you two! Has the party moved here? Can we all join in?"

Nico stiffened.

Tristan's body went rigid against him.

He turned to block her from the intruder's gaze.

The Englishman swayed in the doorway, grinning like a fool.

Nico stepped forward, closing Tristan's door behind him with a deliberate click.

"Go to bed, mate. You've got a big day tomorrow." His tone was mild, but the warning was unmistakable.

The man snickered. "What about you, mate? Shouldn't you be in bed too?"

Nico straightened to full Luc height, letting every inch of his authority settle over him. His voice was like steel.

"That's sir, not mate. You will keep your thoughts and comments about the lady to yourself."

A pause.

The Englishman blinked, swaying slightly. Then, something in his liquor-soaked brain clicked.

"Oops." He snapped a sloppy salute. "Aye aye, sir. Sorry, sir. Good night, sir."

With a stumble, he made it to his own door.

Nico exhaled slowly before stepping back into his own cabin.

The brief contact with Tristan still burned in his veins.

There'd been a shift in her attitude toward him. She'd let him hold her—if only for a moment.

She had better not be falling for Nico.

He was only going to be around for a few more days. If they wrapped this up quickly, he'd be gone.

But holding her? Holding her was like breathing in flowers on a warm summer's day.

His heart pounded. He had to find a way to build a future with her.

Chapter Nineteen

A day in the office was a welcome respite from guiding guests on endless tourist visits. It gave Tristan the chance to focus on her actual duties—processing staff integration, verifying passports and visas, ensuring everything was in order. A sense of control, even if fleeting.

She didn't ask if Nico had joined the tours or made any progress. Didn't want to know.

Her door stayed firmly shut.

Last night, when he held her, she hadn't been prepared for the warmth of his comfort. Her anger had mellowed as she carried out her fritzed phone plan. His reaction had been sweetly reassuring. It made her feel the tiniest bit guilty.

But today, she wasn't ready to deal with him. Not with the knowledge that Nico—who had seemed so inoffensive, so trustworthy—was likely just another layer of deception wrapped around Luc, the playboy. Maybe even one of the people Siena had warned her about.

Her judgment was fraying at the edges.

Was there anyone left she could trust?

Had someone intercepted her call with Siena, as her friend feared? Was Luc—Nico—tasked with monitoring her? Had she walked straight into some kind of honey trap by sleeping with him?

Well, if that was the case, he'd gotten nothing from her. She hadn't spoken to Siena since boarding the ship. If he was looking for collusion, he'd have been sorely disappointed.

A sharp roll of the ship pulled her thoughts back to the present.

She tamped down the unease curling through her gut. The movement of the vessel grew more pronounced as they sailed into the Adriatic, leaving Kotor behind.

Tristan forced herself to focus on her work. Sitting at her desk, engaged in productive tasks, was the only way to keep her conscious mind from fixating on the creeping sense of imminent danger her subconscious had already recognized.

For most of her seven years in the Navy, she'd thrived on storms at sea.

Vibrant. Elemental. Energizing.

Until one fateful night.

A knock at her door.

"Good evening, Ms. Sinclair. Everything alright here?"

Tristan jolted slightly, dragged from her thoughts. She glanced up to see a security detail standing in the doorway.

"Yes, I'm fine," she said, schooling her expression.

"It's getting late, ma'am, and the storm is strengthening. May we escort you to your cabin?" the Second Officer asked.

She hesitated.

The storm was intensifying, its presence pressing against the walls of the ship. She wasn't ready to face it. Not without distractions. But she was a senior member of the crew. She had to keep her composure.

"Certainly," she said, rising smoothly. "I'd appreciate it. I hadn't realized the time."

She projected a self-deprecating smile, grabbed her jacket but didn't bother to put it on.

Stepping over the lip of the doorway into the corridor, she double-checked that her office was locked before turning back to her escorts.

She recognized the Second Officer from the officer's mess, but the junior security guard was unfamiliar.

"Hi, I'm Tristan." She extended a hand. "As the sign on the door says, I'm in human resources."

The guard hesitated for a fraction of a second before shaking her hand. "Ma'am, I'm Zahra Ephrad."

Tristan smiled. "Where do you call home, Zahra?"

The young woman flicked a glance at her supervisor, as if gauging whether it was appropriate to engage in casual conversation with an officer.

At his nod, she turned back to Tristan.

Tristan focused on Zahra, using conversation as an anchor against the storm brewing outside—and the one inside her own head.

"My parents live in Rabat, Morocco," Zahra said. "But my home is whichever ship I'm working on."

"Why did you choose security?" Tristan asked, latching onto the distraction.

Zahra shrugged. "In my culture, it's not appropriate for a woman to stand on her own." A small, wry smile flickered across her face. "But my spirit refused to be constrained. I had to leave. That meant learning to protect myself. Once I did, I realized I could also protect others—and someone would pay me to see the world while I did it."

Tristan smiled at the quiet excitement in the young woman's voice.

"Do you see a career for yourself in security?" she asked.

"Yes, ma'am. Mr. Taylor has been mentoring me." She nodded toward her supervisor, a faint blush creeping up her cheeks. "He's helped me understand the management training I'll need and the extra physical skills I should develop. I'm very grateful."

They reached the corridor leading to Tristan's cabin.

"Thank you, John," she said, turning to the Second Officer. "I appreciate your thoughtfulness. I'll be fine from here." Then, to Zahra, she added, "Good luck with your dreams. I hope you find what you're looking for."

With a final nod, she gripped the handrail lining the corridor and pulled herself forward, step by step.

Once inside her cabin, she breathed a sigh of relief that she'd made it this far, even though she wouldn't sleep tonight. Not until the storm passed.

She peeled off her clothes and stepped into the ensuite. Hot water. Fresh clothes. A reset.

After dressing in a loose tracksuit, she paced the narrow confines of her room—back and forth, over and over—until dizziness forced her still. She dropped into the chair at her desk, clasping her hands together, forcing herself to focus.

Then, the ship lurched.

A wave slammed into the hull. Tristan gasped. Another hit broadside.

The old fear clawed its way up.

A raw, instinctual sound tore from her throat as she bolted upright, pressing her hands flat against the wall. She wedged her feet against the bed frame, as if bracing the cabin itself from collapse.

Breathe.

The self-command did nothing.

The ship pitched again, and her strangled cries filled the room, lost in the storm.

* * *

Nico first dismissed the sounds coming from Tristan's cabin as muffled conversation. Jealousy curled through him. Was she entertaining someone? But like the other night, he heard no other voices—only her.

He hesitated. She'd kept her distance all day. If she wanted nothing to do with him, she wouldn't welcome his intrusion.

Then, another cry—this one sharp, distressed.

His hesitation vanished. Hastily reapplying his beard and moustache, he strode across the hall and rapped firmly on her door.

No answer.

Another low, agonized moan followed as the ship pitched.

Testing the handle, he found it unlocked. Relief warred with urgency as he stepped inside.

She stood, braced against the wall, her body rigid, chin tucked to her chest. Her eyes were clenched shut, her breath coming in short, ragged gasps.

Trapped in something deeper than the storm.

"Tristan." He kept his voice low, steady. No response.

The ship rolled again.

"Tristan." He stepped closer. Still nothing.

Gently, he reached for her hand.

Her reaction was instant. She snapped toward him, eyes wide, wild with fear. Before he could speak, she threw herself into his arms, clinging as if he were the only thing anchoring her to the world.

His arms came around her automatically.

"It's okay," he murmured, guiding her toward the bunk. "You're safe. Nothing's going to happen."

The next swell hit. She stiffened.

"Shh. I'm here. The storm will pass."

She shuddered. "Luc."

His breath caught. Had she recognized him?

"It's Nico," he corrected carefully.

Her grip tightened. "Luc. Hold me."

He was lost.

He gathered her close, tucking her against him, his heaven warding off her hell. She needed Luc right now, not an argument. His past sins didn't matter—only this moment.

Her breathing steadied, but she didn't let go.

"Tristan." He brushed his lips over her temple. "You're a seafarer. You know storms happen. What scared you so much?"

No response.

After a long silence, he shifted back, tilting her chin up.

"Tris?"

Her dazed eyes locked onto his. Then she pressed her face into his neck, clinging fiercely as the ship pitched again.

"Luc," she murmured. "You don't look like Luc, but it's you."

He went still. "I can be Luc," he said, avoiding the admission of his true identity. Her face rubbed against the column of his throat. He closed his eyes, willing his body from reacting.

"Tristan?"

She reached up, fingers tracing his beard. Soft. Searching.

Then, with a deliberate slowness, she peeled the edge away.

"That's better," she whispered, as if she'd known all along.

Her gaze flicked to his lips.

"Now you can kiss me. Make me forget the storm."

She pulled him down, sealing her mouth over his.

His body detonated.

A week. A long, torturous week of resisting her, of keeping himself in check. Of watching, wanting, holding back.

"Cara." His lips roamed, tracing reverent paths over her face—her cheek, the curve of her jaw, the soft dip above her lips. Drinking her in.

She clung to him, her body pressing tight, one hand skimming under his T-shirt, fingers splaying over his chest. "I needed this." Her voice was breathless, urgent. "Soft and strong. Velvet and steel."

Her touch ignited every nerve in his body.

"Take this off." She tugged at his shirt.

He obeyed instantly, yanking it over his head. The second his skin was bared, she pushed him back onto the bed, her mouth following the path of her hands, her lips hot, seeking.

A groan tore from his throat as she closed her mouth over his nipple, her tongue sweeping slow circles over his skin.

"Tristan." His breath hitched. "If we go any further—"

She lifted her head, her gaze molten. "Don't stop." Her fingers dipped beneath his waistband, teasing over the hard length of him. "I want all of you."

His control shattered.

He shoved his pyjama bottoms down, kicking them off. His cock jutted, heavy and thick between them.

Tristan's eyes flared. She wrapped her fingers around him, firm, knowing, her thumb sweeping over the sensitive ridge.

"You're always this demanding?" he rasped, barely able to string words together.

"I don't think so." A slow, teasing smile curved her lips. "But I like having you in my power."

"You certainly do." He dragged a hand through her hair, needing to touch, to claim.

Her fingers skimmed up to his cheek. "Does this come off?" she murmured, tracing the edge of his false birthmark.

"Uh huh, but it's a bitch to put back on."

"And the hair... It's awful. Truly awful," she said, frowning. "But this," she said, grasping his cock, "this is wonderful!" She ran her hands lightly along his shaft as if fingering the notes on a cello staff in a robust classical piece. Sliding her body lower."

He barely had time to chuckle before she dipped her head, her tongue flicking over the tip of his cock, testing, teasing.

"Tris!" His hips jerked. His hands buried in her hair, though he couldn't tell if he was trying to pull her away or hold her there.

She glanced up. "Problem?"

His voice was raw. "We need protection."

A slow, wicked smile curled her lips. "I have some. Courtesy of the last occupant of the cabin." She arched a brow. "Or were you saying 'stop'? You have this whole clear consent thing, if I recall."

His pulse thundered. Damn her. "No. Don't stop." His voice dropped. "Find the condom."

Tristan slid off the bed, steadying herself against the wall as the ship rocked.

Luc sprang up. "I'll get it. Where?"

"Top drawer. Left-hand side."

He yanked it open—and stilled.

A neat stack of silken panties lay beside a pile of colourful foil packets. Hell.

Grabbing a handful, he shoved them under her pillow and turned back to her.

Her gaze devoured him. Naked. Waiting. Wanting.

"You are beautiful," she whispered.

His cock jerked under her gaze. Damn.

"And you," he murmured, dragging his eyes down her still-clothed form, "are overdressed."

She reached for him, but he caught her wrists, pressing her back against the sheets.

"Uh uh." His voice darkened. "You've had your fun. Now, it's my turn."

Her lips parted on a soft O.

Then she smiled—slow, sensuous, inviting.

Welcoming.

Luc slid from the bunk, kneeling beside it.

Burrowing his fingers into her tangled hair, he traced her lips with the tip of his tongue, teasing before dipping inside.

His other hand explored the shape of her—sliding over the loose fabric of her tracksuit, his palm pressing against her hardened nipples.

She moaned as he relaxed the pressure, cupping her breast instead. His kiss deepened into a fierce, possessive claim, while she gripped the slats of the headboard behind her—offering herself up.

An invitation he could not resist.

His hand roamed downward, over the softness of her belly, then lower still—his palm circling the heat between her legs.

"Oh. F-f-far out," she stammered. "Luc."

"I'm here, cara."

He lowered his mouth to her breast, his teeth grazing over the fabric covering her aching flesh.

She cried out, hips arching off the bed.

When he nudged her top aside and latched onto bare skin, she bucked beneath him, a strangled gasp tearing from her throat.

"Ah, cara." He nuzzled against her flesh. "You are a delight. Let me see you."

He slid her tracksuit bottoms down her legs, peeling them away, leaving her bared to him.

Reacquainting his mouth with hers, he swept a hand between her thighs, fingers sliding over the slick seam of her need.

Her breath caught as he parted her, his fingertips finding the precious pearl hidden there. He rubbed. Circled. Pressed.

Her body tensed, head falling back, neck muscles taut as a sharp, helpless cry escaped her lips.

Without pausing his onslaught, he slipped one finger inside her. Slow. Searching.

Then another.

He stretched her, deeper, firmer, his touch unrelenting.

Her body clenched around him, her thighs trembling.

With his mouth devouring hers, he swallowed her cries as she came apart in his arms.

She was still shuddering when she gasped his name.

"Oh God. Luc. I need you inside me. Now."

Ripping open a foil package, he rolled the condom down his length, barely holding himself together as she scooted forward, wrapping her arms around him just as another wave crashed outside.

Her eyes widened in fear.

"You're safer in the bunk," he murmured.

Sliding onto the mattress, he pulled her with him, steadying her as she straddled him, her breasts tantalizingly close but just out of reach.

She rocked against him, her gaze locking onto his. Tempting. Taunting.

Luc snapped.

Grasping her hips, he lifted her just enough before slamming into her, spearing deep.

She cried out, her nails biting into his skin.

Rolling, he twisted her beneath him, his thrusts turning urgent, relentless.

Her body clutched at him, tight, hot, demanding more.

He drove into her, deeper, harder, until her head fell back with a strangled moan.

"Luc." Her voice was pure surrender.

His rhythm faltered, control shredding.

With one last thrust, he let go, his body straining, trembling as he poured himself into her, his world fracturing around them both.

The ship rocked, the storm raging on.

He collapsed beside her, his arm tucking her close, securing her against him as she rested her head over his pounding heart.

Her lips brushed his skin as she whispered, "Storms will never be the same."

He huffed a laugh, pressing a kiss to her hair. "For me either."

A pause.

Then, softer, he asked, "Why do they frighten you so much? You work on a ship. Storms are a part of life."

She buried her face against his neck for a moment before whispering, "Five and a half years ago... I was still in the navy."

His fingers traced slow, lazy circles on her arm. "I know."

"I was on deck with my two best friends. The Mediterranean was a beast that night, the storm massive."

She shifted against him, her breath uneven.

"A freak wave rolled over the yacht. We all went down."

His hold tightened instinctively.

"One of them—she grabbed me. Held on to a pole for dear life." Tristan exhaled. "I had Beth's hand."

She lifted her right forearm, exposing the scar running through a heart-shaped tattoo with three small initials in each corner.

She traced the wound absently.

"If my flesh had been made of Velcro, maybe..." Her voice cracked. "But I lost her."

A hollow silence settled between them.

Luc swallowed.

"I'm sorry, cara," he said softly. "Truly."

She exhaled, pressing closer to him. "I never thought I'd be able to... I mean, storms at sea have always—"

Her words trailed off, but he understood.

His arms tightened around her.

"I'm glad," he murmured. "That tonight, at least, we made better memories."

She sighed against him, body softening, breath slowing.

Then, just as sleep pulled her under, she whispered,

"Tomorrow, you'll explain why both of you bastards deceived me."

Chapter Twenty

The speaker in Tris' cabin crackled to life:
"Officers. Officers. Officers. Bravo. Bravo. Bravo. Delta. Delta. Delta."

Tristan jolted upright, disoriented.

Her brain was fogged with exhaustion, and for a split second, she forgot where she was. But no one ignored this kind of summons—especially not at four in the morning.

At least the storm had passed.

She nudged Luc, who was still sprawled against her, blocking her from the floor.

"We've got to move. Serious incident. Biohazard emergency." She threw the blanket off. "How can you sleep through this racket?"

Luc grinned—completely unbothered—then yanked her down for a quick, heated kiss before springing from the bed. Instantly alert.

By the time she swung her legs off the bunk, he was already half-dressed, moving toward the door.

"Wait."

He pivoted.

Tris held up the fake facial hair she'd peeled from him the night before.

He slapped the prosthetic back on, grinned and shrugged. "I'll explain later." A teasing lift of his brow. "And you'll explain how you knew."

With a quick glance down the corridor, he slipped out, heading for his own cabin.

Tristan sucked in a breath before dashing to the bathroom.

She turned on the tap—nothing.

Strange.

So, the water itself must be the biohazard.

Grabbing a bottle from her shelf, she splashed some over her face for a quick rinse, then threw on fresh underwear, her tracksuit, and sneakers—no socks.

No lifejacket signal had sounded, so she left hers where it was on the cupboard shelf.

She snatched up a hairbrush, ran it through the tangles once, and bolted out the door.

By the time she reached the gathering area near the bar, a small huddle had already formed.

The captain, deck captain, and chief engineer stood together, speaking in low, tense voices.

Tristan dropped onto a seat beside Shelley, the cruise director, in the second row—right where they usually had their dance lessons with Nicholas and James.

"What's going on?" Tris murmured.

Shelley shook her head. "No idea. But I've never seen Argstrom lose his cool, and he looks pretty shaken."

She tilted her chin toward the huddle.

"Could be an engineering issue. Arno's been talking a lot."

Tristan glanced toward the chief engineer, who was gesturing wildly as he spoke.

Before she could process more, she felt someone sit next to her.

She knew who it was before she turned.

Luc was gone.

Nico was back.

The beard, the moustache, the unkempt hair—even the subtle shift in his posture, shoulders hunched just so.

A small ache twisted inside her, but she swallowed it down.

"Good morning, Nico," she said evenly.

He gave her a brief nod, slipping into his usual reserved persona.

She forced herself to look forward as the deck captain stepped up, microphone in hand.

"Good morning, ladies and gentlemen."

His voice was calm, but there was an edge of urgency beneath it.

"We apologize for dragging you from your beds at this hour, but we have an incident that requires your full attention. The captain will brief you."

He stepped back.

The captain's gaze swept the room, his usual composed expression strained at the edges.

"Officers, we have discovered that the major potable water tank has been fouled."

A ripple of unease moved through the gathered officers.

"At this point, we do not know if this was an accident by the engine crew or deliberate sabotage. The investigation is ongoing."

Tristan's stomach tightened.

Sabotage?

The captain continued, "What we do know is that we cannot sustain the passengers—or even most of the crew—on board under these conditions."

A murmur spread through the room.

"We have made full speed toward Dubrovnik and have already alerted the port authorities. They will facilitate disembarkation.

"Some deck officers, maintenance crew, and a handful of catering staff will remain on board." His eyes scanned the assembled officers.

"All other passengers and crew will be re-accommodated."

"In two hours, I will make an announcement over the general system," the captain continued, "informing all passengers and relevant crew that they must have their belongings packed and ready for collection by 0800.

"They will be allowed breakfast, but only with bottled water—for drinking, cleaning teeth, and any other hygiene needs."

His gaze swept the room, shoulders squared with authority.

"We'll keep you updated as more information comes to hand. Be as open and honest with passengers as possible. The Dorata Giulietta is already scrambling in Trieste. She'll need ten to twelve hours to reach us. Passengers will be transferred to her to complete the planned cruise."

A murmur rippled through the gathered officers.

"Shelley," the captain turned to the cruise director, "today's tours can go ahead but must be delayed by two hours to ensure all passengers are off-loaded first.

"In fact, the more people we have on tours and occupied, the better. They won't have time to worry if they're distracted."

His lips quirked in dry humour.

"The serpentine mountain roads of Dubrovnik, paired with the precision driving required to keep buses from plunging off cliffs, should keep them focused on survival."

A scattered chuckle followed, but the tension in the room didn't ease.

"You all know your jobs," he concluded. "Do them well, and do them quickly. There's a lot to accomplish in a short amount of time."

The Deck Captain stepped forward.

"Section heads, report to me every half hour until all passengers are organized for disembarkation. Good luck. That is all."

Tris shuffled from her seat as soon as Nico left the way clear.

"I'll give you a hand with crew accommodations," he murmured, his voice still deep in buzzard-neck impersonation mode. "After I finish preparing account statements for the guests."

"Thanks," Tris sighed. "It's going to be a long day. I just hope there's plenty of coffee. I didn't sleep very well last night. The storm, you know..."

Nico's lips twitched. "Sorry to hear that. It was rough for a while there."

"Uh-huh. Sure was. But..." she gave him a sidelong glance. "It's changed my reaction to storms at sea. I'm actually looking forward to the next one."

A low chuckle escaped him as they descended the stairs to Deck Three.

"You'd better quit now," he murmured, voice dropping to a delicious rumble, "before I break character and drag you back to my cabin."

A shiver of anticipation coursed through her.

"Is that supposed to dissuade me?"

"Tristan..."

"Hi, Shelley," she cut in, nudging Nico just as they reached the bottom step.

Shelley barely slowed as she passed. "I'll have to manage the tours somehow. I'll pull in the spa teams, maybe even some restaurant staff if needed. You two are going to be flat out today."

She turned briefly toward Nico. "Oh, and the captain's authorized today's tours free for all guests. If I arrange extra buses and walking tours, it might encourage more participation. Dubrovnik has plenty to see and do. Hopefully, the rain lets up.

"Good luck!" she called, already striding away.

Nico exhaled. "That just added another pile of work to my morning. I'll have to wrap up twice as fast before statements go to guests."

His eyes glinted at her.

"You'd best stop distracting me, Ms. Sinclair."

She smirked. "Quid pro quo, Mr. Griff."

"Oh, and when you do our accommodation bookings, make sure we have interconnecting rooms, yes?" he added with a glint in his eye.

"No promises," Tris replied, arching a brow. "We might end up in separate hotels."

"Tristan..." His low warning sent a ripple of anticipation through her.

She smirked. "Oh, FYI—I'm still angry with both of you. Have a good day, Mr. Griff."

Before he could respond, she slipped into her office and let the door slam shut behind her.

Only to find him already inside.

"You don't get off so easily, madam," he murmured, tugging her close by the shoulders. His grip was firm, but not unkind. "You've put me through all sorts of hell this week."

"Your own fault." She grinned, pressing her hands against his chest. "I'm not the one playing fancy dress."

"I'll explain tonight," he promised. "If we have a secret way to meet. Like, say...a common door?"

"You drive a hard bargain."

"I believe you understand that I will haggle incessantly to get what I want."

"And I told you—I'm not for sale."

She rose on tiptoe and pressed a kiss to his cheek. "I will not kiss that awful moustache and beard," she said, retreating.

"Busy day, Mr. Griff. Time's a-wasting."

He sighed. "So it is, Ms. Sinclair, but the day will end, and then—you're mine. I promise."

With a slow, deliberate motion, he bowed his head and brushed a kiss against her crown.

Twelve gruelling hours later, Tris slumped into a cushion-covered metal chair on the hotel terrace, barely upright as the setting sun glared in her eyes.

Her arms felt like lead, her entire body drained. Even lifting the champagne glass Nico had ordered for her seemed an impossible feat.

Below, the Dorata Giulietta rested in the harbor, passengers clustered near muster stations, life jackets in hand. Wisps of smoke curled from her chimneys. 'All aboard' was later than it would have been under normal circumstances, to allow for longer tours and re-embarkation.

The transition from one ship to another had been smoother than expected, but still exhausting.

The borrowed Giulietta crew had stepped back on board with no issues, taking required members from the Laura to fill in gaps for those on leave. Shelley's team, the gentleman hosts, and the entertainers had transferred with the passengers to minimize disruption.

The Giulietta's own administration staff remained, which meant Tris and Nico were among the surplus officers housed in Dubrovnik hotels until the Laura was fit to sail again.

A short, sharp blast from the Giulietta's horn startled Tris from her half-doze.

She grabbed the railing and hauled herself to her feet, waving at the passengers enthusiastically swinging their arms in farewell.

"They probably can't see you," Nico murmured beside her.

"If I can see their faces, they can see me." She shot him a pointed look. "The benefit is—they can't see my exhaustion. Now, up you get, lazy bones. Everyone needs acknowledgment. You can sacrifice three minutes of your precious time and energy."

With a long-suffering sigh, Nico shuffled upright, lifting one hand in a half-hearted wave until the bulk of the ship moved past, leaving only the passengers at the stern still visible.

"We're meeting the others for dinner in twenty minutes," Tris said, setting her untouched champagne on the table between them.

"It won't be a late night for me."

"Me either."

Nico stretched lazily, but his hunched posture remained intact. "I'm looking for whatever my bed offers, straight after we eat."

A wicked glint flickered in his eyes.

Tris shot him a stern glance, refusing to engage. Instead, she turned on her heel and headed inside.

Dinner was light-hearted, the atmosphere lively despite the sheer exhaustion settling over them all.

The offloaded crew from the Laura were spread across multiple hotels, but twenty of them had ended up here, gathering to share a meal.

The deck department, treating their unexpected onshore stay like a mini-holiday, were already planning evening entertainment in the city.

Tris, however, was done.

The combination of limited sleep and a full-throttle day had drained her completely.

The moment she finished her meal, she excused herself with a brief farewell, glancing at no one in particular, and escaped.

In her room, Tris let the hot water wash away the exhaustion of the day. After drying off, she unlocked the interconnecting door from her side with an ornate metal key, its heavy tassel swinging against her wrist.

The entry doors were secured with modern electronic keys, but this one—this old-world artifact—felt like it belonged in a forgotten romance, conjuring images of secret assignations.

She crawled into bed, her body still swaying as though she were adrift on water.

A shaft of light reflected off the balcony next door, hit Tris' face. A feathery breeze tickled her neck. Tris stirred, her eyelids fluttering open as she sighed into the dawn—a breath that was cut short by the weight across her ribs.

She lay very still.

A familiar scent surrounded her—Luciano. His breath whispered across her throat, each exhale sending tufts of warm air skimming her skin. The steady rise and fall of his chest against her back was a rocking lullaby, soothing and intoxicating all at once.

She breathed him in.

Was this how it felt to be cherished?

Loved?

Her lips curved as she nuzzled her cheek against the arm cradling her head.

But reality crept in, too.

There were questions to be asked. Answers to be given. Her life was in Melbourne—worlds away from this man and his playboy lifestyle.

She tensed, preparing to slip from the bed.

Luc's breathing changed. His arm tightened around her.

"Don't go," he murmured, voice still laced with sleep. "We missed this yesterday. Let me hold you, cara."

Her heart lurched at the quiet endearment.

Well, heck. Why not?

She eased back against him, pressing her hips into the unmistakable hardness at her spine.

A low groan rumbled in his chest. His lips brushed her ear, sending shivers down her arms.

"In a perfect world, we would wake like this every morning, amore mio."

His arm shifted, cupping her breast, his thumb sweeping slow, idle circles over her skin.

She turned to face him, her gaze locking onto his.

"Good morning, Luciano."

His mouth captured hers, stealing the air from her lungs.

"Ah, bella..." He shuddered, pressing his forehead to hers. "I need this. I need you."

His kiss deepened, igniting something primal, something that had been simmering for far too long.

Tris arched against him, looping an arm around his neck, letting her thigh glide along his.

His erection stiffened against her belly.

He groaned, voice ragged.

"Do you have protection?" she whispered.

"Sì." His lips quirked. "Raided the mini-bar last night. There was a package next to the hangover cure. You have options—ribbed for her pleasure, mint-flavoured, or studded for his excitement."

She laughed, plucking the green foil packet from his fingers.

"This one will do."

With deliberate slowness, she rolled the rubber sheath over his length, her fingertips flexing, teasing.

Her mouth followed.

"Mmm. It's the mint one," she said, licking the length of him.

Luc's sharp inhale was followed by a curse. His hands dove into her hair, tugging gently.

"Wait. I can't—"

She glanced up, then ducked back to lick some more.

But Luciano had other plans.

In one swift movement, he flipped her, bracing over her, his body a taut line of restraint.

And then—he was inside her.

His jaw clenched, the muscles of his neck straining.

"Dio..." He let out a shaky breath. "Thank God you're ready for me."

Tris wrapped her limbs around him, locking her heels at the small of his back, letting him fill her completely.

Her hands stretched above her head, offering him everything.

He took one breast into his mouth, teasing, pulling, until sensation crackled through her like a live wire.

The pace quickened—a driving, relentless rhythm.

Luc's gaze burned into hers, his intensity unwavering.

She could feel it—the coil tightening, her body tensing to the breaking point.

Until he drove into her one last time—

she shattered, splintering apart in a thousand pieces.

There was nothing else on earth that electrified every cell in her body like this. She clung to the moment, holding on as long as she could, like savouring the final dying reverberations of a spoon on fine crystal.

Luc collapsed against her, his body a heavy, delicious weight, his breath ragged and uneven.

His fingers skimmed her skin, tracing lazy, possessive patterns.

"Ah, bella..." he murmured. "When I am with you, I lose control."

"Mmm-hmm," she hummed, still feeling him inside her.

A slow, wicked smile curved her lips.

She shifted, slithering atop him, her nails grazing his chest, teasing the peaks of his nipples.

Luc's breath hitched.

She stabbed her tongue into his mouth, her lips sealing to his, tasting the aftermath of pleasure. A low, needy sound vibrated in her throat, a sound she barely recognized as her own.

Luc bucked beneath her, his hands tightening on her hips.

She wrapped her fingers around his base, applying a rhythmic, pulsing pressure.

His moan was pure sin.

Then his hand joined hers, except—his fingers found the hidden bud between her thighs.

Her gasp turned into a cry, her grip slipping as her body convulsed at his touch.

She had no time to recover.

Luc thrust into her, his pace now reckless, unrestrained.

A guttural growl escaped him as she arched her body, her nipples skimming his chest, her mouth crashing onto his, absorbing the ferocity of his passion.

His body went taut beneath hers, the same exquisite tension building in her until—

She shattered.

They shattered together.

No beginning. No end.

This was more than sex. This was something raw, consuming, infinite.

For the first time in her life, she felt it—the merging of bodies, souls, and spirits. A communion so profound it defied logic, an undeniable unity that left her breathless.

Love.

Unsought.

Unexpected.

His arm tightened around her, holding her against him.

She slid a hand between them, pressing her palm to the steady, powerful beat of his heart.

Luc sighed, his fingers mapping her body in lazy exploration, drifting through her hair, skimming her spine, before finally pressing a lingering kiss to her forehead.

That kiss.

It had mind-erasing properties.

She completely forgot she was supposed to be furious with him—even if Nico had disappeared this morning.

She edged to the side of the bed, watching him.

His face was bare—the beard, the moustache, the disguise... gone.

Her fingers caressed the overnight stubble, her pulse kicking up.

"Why are you not in disguise today?"

Luc's mouth quirked. "Nico will be in meetings all day, conveniently unavailable to meet with anyone. The captain has been informed."

Her brows knitted.

"And Luciano?"

"Luciano must make an appearance." He stretched, his body still humming with the aftershocks of their release. "On the orders of Signor Ricci—to investigate what happened to the jewel of the Dorata fleet."

Tristan froze.

Her stomach tightened.

"Signor Ricci?" she repeated. "As in... the owner of the cruise line?"

"Half of it," Luc said smoothly. "My father and I are equal partners."

A wave of disbelief crashed over her, shattering the fragile sense of bliss she'd been floating in.

She pulled away, her chest tightening.

"You are the renegade playboy son Catalan mentioned?" Her voice squeaked past the constriction in her throat.

Luc's jaw ticked. "I am my father's son, yes."

She inhaled shakily, struggling to process this.

His name, his family, his influence—he'd hidden all of it.

Luc's eyes darkened, as though he could see the storm brewing inside her.

"The playboy persona is a mask," he said quietly. "It lets me work without scrutiny. My parents always know where to find me. I don't live off them. I'm self-sufficient—not the leech Catalan described."

His face tightened, like he was bracing for a blow.

Tris swallowed.

Her mind was spinning, her body still hypersensitive from what they'd just shared.

This changed everything.

She crossed her arms over her chest, her voice low, guarded.

"What exactly is this 'work' you do?"

She lifted her hands, air-quoting the word work.

Luc's gaze flickered, something unreadable passing behind his eyes.

Just like that, the intimacy of the moment splintered into uncertainty.

Luc's gaze held steady, his voice even, but she caught the tension coiled beneath the surface.

"I'm employed by shipping companies to go undercover in different roles," he said. "To expose why disruptions are occurring in what should be smoothly run enterprises."

Tristan's breath hitched.

Her mind reeled.

"Is that what you were doing on the Laura?" she asked.

"You know the issues there yourself." His expression darkened. "The wine, the salaries, the possible sabotage."

A chill slithered down her spine.

Her voice lowered.

"So what am I?" she asked. "Your accomplice—or your prime suspect?"

Luc's entire demeanour shifted.

"Cara..."

In a flash, he was on his feet, as naked as the day he was born, his grip firm but gentle as he grasped her upper arms.

"You are not a suspect," he said, his voice a shade too raw.

Her pulse spiked.

"You're the woman I regretted leaving in Melbourne to take on this job." His fingers tightened, just slightly, like he was afraid she'd pull away.

"What we have is special. I want it to continue," he said.

A storm raged in her chest.

She searched his face, looking for something—anything—that would make this easier.

"I told you on the first day we met," she whispered. "I don't do rich and famous."

Luc's jaw flexed.

"I might not be rich for long." His voice held a bitter edge, his frustration slipping through. "That's what I'm trying to protect with this investigation. One bad experience—one scandal—on a Dorata ship can taint the entire fleet."

His hands dropped from her arms, but the intensity in his gaze never wavered.

"The enterprise my predecessors built from scratch—the thing my father and I have spent our lives maintaining—could fall apart overnight."

Tristan's stomach twisted.

She suddenly saw it—the weight on his shoulders, the stakes behind the playboy mask.

He wasn't just some wealthy heir with an ego.

This was his legacy.

And it was crumbling.

Luc exhaled, his expression softening.

"I'm due on board in an hour," he said. "To find out how the water was fouled—and whether it was sabotage."

His fingers brushed her wrist—a fleeting touch, barely there.

"I'd love to have you with me," he admitted, voice low, almost reluctant. "Because you see things others miss."

Tristan's heart clenched.

"But today," he continued, "I can't."

He hesitated. Then, a slow, crooked smile.

"There will come a time..." His lips slanted over hers, stealing her breath, her thoughts, her willpower.

Without a flicker of hesitation, without even bothering to cover himself, Luc strode through the connecting door, disappearing into his own room.

Tristan dropped onto the bed.

Her mind whirled.

What the heck just happened?

Her pulse pounded as the same question that had haunted her for days resurfaced, demanding an answer.

Who the hell was he?

Chapter Twenty-One

Luc struggled to focus as the captain detailed the problems that had forced the ship to offload passengers. His mind remained on Tristan, on the way he'd left her this morning—naked and confused.

The naked part? He'd love to recreate every morning for the rest of his life.

The confusion? Not so much.

He wanted to explain everything, but until he had the full picture, he had to tread carefully. Even with her.

The connection between them had been instant—ever since they'd collided in Melbourne. With every moment they'd spent together, it had only grown stronger. Even when he'd been in disguise and she didn't know who he was.

For now, there were bigger problems to solve.

Luc stepped over the threshold into the engineering section, the scent of oil and warm metal clinging to the air.

Arno, the chief engineer, stood with his arms crossed, his expression grim.

"Good morning, Arno," Captain Argstrom said. "This is Signor Luciano Ricci. He needs an explanation for what happened two nights ago."

The engineer barely glanced at Luc. "I can't explain it, sir."

Luc lifted his brows slightly.

Arno let out a heavy sigh and continued. "The entire crew was on high alert that night—switching engines in rough seas, running diagnostics. No one slept. By morning, we were all exhausted."

Luc nodded, urging him on.

"We checked and double-checked everything. The engines were fine. Now, I know what you're thinking—maybe one of the junior staff missed something. It's always a risk." Arno's jaw tightened. "That's why I did another round myself after sending most of the crew to rest."

"And?" Luc asked.

Arno's fingers flexed, as if reliving the moment.

"Everything looked good. No pressure drops, no leaks, no oil spills. I just had this...feeling. Like we'd missed something."

Luc stiffened. Instincts. The best engineers had them.

"I walked the floor again. That's when I saw it. The valve tap—it was horizontal, like it should be, but...reversed."

Luc's pulse kicked up.

"The valve acts as a seal between the drinking water and the untreated intake. Someone had positioned it to open."

Luc exhaled sharply. Sabotage.

Arno's expression darkened. "Sea water flooded the entire tank. The whole system was contaminated."

Luc's jaw set hard. "What did you do next?"

"I corrected the valve and ordered the pumps shut down., but by then, the damage was done. That's when I called the bridge."

Luc ran a hand through his hair. "What's the solution?"

"We had to drain and sanitize the entire tank. Refill it with fresh, clean water. Flush every pipe." Arno exhaled. "We got lucky. The contamination hadn't spread further."

Luc nodded, filing the information away.

"Sir," Arno added, his voice steely, "no one on my crew would have done this."

Luc met his gaze.

"These men—" Arno's voice shook with conviction. "They love these engines more than they love anything else in the world. They'd never intentionally cause damage. So don't go blaming them, you hear?"

The unwavering loyalty in Arno's voice was clear. Luc respected that.

"I'm not here to place blame," he said evenly. "I'm here to find out what happened."

Arno nodded stiffly, arms still crossed tight over his chest.

Luc pressed forward. "Was anyone else in this area that night?"

Arno frowned. "No, sir. Only the crew." He blinked. "Well—there was the catering guy—Mills. He brought us some birthday cake around twenty-one hundred hours."

Luc's spine stiffened. "Birthday cake?"

Arno gestured vaguely. "From the party we missed upstairs."

Luc's mind whirred. "Who sent it?"

"No idea."

Luc scanned the room. "Where did he put it?"

Arno pointed. "Right there—against this tank. He had one of those fold-away trays they use in the restaurant."

Luc stared at the spot.

A catering guy.

A cake left right next to the contaminated water valve.

Too coincidental.

His gut whispered a single word.

Planted.

Luc's gaze tracked from the table's position to the valve and back.

The setup was deliberate. If the crew had gathered around the cake, their backs would've been turned—blind to anyone tampering with the valve.

Arno followed Luc's line of sight. His eyes widened.

"Bloody hell." He sucked in a sharp breath. "Pardon my French, sir. Fuckin' mongrel. Wait till I find him."

"Settle down, Arno." Argstrom's voice was firm. "Don't go jumping to conclusions. That'll be all."

"Aye aye, sir." Arno's boots thudded against the metal floor as he stomped off, disappearing around a piece of equipment.

Argstrom turned back to Luc.

"We can't be certain it was sabotage, Signor Ricci. The investigation is ongoing. I'll have Mills found and questioned."

Luc nodded. "Thank you, Argstrom. I expect your report as soon as possible. Good morning."

As he stepped onto the gangplank deck, his mind whirred. Mills—the same man Tristan had seen delivering wine across the corridor. Another piece of the puzzle—but how did it fit?

Luc had been gone less than ninety minutes, but he couldn't wait to get back to the hotel to tell Tristan what he'd learned.

The sight of her smile when she woke had hit him like a gut punch. She was everything he wanted—in a woman, in a partner, in a wife.

Fiery. Determined. Loyal.

And he loved her.

He could admit that now.

He strolled down the hotel corridor, let himself into Nico's room, then into Tristan's.

"Honey, I'm home," he teased, dropping a kiss on her head.

Her reaction was immediate.

She launched herself from her chair, spinning toward him so fast he almost took a step back.

Her eyes blazed, red-rimmed from recent tears.

Her arms were rigid at her sides, fingers curled into fists.

Then she let loose.

"You elitist, self-absorbed, self-serving prick!"

Luc blinked. "Okay. Context?"

"You think because you have money and power, you can walk over people? Rip their lives apart like—" She clawed at the air, as if shredding paper, then flung the imaginary confetti at him. Her voice trembled. "Well, guess what? You don't get to do that to me."

"Tristan…"

"Did you or did you not contact my boss in Melbourne?"

Luc hesitated. "Well, yes. You were working on one of our ships…"

"One I was already hired for. Due diligence was done. I am fully qualified for this position. There was no reason for you to go behind my back—to John Trevethan, of all people." Her breath hitched. "But you had to go getting up people's noses. I was up for a promotion that I've been working my arse off for years to get. I told you about it and why it was important to me."

She sucked in a breath, chest heaving, her voice breaking on the last words.

Luc's stomach tightened.

"Now? Thanks to you?" She let out a sharp, bitter laugh. "I'm out of the running. Hell, I'm out of a job altogether."

Luc stilled.

"Tristan…"

"No." Her hand shot up. "I don't want excuses. Or explanations. Or justifications."

Luc met her glare, his own jaw hardening.

"You must admit," he said evenly, "your arrival on board was… convenient."

Her eyes flashed.

"When we met in Melbourne," he continued, "you gave no indication you'd be traveling to Italy to work on a ship owned by my family."

A beat of tense silence hung between them.

Then—

Her lip curled. "Screw you, Luciano Ricci. I didn't know—nor did I care—who owned the bloody ship. Siena needed my help."

Luc stilled. "McFarlane? You're in cahoots with McFarlane?"

As if trust were a physical thing, he felt it crumble inside him. His soul shrivelled at the thought.

Tristan's eyes flashed. "I'm not in 'cahoots' with anyone." Her voice was sharp, mocking his choice of words. "She warned me not to give out any information because she feared for her life. She thinks she's being framed for embezzlement. With her injury, she couldn't get back on board to check. So she asked me for help." She crossed her arms, her glare piercing. "I was the only person she trusted—not any of your precious insiders." She rubbed a hand across her forehead and glared at him.."

Luc's mind reeled, but before he could form a response, Tristan's voice cut through him like a blade.

"You talk about 'convenient'?" Her lips curled. "What a coincidence that you 'just happened' to bump into me in Melbourne, spilling my coffee so I'd remember you. You 'just happened' to invite me to dinner. To your room. Then—by some miracle—you're in the seat next to me on the plane."

She jabbed air quotes around each accusation.

"I should have known I was falling for a honey trap." She tilted her head, eyes dark with suspicion. "Was I wrong?"

A pit of acid burned in Luc's stomach.

"You're blaming me?" His voice was tight, his patience fraying. "I didn't know who you were—or that you had any connection to Mc-Farlane. If I had, you'd have been off the ship the moment you turned that snooty nose at me with your..." He mimicked her clipped tone, "'Time's a-wasting, Mr. Griff.'"

Tristan's laugh was sharp, bitter.

"Where would you be then?" She flung her hands wide. "You had no clue who the wolves were. You didn't spot the doppelgängers. That was me. You didn't make sure Fowler, Mills, and Watkins stayed on board so we could track them at port." She stabbed a finger at his chest. "The only thing you were useful for was getting extra crew on board. And let's be honest—that wasn't skill. That was Daddy's playboy pulling strings."

Luc's jaw clenched.

Tristan shook her head. "You kept everything from me—in both of your personas. Nico Griff was a lie. Luciano fucking Ricci turns out to be an even bigger one."

Her voice dropped to a low, seething whisper.

"Definitely not someone I should have given any part of myself except maybe a sailor's salute."

She flattened her lips, bounced her palm off her forehead, and glared at him—like she might headbutt him at any moment.

Tears pooled in her eyes, but she dashed them away with a swift hand.

"They say no good deed goes unpunished." Her voice wavered. "I guess I'm living proof. I gave up my holiday to sort out shit on your ship, and I'm repaid by losing every fucking thing I value."

Luc took a breath, trying to ease the tightness in his chest.

"You swear like you're still a sailor," he said idly. The words were out before he could stop them.

Her expression turned ice-cold.

"Proud to be one, arsehole." She cocked her head. "By the way—how the fuck did you know, before I told you that night in the storm, that I was in the navy?"

Luc froze. The ground shifted beneath him.

"Umm... Trevethan might have mentioned it."

Tristan's nostrils flared.

"And what else of my private life did he hand over to you without my consent?"

Luc hesitated. "Not much."

Her gaze bored into him.

He sighed. "That you were in the navy. That you're good with staff. And that you live alone."

Tristan's laugh was hollow.

"Bastards. Both of you." Her voice softened, but her body sagged with exhaustion.

"I spent six years in the Navy doing exactly what I did this week. That's why Siena trusted me to know what I was doing." Her gaze shifted toward the window, away from him.

Luc could see the tremble in her shoulders.

"Siena isn't your criminal," she murmured. "I know that for sure."

Luc's stomach twisted.

"Tristan—"

She flinched and threw up a hand, palm out. A stop sign.

Her voice cracked. "You break me, Luc."

The words gutted him.

"Just go."

A lump lodged in his throat. The roiling in the pit of his stomach was akin to the sensations he experienced if he'd disappointed his grandmother when he was eight years old.

"Tristan..."

Luc's chest ached.

For a moment, he stood there—paralysed. Then, spine stiff, he turned and strode through the interconnecting door.

Behind him, hurried footsteps followed—then the click of a lock.

He sank into a chair, burying his face in his hands.

He needed to fix this.

But how?

Chapter Twenty-two

Tristan plonked herself at the desk, resting her forehead on the bar made by her two index fingers. Luc's betrayal stung—but she could understand it in a business context. John Trevethan's? A whole different level of treachery.

She opened her laptop, scanning her last meeting notes. Then, grabbing the complimentary hotel notepad, she started a list.

With the dot points as her battle plan, she dialled Trevethan's number.

It wasn't quite 6 p.m. in Melbourne. He'd still be in the office.

He picked up on the second ring.

"Trevethan," he said.

Tristan's tone was calm, measured.

"John, it's Tristan Sinclair. Care to explain what the fuck is going on with this email terminating my employment?"

A beat of silence.

Then, indignation.

"You're working for someone else."

She cut in, ice-cold. "Stop right there. Who suggested I was working elsewhere?"

"Luciano Ricci himself contacted me to verify your credentials."

Ah. There it was.

"Uh-huh. And how do you know it was Signor Ricci? Did you see him?"

"It was a phone call," he snapped. "I didn't need to see him."

"So you assumed the person on the other end was who he claimed to be?"

Trevethan huffed. "He had an Italian accent."

Tristan almost laughed.

"So does the fucking maître d' at the hotel. It could have been any-one—even a competing candidate for the job. Yet, you gave out my personal information without my consent. Breach number one."

She checked her list, pen hovering.

"Has the role been filled?"

"Of course," he snapped. "No point waiting around when you weren't coming back."

Her grip tightened on the phone.

"Without informing all candidates of a scheduled interview?" she said smoothly. "Breach number two

"And the termination of my employment? What were the grounds for that?"."

Trevethan exhaled sharply.

"You were goddamn working somewhere else," he insisted.

"How exactly did you determine that?" Tristan asked. "Did you at-tempt to contact me?"

Silence.

She didn't wait.

"I downloaded a summary of our last meeting. In that conversa-tion, I explicitly informed you that I'd changed my leave status to un-paid. And I quote:

'I might end up working on the ship for a few days.'

Your response? 'Okay, that's fine. Whatever you do, stay safe and come back. Get this job and kick ass. Don't do anything stupid—like fall in love with a handsome Italian.'"

She let that hang for a beat.

"Your words, John. I took that to mean you didn't give a shit what I did while I was gone—so long as I came back."

Trevethan floundered. "Well, I—"

She steamrolled over him.

"Company policy requires grounds for dismissal, formal notification, and a chance to respond. You did none of that."

She let the silence simmer, then drove the final nail in.

"Breach number three."

Trevethan's breathing turned ragged.

Tristan's voice dropped to lethal calm.

"I'm offering you a right of reply before I move forward with legal action. How would you like to respond to a wrongful dismissal lawsuit?"

A beat of dead air.

Then, Trevethan swallowed audibly.

"In that meeting before I left," she continued, "you said, 'Sometimes people you trust let you down when you don't expect it.' You were talking about Michael."

She let her next words slice through him.

"Now I'm talking about you."

Trevethan made a strangled sound.

Tristan didn't stop.

"My next call will be to Jennifer Mellor. You know of her?"

A sharp intake of breath.

"Shit, Tris," he rasped. "She'll shred us."

"She's the she-lion of industrial disputes," Tristan agreed. "And she doesn't settle quietly. Expect an email from me soon. And a call from Ms. Mellor. Consider how you'd like to respond."

She let the weight of that settle.

Then, voice calm and final—

"Goodbye, John."

"Tris—"

She cut off his plaintive mewl with a sharp tap on the red button.

* * *

Argstrom recalled the staff and crew to the Dorata Laura the next morning.

The night before, Tristan kept to her room, ordering room service and indulging in much-needed quiet—time she spent responding to Jennifer Mellor's rapid-fire questions.

As for Luc?

When he'd attempted contact, she'd shut him down with a text to the number he'd given her in Melbourne: "Stop the harassment. Our relationship is strictly professional. Contact me only for work-related matters."

Her already cracked heart shattered into smithereens.

True to her request, his messages became professional—standard accountant-to-crew-purser exchanges.

Until the afternoon before they arrived in Naples.

"Please be informed, payments to (listing a dozen of the doppelgangers) are forwarded to an account at Napoli Mega Bank in the name of Siena McFarlane; payments to (listing the remainder of the fake identities) are forwarded to a second account at Napoli Mega Bank, also in the name of Siena McFarlane.

I will recommend to Signor Ricci that warrants be issued for this person to recoup lost revenue.

Yours sincerely,

Nico Griff."

Tristan's chair scraped back violently as she stormed next door.

"This is bullshit." Her voice cut through the office. "None of this fiasco is Siena's doing."

Nico barely looked up. "Good afternoon, Ms. Sinclair." He handed her a stack of spreadsheets. "Here's the data."

She barely glanced at them. "Easily fabricated. I don't know why you're setting Siena up, but I will fight to prove you wrong."

Nico remained unmoved.

"She warned me people like you were after her. That her life was in danger. I trusted you. I thought you were actually searching for the real culprits—but all you wanted was a scapegoat."

"The numbers don't lie." His expression didn't flicker.

"Then the operator does," she shot back. "Have you ever met her? Spoken to her directly? Or is that too human for the likes of you people?"

"I follow the inquiry, weigh the facts, and draw conclusions." His tone was mechanical. "I didn't put your friend in this situation. She did." His gaze sharpened. "Are you here to cover it up?"

Tristan saw red.

"Bastard. You haven't even explained the wine shipments, have you? Why do our three musketeers of Mills, Fowler, and Watkins all refer to Mr. Davis? None of them mentioned Siena as the recipient."

"The merchant did." Nico leaned back, unshaken. "This lot is for Miss McFarlane, remember?"

"I don't believe it."

Her blood boiled.

"You've wrecked my life. And now you want to do the same to Siena? You're a fucking mongrel. A fucking elitist mongrel."

She spun on her heel, stomping back to her office, yanking out her phone.

Nico appeared in the doorway, voice cool as steel.

"I wouldn't bother." He slid his hands into his pockets. "I can have people there before she even picks up."

Tristan's stomach plummeted.

Her shoulders sagged.

"Why?" Her voice cracked. "Why Siena? What's in it for you? Who are you protecting?"

Nico's expression didn't change.

She narrowed her eyes.

"Or is this some elaborate stunt to win your father's approval? Riding in on your white horse to 'save the day'?"

That got a reaction.

Nico's head jerked like she'd slapped him.

"I follow the leads," he said stiffly.

"This time, you're wrong," she bit out. "You're monumentally wrong. You've had the wool pulled over your eyes, and you don't even realise it." She dragged in a breath, then straightened.

"Give me until lunchtime tomorrow," she said. "Let me talk to Siena. Face-to-face. I know her. Better than you."

Nico remained silent.

"In fact, why don't you join me?" she continued. "Look her in the eye before you throw her to the wolves. She might even have insights you've missed."

"Why should I?"

"Because if you don't, you're about to face a shitload of embarrassment and bad press."

She leaned in.

"I will not hesitate to tell the world that your fancy cruise line is being ripped off right under your toffy noses, and instead of investigating the real criminals, you're pinning it on the person with the least to gain and the most to lose—all because she started asking questions."

Nico's jaw tightened.

"You'd do that?"

Tristan's fury burned white-hot.

"Bloody oath. You go after my friend without cause, I'll go after you and yours, buster."

The tension snapped like a drawn wire.

Her body hummed with adrenaline, muscles taut to breaking point.

Her heart thundered.

Then—

He smiled.

The bastard smiled.

A Luc smile—in a Nico face.

The exact same smile that once made her melt at Luc's feet.

"You are a tiger, cara." Nico's voice was almost amused. "Alright. I will meet your friend. But understand this—if I'm not satisfied, the police won't be far behind."

"Good." Tristan's voice was cool, but her pulse pounded, she settled back into her chair.

"You might find this interesting." He slid his hands into his pockets. "An underworld contact just reached out. Said he's heard about premium wine going cheap in a warehouse near the docks—ECM signage on the front."

Tristan's brow furrowed. "That can't be Siena. She doesn't know anyone in the underworld—except the ones she's afraid of. And she has no names."

Her gaze locked onto his, past the coloured contact lenses, trying to find the man beneath.

"How do you know this guy?" She tilted her head. "Or is that a silly question?"

Nico's mouth curved slightly. "He's my zio. My honorary uncle."

Tristan let out a short, dry laugh. "Right. I guess every Italian family needs one."

He chuckled. "Not everyone. My zio is an honourable man—as far as his profession allows. He protects his own. Like you do."

A flicker of something unreadable crossed his face.

"That's why he came to me. Someone's trying to steal from us."

Tristan's stomach knotted. "What's his name?"

"Guido Marconi."

A name with weight.

"He's well-known in Naples," Nico continued. "See if your friend knows him too."

Tristan narrowed her eyes. "And if she does, that makes her guilty?"

"Perhaps." He shrugged. "You told me to keep an open mind. I'll try."

He pivoted toward the door, but hesitated, glancing back.

"Why is she so important to you?" His voice was quieter this time. "This Siena McFarlane?"

Tristan exhaled slowly.

Without a word, she rotated her arm, exposing the underside.

The scar.

"She's the one who held me safe when Beth went overboard." Her voice was steady, but the memory wasn't.

"She's saved my life—literally and figuratively—more than once. As I've saved hers."

Her eyes met his.

"She's never stabbed me in the back. Never deceived me. Unlike you."

Nico's face fell.

"In fact," she added, "Siena is the only person left in the world I can truly trust."

His jaw tightened.

"So," he murmured, "between her and me, there's no contest."

Tristan moved her head from side to side, lips pressed tight.

He nodded once, as if accepting defeat.

"Well then, cara," he said quietly, "I hope she doesn't disappoint you."

And then, he walked out the door.

Chapter Twenty-three

Tris needn't have worried about Luc meeting Siena. Her lovely friend won him over immediately with her sincerity.

Luc wasted no time. "Do you know Guido Marconi?"

Siena frowned. "I don't 'know him' know him. I know of him. He's a philanthropist, isn't he? Recently donated a million euros to expand the hospital's ICU in honour of his mother." She raised her brows. "Sounds like a nice guy."

Luc's gaze sharpened. "You've never met him? Never phoned him?"

"Crikey, no." She gave a light laugh. "I don't move in those circles—except with our passengers."

Luc studied her for a beat before stepping out onto the terrace to make a phone call.

Tristan poured glasses of red wine to go with the antipasto Siena had prepared. Luc could join them or not.

Her anger with him hadn't gone away. The problem was, the man still turned her into a puddle of want and need, no matter how hard she tried to box him as a heartless, privileged elitist.

When he strolled back in, his gaze locked onto hers.

Her heart somersaulted—against both her will, and her better judgment.

No. She cranked up the anger simmering in her gut, meeting him with an icy glare.

Luc bit his lip, glancing up at her from under his brows. "The call came from Peter Davis."

Tristan stiffened. "But you were all ready to—"

Siena cut her off. "Him, I know." She took a sip of wine. "He applied for the HR role and lost to me. Wasn't happy about it. Made my life hell." She huffed. "His girlfriend, Freda, hated me too. I avoided dealing with her. She was the one I sent Tris' deets and payment info to."

Luc's jaw tightened. "There are two accounts at Napoli Mega Bank in your name. By my calculations, they've got substantial balances."

Siena blinked. "Excuse me?"

Tristan's hands shot to her hips, chin jutting forward. "You arrogant—"

Siena held up a hand. "Hold on." Her voice was calm, but her knuckles whitened around her wine glass.

"I have one account there, where my ECM salary goes." She let out a breath. "If it suddenly has a 'substantial balance,' that would be a bloody miracle. Don't get me wrong, I'm not povvo, but I'm not exactly rolling in it either."

Luc's gaze slid to Tristan. "Povvo?"

Tris tipped her head back. Through gritted teeth, she muttered, "Another expression for your list, 'Mr. Griff.' It means poverty-stricken."

The intimate smile he gave her nearly buckled her knees.

Siena's eyebrows lifted as her gaze bounced between them.

"Ahem." She smirked at Tristan before turning to Luc. "How about I go to the bank tomorrow and verify these accounts? If someone's funnelling money in my name, I'd like to know."

"I'll go with you," Tristan said. "If those accounts are as big as Luc implies, you might need backup if things go pear-shaped."

Luc chuckled.

Tristan frowned. "What?"

"Pear-shaped?"

She rolled her eyes. "You've got a lot to learn, Luciano. And not just about the language." She raised a brow. "You should stick around."

Luc leaned in slightly, voice low and smooth.

"It would be my pleasure to stick with you, cara," he said, raising a single brow."

Siena let out a low whistle.

"Huh. I take it back," Tristan said. "You're gonna have a shitload of grovelling to do, mate. Even then…" She shook her head. "Forget it."

Luc's smouldering glance burned through Tristan's defences.

"Tristan, please." He hung his head for a beat before he met her gaze, jaw flexing. "I would walk over hot coals to apologise for destroying your dream job. If that's not good enough, tell me what I must do." He folded his arms.

"But not today. Right now, my focus has to be on whoever is trying to destroy the business. Do you understand?" His voice roughened. "This is personal. They're attacking my family, my father, everything we've built. The meet with Zio is set for ten in the morning. When it's done, you can ask whatever you like of me."

Tris swallowed hard.

Could she deny this man anything?

Damn him. Damn him for being right to keep the focus sharp.

She had been just as determined to find the culprits. Her resolve softened. "Okay. What do you need me to do?"

Luc let out a breath. "Thank you." He turned to Siena. "Do you still have the master key? If this is an ECM warehouse, it might work."

"I do." Siena dug through her handbag. "I didn't have time to return it before they stretchered me off the ship."

She fished out a plain white plastic card, holding it up between two fingers. "Oops. Does that make me a suspect? Too bad." She shrugged, then handed it over. "Here you go."

Luc turned it over in his palm. "This is it?"

"Yep." Siena smirked. "Could be anything, huh? Just don't lose it. I need it back to log it in."

* * *

Tristan and Siena stepped into the bank, uncertain if their plan would work—or how it might unravel.

The morning rush had passed, leaving behind a lull before business customers trickled in after lunch.

Tris scanned the room.

They waited at the head of the queue while a teller chatted with an elderly woman. The conversation, full of warmth and familiarity, sounded like a well-rehearsed exchange of family updates.

At the next counter, a businessman in a crisp suit argued over the exchange rate for a bank cheque in pounds sterling, railing against what he considered an exorbitant fee. His teller, unfazed, barely lifted a glance from the screen, her fingers moving methodically across the keyboard.

At the final counter, a bank employee furiously keyed in data one-handed, flipping pages with her free hand. Her posture radiated, 'Go away. You can see I'm busy.'

The elderly woman at the first counter wrapped up her conversation with the teller in a tone signalling sage advice.

"Grazie, Zia. Ciao!" the teller responded.

"Ciao, Ragazzina," the older woman said before shuffling off.

With a lingering smile, the teller waved Siena forward. Siena handed her a slip with her account details. "I'd like to check my balances, please."

The teller verified the name and photo on the screen, printed out the balance slip, and slid it across.

"Is there anything else I can do for you, Miss McFarlane?" she asked, her English flawless.

Siena smiled. "Yes. I'd like the balances for these accounts as well."

The teller repeated the process but stopped mid-motion. Her frown deepened as she glanced between the screen and Siena.

"One moment, Miss McFarlane. I must check this."

She hurried across to a man in a tailored suit and cravat. His slicked-back hair gleamed, and his small, precise moustache gave him the air of either a caricatured banker or a barber from the early twentieth century.

The moment he heard the teller's whispered explanation, his sharp gaze snapped to Tris and Siena. Without hesitation, he issued a quiet but firm directive.

The teller's face had paled by the time she returned.

"I'm sorry, Miss McFarlane," she said. "Could you please accompany me? Signor Ancillieri, our customer service manager, will assist you."

Siena's shoulders stiffened.

Tristan's instincts flared. "What's the problem, Stefania?" she asked, her voice level as she read the name on the woman's tag.

The young teller darted a nervous glance at Tristan, though it wasn't clear what had spooked her.

"It's the photograph, signorina," she murmured. "It does not match."

Tristan exchanged a glance with Siena. Interesting.

"Ah. We'd best meet with Signor Ancillieri, then," Siena said smoothly.

The teller's hands trembled as she gestured them forward. "Follow me."

Tristan focused on the customer service manager as they approached. His eyes flicked over their clothes and jewellery, as if calculating their worth down to the euro before they reached him.

He didn't bother with a greeting. "Which of you is Miss McFarlane?"

"I am," Siena said, standing tall.

His gaze snapped to Tristan. "And you are?"

"Security," she fired back.

The banker flinched, his head jerking as though an unseen string had been pulled taut.

"Whom do you work for?" he demanded.

"Miss McFarlane," Tris said flatly, stilling the muscles n her face.

The man's lips thinned in displeasure. "Please sit down, Miss Mc-Farlane," he said, though his gaze never left Tristan. "Are you carrying a weapon? We don't allow guns in here."

Tris gave him a slow, deliberate once-over, then murmured, "I don't carry a weapon, Ancillieri. I am the weapon." She widened her stance and folded her arms.

Siena raised her face to Tristan. "Marconi, you're scaring the man. Sit down."

Ancillieri visibly paled at the name.

"No, thank you, ma'am. I'll wait here."

Ancillieri regained his composure and turned to Siena. "Miss Mc-Farlane, there is an issue with the accounts you are inquiring about."

Siena's expression remained neutral. "I don't see why. They're in my name, are they not? You've confirmed I am Siena McFarlane. What's the problem?"

"The problem, signorina, is that these accounts contain large sums of money—and the photo ID used to open them does not match you." He reached for the phone on his desk. "I must call the police."

Tristan moved in two swift strides, her hand closing over the receiver before he could lift it—not touching him, but close enough that the threat was implicit.

Her voice dropped into a purr. "That would be the right call, Ancillieri... if you were certain of your facts."

"I am. This woman does not match the identification."

Tristan bent towards him, her voice smooth but lethal.

"Ms. McFarlane has been banking with you for over five years. When were these accounts opened? Who is the woman claiming to be her? Are you colluding with her for personal gain? Do you understand the penalties for identity theft, fraud, and embezzlement, Ancillieri?"

Each question landed like a hammer blow, and with every strike, Ancillieri shrunk deeper into his seat. By the final accusation, he was whimpering.

"But... but what can I do?" he stammered.

Tristan didn't blink. "You have one verified Siena McFarlane standing right here. Call the other one. Tell her there's an emergency. She must come in within thirty minutes to re-validate her accounts—because the finance department is sweeping up all non-compliant funds to resolve the financial crisis."

Ancillieri's jaw went slack.

"She'll come," Tristan continued. "Remind her she's received multiple warning letters about this. Now, given her status as an 'important client,' you decided she deserved a direct call from you."

Tris issued the command with no emotion, no hesitation.

Ancillieri swallowed hard. "Sì. I will do it."

Tris resisted the urge to exhale in relief. So far, so good. Siena projected an air of concerned effrontery so well that Tris nearly applauded.

Across the desk, Ancillieri dialled the first number.

Siena's handbag vibrated. She fished out her phone. "Hello?"

Ancillieri huffed and slammed the receiver down.

"Oh. That was you, Mr. Ancillieri?" she asked, feigning surprise.

The banker's scowl deepened as he stabbed at the keypad again and put the phone on speaker.

"Freda speaking," a clipped English accent answered.

"Freda? This is Signor Ancillieri from Napoli Mega Bank. I must relay an urgent message to Miss McFarlane."

"Oh, oh. Of course," Freda chirped. "I am Miss McFarlane. I use Freda so I don't get confused with my sister-in-law."

Siena's fingers curled against her skirt.

"I see, Miss McFarlane. We have sent several letters regarding an urgent issue. Have you received them?"

"Oh, probably. I figured they were statements and tossed them in the trash."

Ancillieri's face turned a dangerous shade of red.

"Miss McFarlane, you must keep bank statements for seven years."

"He-he, who's going to check?"

Ancillieri's jaw clenched. "The Finanza."

The light-hearted giggle on the other end died instantly.

"Which is why I am calling," he pressed. "The Finanza is sweeping all accounts not verified in the last six months. If you don't want to lose the funds in both of your accounts—which now total close to one million euros—you must come to the bank immediately to validate your details."

Tris and Siena exchanged a sidelong glance.

"Surely you can email it to me or something," Freda said.

"No." His voice hardened. "We need your original signature. That is why we sent the letters. You must be here within thirty minutes." He paused for effect. "At the branch near Termine Centrale."

Silence.

Then, a clipped, "Sì. Grazie."

Ancillieri hung up.

Tris let the silence hang for a beat. "Excellent, Ancillieri. Now, Miss McFarlane would like a cappuccino while she waits for her impostor."

The banker jerked upright. "Certainly. Excuse me." He scuttled away.

Siena's breath came out in a hiss. "Freda." Her voice shook. "Freda is Peter Davis's partner. I told you about her. She works for the recruitment agency ECM uses—she'd have access to all our files." She swallowed. "A million euros, Tris. They'd kill for that kind of money."

Tris' voice was low. Controlled.

"Settle, Siena." She kept her posture rigid, eyes sweeping the room. "We have an audience."

In her earpiece, a buzz.

Luc's voice came through.

"Musketeers at the warehouse," he said, giving the wine delivery men the nickname Tris had used. Tris hadn't asked where Luc had sourced their comms gear. It was top-tier equipment. Better even than what they'd used in the navy.

"Roger," she acknowledged. "FYI, a 'Freda' has been contacted. ETA thirty minutes. Marconi out." The name-drop was deliberate. A signal.

Less than fifteen minutes later, a short blonde woman in towering ten-centimetre heels tottered into the bank.

Siena's breath hitched. "That's her," she whispered.

Tris' posture stiffened. She tapped her earpiece. "Target arrived."

The bank's concierge guided Freda toward Ancillieri's desk.

"Miss McFarlane, please be seated."

Ancillieri's tone had transformed—a practiced obsequiousness re-served for high-value clients.

Freda glowed under the attention, tossing her hair back as she lowered herself into the chair. She paid zero attention to the two women lurking nearby, instead taking great care in placing her expensive tote on the floor.

Tris casually moved behind her, arms folded.

Ancillieri's sweat-slicked forehead gave him away.

Siena drifted closer. Freda's smug smile faltered. Her face drained of colour.

"Hello, Freda Higson." Siena's voice was deadly calm. "Would you like to explain why you're pretending to be me?"

Freda snapped upright. "You—? What the hell are you doing here?" Her gaze flashed to Ancillieri. "And you, you little worm. This was a setup. You'll pay for this."

She shoved at her chair.

Tris blocked the movement effortlessly. Like before, she didn't touch the person—just the environment.

"You may now make the call you planned earlier, Ancillieri," Tris said smoothly.

Freda slumped back down, defeated. Then, with venom: "Bloody Peter and his grand schemes." Her lips curled. "And you, you bitch—" she spat at Siena. "Peter was entitled to be the onboard HR. I only let your application through so they'd see he was the better choice. Idiots. The lot of them. Well, they got what was coming."

Tris leaned in, her breath against Freda's ear.

"In the interest of fairness, Ms. Higson—" Tris murmured, tilting her head toward Siena's phone. "You should know your confession is being recorded."

Freda's glance flicked down.

Siena twirled the phone between her fingers, its screen glowing.

Silence.

"Well, fuck," she said, snapping her mouth shut.

Chapter Twenty-four

Nico arrived early at the warehouse, letting himself in with the master key. He moved silently, scanning the logical entry and exit points for those coming to the meeting.

His gaze swept over the towering stacks of wine crates. This wasn't just from one cruise. This was an ongoing operation. Premium stock—all of it likely paid for by ECM.

If Guido followed through, he was in for a bargain.

With minutes to spare, Nico secured a hidden vantage point—a nest where he could observe without drawing attention from either Davis's men or Guido's security.

Fowler, Mills, and Watkins arrived first, trailed by another man—dressed sharper, moving with authority.

Davis? He'd never met the man, but given the deference the others showed him, it was a logical guess.

Nico watched as Davis directed his men to lower a carton, open a bottle, and set out glasses. A performance—a show of hospitality before the deal.

Then, Guido's men strolled in.

The shift in power was immediate. The four Englishmen instinctively huddled, like water buffalo facing a lion.

Salvatore stepped forward, his voice a gravelly demand.

"Which of you is Davis?"

Nico observed with interest. He'd grown up with Salvatore keeping him out of mischief. Guido's chief enforcer—not a man to take lightly.

The man Nico had picked as Davis, swaggered forward. "I am."

Salvatore gestured, and six men fanned out, methodically searching the warehouse. One of them paused at Nico's hiding spot, gave the briefest flicker of recognition, then moved on—choosing to stand nearby instead.

Minutes later, a black car pulled up outside the north-side roller door opening.

Guido entered.

He didn't rush. He didn't speak. He simply absorbed the room, flanked by two men.

Davis plastered on a smile, extending a hand. "Signor Marconi, a pleasure."

Guido didn't take it. His gaze drifted—the stacks of cartons, the makeshift table, the glasses, the wine.

Davis recovered quickly. "Shall I pour you some of this wonderful red, signor?"

Guido's expression remained unreadable. "You may," he said, at last. "From a fresh bottle, if you please."

"I opened this one to breathe for full flavour," Davis said.

Guido said nothing, staring the man down.

Davis hesitated, then gestured to Fowler. "Of course. A fresh bottle."

Guido barely moved, but Salvatore understood the signal.

With a snap of his fingers, he had one of their own men uncork the bottle, rinse the glass with wine, then dump it unceremoniously on the floor before pouring a fresh sample.

Guido took the glass. Sipped. Swilled.

Then, without breaking eye contact, he spat the wine at Davis's feet.

Davis flinched.

Guido set the glass down. His voice, when it came, was smooth. Measured.

"It is a fine wine." He paused. "How many cases do you have?"

Nico's watch buzzed.

A message flashed on the screen. His father, ECM security, and the police were entering the dock.

Shit. Zio had to go.

Not for nothing had Nico spent half his life learning at the man's feet.

Luc tapped five times on the crate beside the guard's ear, followed by two scrapes.

The guard stiffened. Listened.

Luc repeated: Tap, tap, tap, tap, tap. Scrape, scrape.

The guard rubbed his nose, then flashed five-two with his fingers toward Salvatore.

Salvatore leaned close to Guido. "Cinquantadue, signor."

Guido's gaze lifted, locking onto Davis. A slow, deliberate stare.

"For your future reference, signor," he murmured. "I do not steal from my friends."

Davis frowned. "Huh? Friends? Fifty-two? What do you mean, fifty-two?" He let out a forced chuckle. "I have thirty cases of this stuff. Maybe fifty-two of the white—"

He was talking to thin air.

Salvatore had already hustled Guido toward the south exit. The black car rolled to a stop, its door swinging open. Guido slid inside.

Gone.

A beat of stunned silence.

Then: "What the fuck are you doing here?" Fowler demanded. His eyes flicked toward Nico, who'd stepped from his hiding place.

He jerked a thumb at him. "This is the guy who took your place this time around, Pete. Always snooping. Him and that bloody HR woman."

Davis tilted his head. "Then perhaps we need to have a chat with him." He smirked. "What did you say his name was?"

The trio of henchmen marched toward Nico. They never made it.

A thunder of footsteps. Mere moments later, the warehouse swarmed with armed personnel.

Davis froze.

Ettore Ricci strode through the chaos, his presence turning heads and silencing whispers.

"Ah, Davis," he said smoothly. "You have found my wine. How clever of you." His gaze flicked toward the other men. "These are the ones working with Siena McFarlane, yes?"

Davis hesitated only a moment. "McFarlane, aye, sir."

Fowler's face reddened. "Wait a gorblimey minute, ya mongrel—are you landing us in it?"

Davis said nothing.

Ettore ignored the outburst, his eyes now on Nico.

"Would this be the real Siena McFarlane?" Nico asked. "Or one Freda Higson posing as Miss McFarlane?"

Davis's shoulders slumped.

Game over.

Ettore nodded to his security lead.

"The police will deal with these four," he instructed. "Liaise with the senior officer to secure the area and the wine. Change the keycode on the doors immediately."

He'd barely finished before a scuffle broke out among the Englishmen.

"Filthy bastard." Mills snarled, swinging a roundhouse punch at Davis. Watkins and Fowler jumped in.

Police pounced, dragging them apart.

Mills fought against the grip of two officers, spitting profanities at Davis, screaming dire warnings of retribution.

Davis didn't even look at him. He knew he was done.

Nico swallowed, then turned to Ettore. "Can I show you out?"

Ettore gave a small smile. "Grazie, Signor Griff."

Once out of earshot of the chaos, Ettore's voice dropped to an amused murmur.

"A good outcome. We won't need to buy wine for the next cruise. Or the one after that."

"There's also the matter of the embezzled funds," Nico continued. "From what Siena McFarlane said yesterday, Davis was bitter about missing out on the HR job. That means her arrival was likely the trigger—just like you thought. But she wasn't the perpetrator. That's why they worked so hard to frame her."

His father gave a small nod, absorbing the confirmation.

Before he could respond, a group of ECM security personnel strode out of the building, cutting into their conversation.

Ettore glanced at Nico. "Come to dinner tonight. And bring the HR women."

"Certamente, Signor Ricci. Grazie."

Nico dipped his head in exaggerated compliance, jerking his shoulders in a nervous spasm. Grief, it would be good to drop this persona for good.

Ettore smirked, catching the antics for what they were. Without another word, he climbed into the back seat of the car.

Chapter Twenty-five

Beautiful. Stubborn. Passionate.

The words tumbled through Luc's mind as the limousine door opened, revealing the woman who had haunted his thoughts since the first moment he saw her.

Tristan.

Her auburn hair fell down her back. Her stylish knee-length cream dress accentuated every perfect line of her body.

Getting her here tonight had been no small feat. She was still furious at him for costing her job. He'd spent the day trying to make it right, though part of him hoped she wouldn't accept the offer.

Tris adjusted the square neckline of her dress, her gaze flicking to the stone façade of his family's home. She swallowed, pressing a hand to her midriff.

She didn't smile. If anything, she looked ill at ease.

Beside her, Siena—balanced on her crutches—had no such hesitation.

"Wow." Siena's voice was filled with wonder. "This place is something else, eh? Could you imagine living here, Tris?"

Tris barely glanced at her. "I don't think so. Do you need a hand?"

Luc stepped from the shadows.

"Welcome. Both of you." His voice was warm as he air-kissed Siena's cheeks. Then he turned to Tristan.

Resting a hand on her shoulder, he met her gaze before resting his lips first on one cheek, then the other. He inhaled her scent—a sharp hit to his senses.

Every time, she did this to him.

Would it be the same in twenty years?

A soft voice interrupted his thoughts.

"Good evening." His mother approached. "We're so pleased you are here." She glanced at him, eyes twinkling. "I am Isabella Ricci—since my son is distracted and has forgotten his manners."

Tristan's sharp blue gaze flicked to his, then away, as if dismissing him outright.

She straightened. Shoulders squared. Chin lifted. Military precision. Defying the world.

"Tristan Sinclair, ma'am. Thank you for your kind invitation." She extended her hand.

Isabella took it, studying Tristan the way only a mother could.

Luc stood between the two women he cared about most in the world as they assessed each other.

Then, Isabella released her hand and gave Luc's shoulder a brief, knowing squeeze.

"Bene," she said softly. "Bene."

Her attention shifted. "And you are Miss McFarlane?"

"Siena. Yes, ma'am."

"Then, Siena, you must let me show you the garden. It is a hidden jewel in the heart of Naples, don't you think? And please—call me Isabella. 'Ma'am' is awkward, no?"

Siena grinned. "Definitely awkward."

They strolled away, leaving Tristan and Luc alone beside the car.

Tris tucked a stray strand of hair behind her ear. "I had an email from John Trevethan, my former boss, this afternoon.

The anger in her face was gone, but so was the fire. The band around Luc's chest tightened.

"Sì?"

"He offered me a different job," Tristan said, her voice flat, emotionless. "A promotion, actually—to manage the new, highly lucrative dockside contract I secured with ECM."

Luc's brows lifted.

"There was also an apology," she added, her tone still neutral, "for his earlier comments. Apparently, it was all a misunderstanding when Signor Griff contacted him previously."

She exhaled slowly, shifting her weight. "But it's not the job I'd been working towards. They moved fast to fill that position the second I was out of the running." Her lips pressed together before she continued. "John said you, Signor Luciano Ricci, personally commended my work—and that the contract depends on me being the one to run it."

Luc studied her carefully. "That pleases you?"

Tristan shrugged. "It's a job." The tightness in her expression betrayed her indifference.

"I've known John a long time," she continued, her voice steady, but something brittle lurked beneath. "For him to turn on me without waiting for an explanation... That bit hard."

Luc said nothing, letting her speak.

"It's not hard to see why he did it," she mused, as if talking to herself. "He saw my supposed 'defection' as a betrayal. First, his partner, Michael, let him down. He couldn't fire Michael. But me?" She gave a hollow laugh. "I was the scapegoat for his frustrations. I expected more loyalty. But people aren't always what they seem, are they?"

The jab landed like a punch to Luc's gut.

He guided her to a stone bench in front of the ornate fountain, its gentle trickling the only sound between them.

"You want an explanation," he said, rubbing the back of his neck.

She shook her head. "I don't need one."

Her voice was too firm, too resolute. "I have a few days before my flight home," she continued. "I'll spend them with Siena. Then the rest will be history."

A flicker of vulnerability betrayed her—a tremor in her chin, a slight flick of her gaze toward the fountain.

Luc took her hand, his heart pounding.

"Bella, please."

She didn't pull away.

He laced their fingers together, his thumb brushing over hers. "Since I was a teenager, I've done all kinds of undercover work on ships. Different disguises, different personas. Nico was just another one."

She inhaled.

"The disguise had to be foolproof," he went on. "People on our ships have known me my whole life. If they knew the owner was around, they'd clam up. There was no way to uncover why the Laura was losing money unless I went incognito. So, I became Nico. Someone inconspicuous. Non-threatening."

"I liked Nico." Her voice was soft.

Luc stilled.

"He wasn't arrogant," she continued. "He had an intelligence he didn't want people to notice. And he was kind." Her breath hitched. "Yeah. Lovable."

She turned her gaze to him, eyes sharp.

"But he wasn't real, was he?"

Luc's throat tightened.

"What about Luciano Ricci?" she asked, her voice cool now. "The playboy billionaire? Is he real?"

He let out a slow breath.

"It suited my purposes for people to see me that way," he admitted. "It explained my long absences. They could imagine I was off drunk in the Caribbean or having orgies in the Alps when, in reality, I was sorting problems for shipowners across the world. My parents always knew where I was. They always knew what I was doing."

Her expression didn't change.

"Why?" she asked. "Why not just stay here and learn the family business?"

Luc met her gaze.

"I inherited half the line directly from my grandmother. The oldest grandchild. The only one alive when she died. Papa runs things until he says otherwise."

Tristan canted her head, as if considering that.

"I have been learning the business," he continued. "Since I was a child. Like he did. I've worked nearly every position on board—except senior management." His voice lowered. "I am the business."

A long silence stretched between them.

She sighed, twisting her mouth to the side.

"Will you take the job in Melbourne?" he asked.

"I'll go home." She pulled her hand away, placing it in her lap. "But I'll find work somewhere else. I can't work with John anymore."

Luc frowned. "Without you, they'll lose the contract."

She shrugged her shoulders, curled her lips almost amused.

"That's for you and them to sort out," she said simply. "It doesn't affect me. The illusion that I'm indispensable to anyone is well and truly shattered."

Luc's jaw clenched.

"You're indispensable to me." His voice was hoarse. "Essential to my happiness. My life."

Her shoulders squared. "One-night stand, remember?"

A muscle ticked in his jaw.

"There were a couple," she amended, her voice sharper now. "But the rules apply. No involvement. When it's done, we walk away."

She pushed to her feet, walking to the fountain's edge.

He followed.

"Bella—"

He caught her arm, turning her toward him.

"I broke the rules the very first night," he whispered. "I fell in love with you."

She stiffened.

"When I saw you on the ship," he continued, voice rough with emotion, "my heart sang—because I hadn't lost you after all."

Tristan pulled back.

"But you did lose me." Her eyes darkened. "You emailed my boss to check up on me."

Luc dipped his head.

"You were prancing around in your world of make-believe, yet you didn't trust me enough to take me at face value." Her voice shook with anger. "That's ironic, don't you think? Since you were the one playing pretend."

Luc furrowed fingers through his hair..

"My only defence is that I was doing what I thought was best for the company," he said. "I couldn't have foreseen the impact a simple query would have on your dreams." His voice was raw, scraping past the boulder in his throat. "For that, I'm truly regretful. You did everything to uncover the villains, only to be repaid this way." He swallowed. "Can you ever forgive me?"

Tristan's laugh was hollow.

"As I said minutes ago—in less than a week, all of this will be 'once upon a time, in a far-off land' stuff." She met his gaze. Hard. Unwavering.

"You don't need absolution from me to get on with whatever the hell you do in your life," she said. "And I sure as heck don't need you."

Luc felt the air leave his lungs.

She turned her head away.

He took a step closer. "Barefoot on hot coals, cara. I'm standing in the middle of an inferno for you." He held his hands out to the side. "Please hear me out. You're the only woman in the world who has turned me around, so I don't know which way is up, the only one who cared about me without the trappings. I love you. I want to spend my life with you—every single day."

Her glance skidded away from him to the villa, the grounds, the tree-lined driveway. She swallowed. "It wouldn't work," she said, stepping away. "We're worlds apart."

"Is that a polite way of saying, 'it's not you, it's me', and that you don't care for me at all?"

She slumped her head. The anger seemed to seep from her into the earth beneath her feet. She raised sad eyes to him.

"Is it Siena? Is she the one you love?" he asked.

Tris jolted. "Not in that way," she said, her expression firing to life. "I told you she saved my life? The first time was when we were in a foster home when we were twelve years old. Twelve. The man of the house decided he would teach me about sex and how to please a man. I was shy. I didn't know what to do, how to fend him off.

"Siena stormed into the room and dragged me out, yelling 'Put your fuckin' dick back in your fuckin' pants, pervert!'" She chuckled. "She doesn't mince words. Our foster mother came screaming up to see what was happening. The guy said, 'She wanted to see it.' 'She' being me. Children's Services transferred us out that afternoon into different foster homes."

She glanced up at the moonlit sky, then back at him.

"When we were fifteen, Siena and I ended up in another foster home together." Her voice was quiet, edged with memory. "That time, there was Beth."

Luc said nothing, just watched as her gaze turned inward, lost in the past.

"The family was good to us. And when we turned eighteen—give or take a few months between us—we enlisted, and went into officer training at the Defence Force Academy. Our foster parents were former Navy. They said it was the best way to get an education and serve our country."

Her arms tightened around herself.

"The three of us joined the Navy together. Sometimes, we were sent undercover—to the places sailors go, listening for whispers of trouble, potential threats." Her lips pressed into a thin line. "We pulled each other out of danger more times than I can count."

She rubbed her arms, as if the memories clung to her skin.

"And then came the storm. The one that took Beth."

Luc reached for her hand but instead took her arm, turning it gently to expose the long scar from her elbow to her wrist.

"Beth did this?"

She hesitated. "I did it to myself, I suppose." Her voice dropped to a whisper. "If I'd grabbed her shirt. Her belt. The way Siena grabbed mine... maybe she'd still be here."

"Siena saved your life then too, didn't she?"

A small, wistful smile ghosted across her lips.

"She did." Her fingers traced the edge of the scar. "I love Siena. She's the only person I've ever been able to rely on. That's why, when she asked me to come to Italy—to find out who was trying to frame her—I came."

Luc's chest tightened. "And you saved her." His eyes flicked to the tattoo on her soft skin. "What does it mean?"

She turned her arm over, studying the faded ink.

"The sword and shield around the heart? Our promise to always protect one another. Whenever, wherever, whatever the cost. Three initials inside it? E.S.T. Elizabeth, Siena, Tristan. A bond—one heart forever." Her breath hitched. "Until the storm tore us apart.""

For a long moment, she simply stared at it. Then she wrapped her arm around herself, as if shielding the wound from sight.

Luc swiped a hand over his midriff calming the tension there.

"If not Siena... then who?"

Her eyes met his. Unflinching. Raw.

"There's no one else." Her voice was steady. "There's only you. I wouldn't react to you the way I do. I wouldn't have known it was you in that god-awful disguise unless I loved you."

Luc didn't hesitate.

"Then marry me." His fingers curled around hers. "Give us a chance. Let's build something together. A family. Our own mark on the ECM legacy."

Her hand went cold in his.

She shook her head.

Rejection hit him like a freight train rolling over him.

"Why?" His voice was rough. Her refusal, when everything between them felt right, burned like acid in his veins.

She gestured vaguely toward the grand estate around them.

"This."

"What do you mean, this?"

Her laugh was brittle. "I don't do rich and famous, Luc. I don't trust people with wealth who think the world belongs to them." She exhaled sharply. "The one guy I was serious about? He was from a well-off family. Promised me the world—then introduced me to his bloody wife. Wealthy people don't impress me much."

Luc clenched his jaw.

"That's why you're turning me down? Because I have money?"

She didn't answer.

His heart slammed in his chest. Hope flickered. If that was all...

There had to be a way.

She exhaled softly. "I'm afraid so."

Luc stilled.

"I grew up in the foster system." Her voice was steady, but there was a shadow beneath it. "All I know about my background is that my unwed mother died young. My grandparents saw me as a liability to their lifestyle and left me in the system."

She shrugged, but the movement was forced, hollow.

"So, if that makes things awkward for you, and you'd rather have the driver take me back to Siena's... I'd understand."

A thousand rabbits stomped in his chest.

"Please stay." He stepped closer, wrapping an arm around her waist. When she didn't pull away, his heart leapt. "My parents have been looking forward to meeting you."

She didn't argue, but her shoulders were still tense.

Luc hesitated, then asked, "Would you love me if I had no money?"

Her gaze lifted to meet his.

"I do love you." The words were quiet but firm. "If you had no money—if you were just Nico Griff, doing the job—we'd be equals. Do you understand?"

Luc smiled, relief washing over him.

"Our differences are what make our love special, don't you think? It works." His fingers brushed along her back. "You'll soon see—not everyone in my family comes from money. We don't judge people by their bank balance. Let my mother tell you her story."

He turned her gently to face him.

"My proposal stands. I love you. I want us to be married." His eyes searched hers. "If you ever change your mind... just give me a sign. I'll know."

Then he kissed her, light and fleeting—but full of promise.

"Agreed?"

Tristan shook her head, but there was a trace of a smile.

"You don't give up, do you?"

His grin deepened. "You know that about me already, cara."

He held out his hand.

"Shall we go in?"

Chapter Twenty-six

She shouldn't let him hold her like this.

She had turned him down—not because she didn't love him, but because she loved him too much. Too much to let her past humiliate him when the world learned who she was.

She wasn't ashamed. Her history shaped her. It made her independent, taught her right from wrong, built a loyalty in her so fierce, it bordered on reckless. But not everyone would see it that way—especially people like Luc's family, the elite, the untouchable.

Still, she stayed close.

Because this was the last time.

She'd store away this moment, press it into her memory like a flower between the pages of a book.

She could give him a sign she'd changed her mind? If only that were possible.

The sala held a small gathering of six people.

Siena stood with a glass of bubbly wine, engaged in conversation with a man younger than Luc.

Her body language spoke volumes—she wasn't impressed by him.

"This is my brother, Sebastian," Luc murmured. "If you thought my disguise was bad, at least it worked. Seb didn't recognize me."

Sebastian's eyes narrowed. "What disguise?"

"It doesn't matter." Luc moved on. "And here's the man whose name you borrowed this morning." He gestured to a portly man with an open smile—but eyes sharp as a blade.

"Tristan, meet Guido Marconi."

The man shook her hand, grip firm, assessing gaze.

"Signorina, it would be an honour if you truly were a Marconi," he said with a chuckle.

A round-faced woman joined them, slipping her arm through Guido's.

"My wife, Margherete," Guido said.

"Piacere," she said warmly.

"I'm pleased to meet you, too," Tris responded.

Luc moved on. "You've met Mama. She recognized me—even in disguise."

"Not at first," Isabella admitted. Her smile was knowing. "Your father nearly crushed my fingers. That's when I knew something was off. Then, the mark on your hand..."

Luc grinned. "You were good, Mama. Very good."

"And Papa," he said, indicating the final member of the group. "Ettore Ricci."

The older man's expression was warm, yet regal.

"Tristana, it is so very lovely to meet you in the flesh, finally." His voice held weight, sincerity. "You are a remarkable woman. I thank you from the bottom of my heart for flushing out the vipers in the nest."

Tris inclined her head. "I couldn't have done it alone. Siena had her suspicions before I joined the ship, so I had a starting point. Then Mr. Griff connected the sabotage to the embezzlers—and their reason for wanting the ship back in Naples early."

"You were an excellent team." Ettore's eyes gleamed. "Perhaps you might reprise your roles someday?"

Luc chuckled. "Oh no, Papa. Tristan wants life to settle into its proper place. And as for Mr. Griff... he's retired. Permanently."

Sebastian frowned. "Griff? Wasn't he the guy on the quay? The one with the awful birthmark?"

Luc smirked. "He was me."

Sebastian blinked. "Huh?"

Guido chuckled. "Umberto is a master technician."

Tris arched a brow. "That's how he also managed a passport in Griff's name?"

Guido's grin widened. "Now, bella... we don't discuss such things. People become upset."

Tris laughed softly. "Enough said."

Across the room, Isabella called, "Luciano, help me with the wine, please."

Luc sighed theatrically but gave Tristan a quick squeeze before stepping away.

She watched him go, heart torn between longing and logic. For now, she could only hold onto the moment.

"He is a good boy," Guido mused.

Her heart thumped. A good boy? Maybe. But he was also one hell of a man.

"Sì," she murmured.

Ettore studied her. "What are your plans, Tristana? Will you continue working with us?"

She shook her head. "My role here was temporary. Siena couldn't be onboard because of her injury. She needed someone she could trust to unravel the mystery before her head ended up in a noose. She asked. I answered."

"I see." Ettore's brow furrowed. "You dropped your life to help your friend?"

"We have history."

Tris caught Siena's glance and smiled. Siena raised her glass in silent acknowledgment.

"We shared foster homes—at different times as children, then again as teenagers. Later, we joined the Navy together." She paused, swallowing the tightness in her throat. "She's worth fighting for."

Siena's eyes widened.

"Tris?" Siena's voice was gentle, questioning.

Tristan shook her head. Not now. She'd explain later why she'd revealed their past. If she tried now, she might burst into tears.

Isabella returned, Luc at her side.

"Please, come to the table," she invited.

Tris took a seat opposite Luc, positioned between Ettore at the head of the table and Guido to her right.

Two waitstaff served the first course—a rich, steaming cioppino with prawns.

It smelled delicious, though Tris found it difficult to eat with Luc catching her gaze every time she glanced up.

Siena broke the moment. "I read about your bequest to the hospital, Signor Marconi. You are very generous."

Guido waved off the praise. "Not so much. My father and Isabella's both died to random violence when we were very young. Our mothers raised us for as long as they were alive. They were wonderful women. It is only right to honour them."

"Sì," Isabella said. "Guido and I grew up on the back streets of Naples, Siena. Not exactly a respectable part of town. We looked out for each other, eh, Guido?"

Guido chuckled. "Do you know, once, when we were eight, some older boys were hassling me. They were big. One of them punched me. Broke my nose. The leader was about to hit me again when Isabella—"

He glanced the length of the table, grinning at his friend. "She threw a rock and knocked him out cold. Then she grabbed my hand and dragged me away. The boys never bothered us after that."

"Because you became one of the tough kids," Isabella said, "with your own gang."

Guido shrugged.

"I survived. I've had more than my share of run-ins with the authorities—and would have had another one today if Luc hadn't warned us."

He turned to Luc, eyes amused. "You remembered the old signal, eh, Luciano?"

Luc lifted a shoulder.

"Ooh, a secret signal?" Siena leaned in, eyebrows raised. "What is it?"

Guido bumped Tris's arm. "Can we trust her, do you think?" he asked, winking.

Siena gasped. "You can trust me. It's Tristan who's reckless with secrets." She shot Tris a teasing grin.

Tris batted her eyelashes. "Only our shared ones—for good reason."

A low rumble emanated from Guido's chest before he continued.

"My mama raised me to be a good boy, you know? She tried. But times were tough when I got into my line of work. In the middle of the night, when it was just me and my conscience, what I did would bother me.

One night, I asked God for a sign that I was doing the right thing. He directed my gaze to my bedside clock. The time read 00:52."

Siena's brows knitted. "The 'fifty-two'—like on your pendant?"

"Sì." Guido nodded. "You see, on an old digital clock face, if you square off the numbers just right, fifty-two becomes a symbol—figure and ground, you know? The figure was a crucifix. The ground—a chalice. God's blessing."

He made the sign of the cross.

"From that moment on, I decided to help people. I take from those who can afford to lose or those who are too stupid to be worth saving and redistribute sustenance."

Siena's gaze narrowed.

"What did you do, Luciano?" She raised a fist. "Did you just jump up and yell, 'Fifty-two!'?"

Luc chuckled. "I couldn't exactly do that. It would have given away my position."

Guido's grin widened. "He improvised. Five taps, two scrapes. My men understood the signal and got me out of the warehouse."

His smile turned sly.

"We passed the police cars on the way out. Thank you, my boy."

Luc's expression hardened. "I would have let things play out if I believed you were in it with Davis."

"Of course." Guido's voice carried an undertone of pride. "Always the businessman."

Siena wasn't done. "Did most of your friends end up on the wrong side of the law?"

"Not all." Guido's glance flicked to Isabella again. "Isabella was clever. She studied hard, won a scholarship to secretarial school." His tone softened. "Her mother was so proud she'd found a way to escape."

As the waitstaff cleared the soup course, they replaced it with orecchiette pasta tossed with capers and tomatoes.

The conversation paused, then Isabella picked it up again.

"My mama died of lung disease before I finished my course," she said quietly. "In the middle of my grief, our landlord tossed me out. I had nowhere to go."

She directed a glance at Guido, eyes warm.

"He brought me to live with him, found me work so I could finish my studies. He was already a successful entrepreneur at a young age," she added, her lips quirking.

Siena's eyes twinkled. "What did the old biddies have to say about that?"

Luc frowned. "Biddies?"

He shot Tris a questioning glance.

"We all learned English when we were young, but your Australian slang still catches me off guard."

His lips tilted, sending warmth flooding through her. She shouldn't feel that way.

She. Had. Turned. Him. Down.

"The old gossips," Siena explained. "Women with strong opinions on what's right and wrong. I'm guessing Italy has its fair share."

"Oh, we have them, but they never bothered with us," Guido said.

"My living with Guido worked out well..." Isabella canted her head, smiling wryly. "Until the night he brought Margherete home to visit."

"Sì." Margherete's tone turned theatrical. "He invites me to see his house, and what do I find? Another woman!"

She wagged a finger.

"No, no. I will not have another woman around. He says he loves me—so why is she here? I left and told him to stay away."

She cast a mock-glare at Guido, but her eyes twinkled.

"Then what happens? The very next day, his woman," she spat the word playfully, "arrives at my door. And she says—"

Margherete squared her shoulders, deepening her voice in a passable imitation of Isabella.

"'I will tell you something, you stupid girl. Guido is my friend. He is my brother. He is not— and never has been —my lover. I love him, always have. And he loves me. But now—he loves you.'"

The table erupted in laughter.

Margherete shook her head. "Isabella took a step forward. I took a step back. She was scary."

She wiggled her shoulders in a shudder, then grinned.

"Then she says, 'I'll tell you now, if you ever hurt him again like you did last night, I... will... hurt... you.'"

Margherete threw up her hands. "What could I do? I ran straight into Guido's arms—and I have been there ever since, eh?"

The retelling seemed like a well-rehearsed family favourite that had the table chuckling again.

A server placed another dish in front of Tristan, clearing her white wine glass and replacing it with red.

"That's such a lovely story," Siena sighed. "So romantic."

Her gaze flicked between Ettore and Isabella. "If it's not rude, how did you two meet? I mean, if one of you came from wealth and the other not so much, how did your paths cross?"

Ettore and Isabella exchanged a glance—one filled with an eternity of affection, far beyond what years could measure.

"In my family," Ettore began, "we insist our young people learn all there is to know about our ships. They must be able to step into any role if needed—to protect our people, to ensure the company's success. We learn the business from every angle, so we truly understand the people we work with—their motivations, their struggles. They depend on us, just as we depend on them."

His gaze flickered to Sebastian. "Of course, we get some pushback from our children now and then."

"Blah, blah, blah," his younger son muttered, voice bored.

Siena shot Sebastian a sharp side-eye. "You were saying, Signor Ricci?"

Ettore sipped his wine, amused. "Ahem. Yes, our children working onboard. That experience is why Luciano is so successful in what he does—undercover work, all over the world. He's been a cleaner, a mechanic, a room steward, a galley hand—many things. This time, he used his accounting degree."

Tristan arched a brow at Luc.

"And Isabella?" Siena prompted.

Ettore's smile softened.

"I was working as a stevedore when this beautiful young woman joined the pay office as a secretary. I fell in love instantly."

His voice held a quiet reverence.

"I spent twice as much time on the docks as I should have—just to be close to her."

Isabella smiled. "I fell in love with him too. He was hardworking, reliable. I loved him for his sparkling eyes, for the way he made me feel. He was my forever love, until..."

"The day before our wedding," Ettore grinned, "I confessed to her that I wasn't only a stevedore—I was an owner of the shipping group."

Isabella shook her head, lips pursed. "I was not happy. I couldn't marry someone like that," she admitted. "He was too rich. I was a poor girl from a working-class background. I would never fit in."

"Nonsense, of course." Ettore's voice softened, his gaze lingering on his wife. "Just look at her. She's perfect in every way. I didn't need her to 'fit in.' I wanted her exactly as she was, and is. I asked her, 'Are you refusing to marry me because of my money?'"

Isabella picked up the thread. "I told him, 'I am not a gold-digger. I want to work hard with my husband so we can be well-off in time.'"

"And I told her," Ettore continued, "we could skip that step. Because we had more important things to build—like our life together. Our family."

His smile deepened. "So I said, 'If you love me, but will not marry me for my money, then marry me against my money. If I had a rotten brother, would you refuse to marry me because of him? Wealth is like that brother—it's just a fact of life.'"

He chuckled, raising his glass toward Isabella. "And it worked."

Tristan barely heard the laughter rippling around the table.

Luc held her gaze, steady and unwavering.

Her pulse thundered. Tears pricked her eyes.

A life with someone who loved her as much as she loved him? A family of her own? With people who wouldn't judge her because of her past? A love like Isabella and Ettore's?

Yes.

Heat bloomed through her chest, her stomach a wild storm of butterflies.

Luc tilted his head slightly, questioning.

Tristan pressed a hand to her midriff to steady the trembling there. She nodded.

Luc exhaled, his shoulders slumping as if releasing a breath he'd been holding forever. He grinned, mouthed, 'Thank you,' and lifted his glass.

She mirrored the gesture, sipping, never looking away. The butterflies didn't settle. Instead, they were joined by a tightness in her throat—an overwhelming pressure of happiness.

If anyone so much as looked at her the wrong way, she'd burst into tears.

"ECM has an 'Isabella' and a 'Margherete' in its fleet. Are they named for you?" Siena asked.

Tristan barely heard.

She'd had an entire conversation with the man she loved—questions asked and answered—without a single spoken word.

She'd made the most momentous decision of her life while the conversation around her had continued as if nothing had happened.

Surreal.

Ettore nodded. "We name our ships after the important women in our lives. My great-grandmother was Margherete—a happy coincidence, as it is also the name of our dear friend. Paola was Isabella's mother. Laura, mine. Donatella and Giulietta are our daughters. And, of course, Isabella."

He paused. "We must find a name for the new one we're building. She'll be the most luxurious ship we've ever launched. She must be named well."

Luc set down his glass. "We have a name, Papa."

The room fell silent.

"Two minutes ago, Tristan agreed to be my wife." His voice rang with quiet triumph. "The new ship will be the Dorata Tristana."

The table erupted.

"Two minutes ago?" Margherete gaped. "We were all sitting here together! How did we not hear a proposal?"

"Because it was private," Isabella murmured, her eyes glistening. She glanced at Tristan. "You will do well, raggazzina."

Tristan still hadn't found her voice.

"You've got some explaining to do, my girl." Siena's voice was half-growl, half-laugh.

Luc rose, glass in hand, and moved behind his father. He offered Tristan his hand, guiding her to her feet, slipping an arm around her waist.

"Ladies and gentlemen," he announced, "I give you my partner in life and love—the beautiful, feisty, loyal, superb Tristan Sinclair. To Tristan."

"To Tristan!" the chorus rang out.

Luc turned to her. "Your turn, my sweet."

She bumped her head lightly against his shoulder. "Thirty minutes ago, I turned down a wonderful proposal of marriage from this man."

Gasps.

She took a breath then continued, voice steady, but full of emotion. "I didn't believe I was good enough. Bold enough. Well-bred enough to be his partner."

Her eyes flicked toward Isabella. "Your stories changed my mind."

A knowing smile.

"I suspect there was some collusion?"

Isabella shrugged, not bothering to deny it. "Perhaps. These were stories we have not shared in a long time. Tonight... we remembered them," she said.

"Thank you," Tristan said, lifting her glass. "To Luciano—chameleon, friend, egalitarian. You might be wealthy, but you understand people. Tonight, I learned why."

She met his gaze, voice steady but full of the love she had for him.

"You saw the stewards struggling—understaffed, exhausted—but you understood them. You handled a sticky situation without giving the game away. Then you saw Siena for who she truly was—the hero, not the villain."

Luc's expression softened, absorbing every word.

"You listen. You learn. You adapt. And you've done the same with me." Tristan's throat tightened, but she pushed through. "I love you for it. I always will. You are the love of my life."

She lifted her glass higher. "To Luciano."

The salute echoed among the guests.

As the toast settled, Ettore leaned forward, eyes gleaming. "When will you marry?"

Luc didn't hesitate. "Before the Laura comes out of dry dock."

Siena choked on her drink. "Six weeks? Better get busy, hon'." She grinned, shaking her head.

Tristan spun to Luc, narrowing her gaze. "What's the rush?"

Luc's smile was so wide it nearly split his face.

He nuzzled her ear, his breath warm on her neck. "Time's a-wasting, Mrs. Griff," he murmured, his deep voice sending a slow, delicious shiver through her.

Before she could respond, he plucked the glass from her hand, set it alongside his on the table, and gathered her into his arms.

Then, with a deep, slow, utterly consuming kiss, he sealed their engagement and their future.

Dear Reader

Dear Reader,

Thank you for picking up my book.

I wrote the first version of this story a decade ago, just after my first cruise—one that began in Venice and finished in Naples.

The tale has changed over time but some concepts remain constant. The places visited by my characters, Nico and Tris, came from my experiences during that cruise including: the cats at Paleokastritsa Monastery; the crowded, narrow streets leading to the Ancient Greek Theatre in Taormina; and 'hearing' coffee being made in an alleyway in Castelmola which drew me past the baskets of colourful phallic keyrings and accidentally into the now infamous café you'll encounter in the book. Life is full of weird and wonderful happenings and, through my stories, I love sharing a few I've met.

I hope you enjoy the novel. Please let me know through the contact page of my website: www.caenyskerr-author.com or leave a review on Amazon or Goodreads.

With love,

Caenys (think Denise with a K)

What's next on your reading list?

Other stories written by Caenys Kerr:

Return to Calypso Station
Merry Christmas Liebchen
Her Holiday Fling
Happy with the Millionaire (due for release 2026)
The Salignac Legacy
The Beaulieu Birthright

There's always another story being written. If you'd like to keep up to date with new releases, please find Caenys's website at:
www.caenyskerr-author.com